STARGÅTE SG·1™

KALI'S WRATH

Keith R.A. DeCandido

FANDEMONIUM BOOKS

An original publication of Fandemonium Ltd, produced under license from MGM Consumer Products.

Fandemonium Books
United Kingdom
Visit our website: www.stargatenovels.com

STARGÅTE
SG·1

METRO-GOLDWYN-MAYER Presents
RICHARD DEAN ANDERSON
in
STARGATE SG-1™
MICHAEL SHANKS   AMANDA TAPPING   CHRISTOPHER JUDGE   DON S. DAVIS
Executive Producers BRAD WRIGHT   MICHAEL GREENBURG
RICHARD DEAN ANDERSON
Developed for Television by BRAD WRIGHT & JONATHAN GLASSNER

Print ISBN: 978-1-905586-75-2   Ebook ISBN: 978-1-80070-035-2

Dedicated to the memory of Leonard
Nimoy. He lived long. He prospered.

Historical note:
This novel takes place late in the fifth season of STARGATE
SG-1, between the episodes "The Warrior" and "Menace."
It is shortly after Imhotep attempted to break the Jaffa
rebellion by posing as Kytano, and not long after Anubis
made his presence known openly to the System Lords.

PROLOGUE

P3X-418

CAPTAIN Kirti Patel had thought it to be a good day up until the blast came out of nowhere and made a smoking hole in Sergeant Castro's chest.

The rings had deposited them in an area that was covered in deep snowdrifts and sheets of ice. Unlike the area by the Stargate, it wasn't actually snowing here. Major Steven Lagdamen, SG-7's commanding officer, bellowed, "Take cover!" even as he dove behind a drift. "Johnson, check on Castro!"

Patel dove behind another drift, while Airman Anwan Johnson ran over to the sergeant's body. She wasn't sure why the major had given that order — there was no way that Elena Castro could have survived that.

Another bolt flew from nowhere and blew up the snow in front of Lagdamen.

Aiming her P90, Patel fired at full automatic on the spot where the blast had come from. The rounds just flew straight through the air at nothing, even as Lagdamen shouted, "Hold your fire, Patel!"

After Patel ceased firing, she gave her CO a questioning look. "You know what it is, sir?"

"Looks like a Reetou." Lagdamen had slid over to better cover. "Actually, it looks like nothing, which means invisible, which means Reetou. You agree, Johnson?"

The airman had at this point taken up position behind his own pile of snow. "Sergeant Castro's dead, sir. And yes, those look like the same weapons they used in the SGC three years ago, sir."

Patel nodded. She remembered the file on the Reetou, who somehow existed 180 degrees off from the rest of the universe — or something. Physics wasn't her strong suit. The point was, they were invisible, making them damn near impossible to kill — especially since the weapon that worked best on them wasn't standard issue for regular offworld missions. Stargate Command only had a handful of the Transphase Eradication Rods.

"They took out some good people," Lagdamen said. "But a P90 won't cut it. We've got to get back to the rings."

It had been a straightforward recon mission. SG-7 had been assigned to the next planet on the Abydos Cartouche that Dr. Daniel Jackson had provided to the SGC five years earlier. The MALP had gone through the Stargate to find a habitable world, albeit one that kept its gate on an island in an area that was in its winter season. The island was very small, but did have a collection of rafts. Lagdamen, Patel, Castro, and Johnson had donned their winter gear and gone through the gate.

Castro had discovered a set of markings that indicated a ring transporter, and she figured out the controls while the others stood watch. Lagdamen, a Philadelphia native, had been complaining about the mess hall's version of a cheesesteak, which the major had declared to be an abomination, while Johnson had said that they actually tasted pretty good, which had earned him a dirty look from Lagdamen.

Once Castro had deciphered the ring code sequence and showed it to each of the other three, they had gone through, weapons at the ready.

And then Castro had been shot two seconds after the rings dropped back belowground and Patel was now staring at the sergeant's dead body.

Her career in the Air Force in general, and her time in combat in particular, had made it easy for Patel to compartmentalize and not think about Castro's husband and son in New York City.

Or think about the fact that she died on an alien world. That part of her assignment to Cheyenne Mountain was something she still wasn't quite used to yet.

Another bolt flew from midair — from a different spot this time, and Patel cried out, "Sir!"

Lagdamen flung himself to the side, but the bolt struck Johnson on his shoulder.

Johnson cried out in pain. Lagdamen crabwalked over to him. "Easy, Johnson, it's just a scratch."

Patel shook her head. The major was saying that to make Johnson feel better, but the wound was pretty bad. At the very least, he wasn't likely to be able to use his right arm for many months. His days in combat were over.

Then a large insect-like creature suddenly *appeared* about a yard in front of her.

Just as she raised her P90 and squeezed off several rounds, a blast from a staff weapon slammed into the creature's side.

Looking to her right, Patel saw a tall man who looked very much like her uncle Rajesh: huge muscles, close-cropped hair, and a dot in the center of his forehead. The dot was bigger than usual, though, and black rather than red. His staff weapon had a T.E.R. attachment. He wore tan knee-length robes with a red sash as a belt, which covered metal neck-to-boots armor.

"So," the large man said, "the Tau'ri have invaded Imphal as well. Are you in league with the Reetou?"

"The Reetou killed one of my — " Lagdamen started.

"No matter." The man held up a hand. "You are prisoners of the Mother Goddess Kali, and will be brought to her immediately."

Lagdamen shook his head and held up his P90. "Not a chance, Jaffa."

Before the conversation could continue, another bolt flew through the air and struck the Jaffa right in the belly, no doubt vaporizing his Goa'uld larva.

As the Jaffa fell to the snow, Patel broke cover to grab the T.E.R./staff weapon hybrid that he'd just dropped. She immediately did a sweep with the modified weapon, trying desperately to remember the files she read on her first day in Cheyenne

Mountain. The Reetou tended to attack in groups of five, and she and the Jaffa had killed one.

The T.E.R. showed her two more about ten yards away, and Patel immediately fired the staff weapon at them, even as one of them fired a weapon of its own. She again dove for cover after firing.

A fist of ice that was even colder than the snow she was now lying in gripped her heart at the sound of screams from behind her. Gazing over the snowdrift, she saw the bodies of both Anwan Johnson and Steven Lagdamen. The major didn't even have a face anymore, and half of the airman's torso was on fire.

Gritting her teeth, she detached the T.E.R. from the staff weapon, held it with her left hand while hefting the P90 with her other, bracing it against her shoulder and hoping that the thick fleece jacket she wore over her fatigues in deference to the weather would do enough to retard the weapon's kick while held one-handed.

She broke cover and again swung the T.E.R. around. One of the Reetou was dead, but its comrade was advancing on their position, along with another that was just coming into view. Squeezing her right index finger, dozens of P90 rounds sliced into both Reetou. Their inhuman screams lasted only a second.

That was four. There was still one more.

Or perhaps more. She wasn't a hundred percent sure she was remembering the mission report properly. There had been *so many* from the various SG teams over the years, she hadn't been able to keep track of them all since her transfer.

A voice from the distance cried, "Jaffa! *Kree!*"

Patel winced. She *hated* hearing those two words in succession.

And then suddenly she saw a dozen Reetou at least. So much for only five attacking at a time.

Taking advantage of having a target to fight, she squeezed her P90 until the magazine ran out, then she took cover to reload. Even as she did so, five Jaffa came over a nearby ridge, firing their staff weapons which were — like her late would-be jailer's — combined with T.E.R.s. Four of these Jaffa were also dressed in knee-length robes of either white, blue, or tan, all with red or gold sashes for belts, and all with the black circle in the center of their forehead.

Between her own P90 fire and the Jaffa staff weapons, the dozen Reetou were all taken care of.

When it was over, the fifth Jaffa stepped forward. He was even larger than the Jaffa who'd tried to take SG-7 prisoner, and the circle on his forehead was gold, indicating that he was First Prime. That circle was partly obscured by his shaggy dark collar-length hair. His robes were gold, and he wore a shoulder sash rather than a belt sash, which was red.

He frowned down at her and spoke in a surprisingly gentle voice. "I was unaware that any of the *Kali Kula* were among the Tau'ri."

"I'm sorry?" Patel slowly got to her feet, but did not lower her weapon.

"You must come with us."

"Like hell. My teammates are all dead thanks to the Reetou, and I need to ring back to the Stargate and report in."

The First Prime smiled widely. "I cannot permit you to go to the *chappa'ai, Kula*."

"My name is Captain Kirti Patel, and I want to —"

"Thakka!"

The First Prime — who was apparently named Thakka? — turned and Patel did likewise. Then all the Jaffa doubled over in pain.

Four more Reetou were bearing down on their position. Patel recalled from the file that the Reetou's presence had an adverse effect on a symbiote — that meant that Goa'uld, Tok'ra, and Jaffa were all vulnerable.

She took all of half a second to mull. Yes, these were Jaffa, but the Reetou had just killed her entire team.

She squeezed the trigger on her P90.

The Jaffa recovered enough to return fire too, but four of the five Jaffa were killed in the ensuing firefight.

In the aftermath, Thakka looked around. "That is sixteen of these creatures that we have killed."

"My team and I took three out," Patel said, preferring to give more credit to her deceased comrades than the Jaffa who tried to imprison them.

"Then there is another," Thakka said grimly. "Three teams of Reetou attempted to destroy this base, but the Mother Goddess, in her great wisdom, provided us with weapons that would detect their perfidy."

Patel might have laughed under different circumstances. Until she joined the SGC, she didn't think anyone talked like that outside of comic books.

Thakka turned to her. "You fought bravely. Truly, you are *Kula*."

Looking at all the dead Jaffa, as well as Thakka, she saw that each of them looked like they were of Indian descent, same as she was. Never mind that she herself was born and raised in Los Angeles — it wasn't as if any of these folks had ever seen New Delhi either. Probably when Kali left Earth, she took a bunch of people from India and its environs with her to seed her worlds, just like many other Goa'uld did when they abandoned the planet thousands of years earlier.

The First Prime continued, "I will allow you to do as you requested, *Kula*. You may return to your fellow Tau'ri and tell them what has happened this day."

Blinking, Patel said, "Ah, thank you." She quickly went to the bodies of Lagdamen, Castro, and Johnson and removed their dogtags, placing them in one of her fleece's Velcro pockets. No way could she bring their bodies back, but she wanted to give *something* to their families.

Solemnly, she walked to the ring platform, removed her gloves, now stained with the blood of her teammates after removing their tags, and started to enter the coordinates to bring her back to the island that had the gate.

"*Kula!*" Thakka cried, and he leapt in front of Patel as she was pressing the last control. A Reetou bolt slammed into Thakka's side as he blocked her. Patel's eyes went wide — the blast would surely have killed her if he hadn't done what he did.

Thakka landed at her feet, and then the rings sprung up out of the ground and brought them both to the island.

When the rings lowered again, Patel was hit by a gust of wind and pelted by heavy snow.

She looked down at Thakka, writhing in agony on the ground. The blast had hit near the symbiote pouch. If the symbiote was damaged it wouldn't be able to heal Thakka and he might die. And he was only wounded at all because he saved her life from the last Reetou left on this world.

Walking to the DHD, she dialed Earth, then entered SG-7's code into her GDO. Shouldering her P90 and putting her blood-stained gloves back on, she grabbed Thakka underneath his arms and started dragging him slowly toward the gate.

She almost gave up just because he was so damned heavy — what with his size, plus the armor, he probably weighed at least three hundred and fifty pounds — but dammit, he *did* save her life. She owed him a trip to the SGC's infirmary.

CHAPTER ONE

Stargate Command

"UNSCHEDULED off-world activation!"

Colonel Jack O'Neill heard the alert over the SGC's speakers as he exited the men's room. It was rarely a good thing when Master Sergeant Walter Harriman spoke those words. Still, there was always a chance this would be one of those rare good things. Or at least a not-actively-bad thing.

Or maybe it'd be some snake-head trying to kill them, or a rebel Jaffa or a Tok'ra showing up with bad news…

Either way, it was an excuse for O'Neill to put off doing the paperwork on the whole Imhotep disaster. He hated writing mission reports. For starters, Carter, Daniel, and Teal'c were all so much *better* at it. Carter and Daniel always included way more detail than O'Neill, and Teal'c's reports were downright meticulous.

O'Neill entered the control room to see that General Hammond was already there, standing over Harriman. Peering through the window, O'Neill saw that Captain Engenbe's platoon of Marines was surrounding the ramp. The iris was closed, but O'Neill could see the glow of the active gate behind it.

The sergeant looked up at Hammond. "Receiving SG-7's IDC, sir."

"Open the iris," Hammond said quickly. "They only embarked half an hour ago." The general looked over at O'Neill. "You feeling all right, Colonel?"

"Hm? Oh, no, just a little upset stomach. It was cheesesteak day in the mess."

Hammond nodded knowingly.

The iris cycled open, and a few seconds later Captain Patel came through, dragging a large man onto the ramp. "Need a medical team, stat!" she was shouting as she dropped the man with a resounding metallic thud. The captain's hands and arms were covered in blood.

"That's a First Prime," O'Neill said, noticing the gold circle on the man's forehead.

"I can see that, Colonel." Hammond leaned forward and spoke into the microphone. "Medical team, report to the gate room. Captain Engenbe, remain as you are."

O'Neill nodded his approval.

Patel turned and shot a look up at Hammond. "General, I know this man is a Jaffa, but he was wounded saving my life. And he and I are the only ones who survived the Reetou attack."

"Reetou?" O'Neill tensed. They hadn't heard much from those overgrown invisible insects since stopping the team that tried to destroy the SGC, but there'd been reports from the Tok'ra of other attacks on Goa'uld worlds.

"Seal the room!" Hammond cried. Immediately, Harriman closed both side doors. "Captain, T.E.R. scan now!"

Engenbe said, "Yes *sir*," and then nodded to one of the other Marines in the gate room, who immediately whipped out one of the three T.E.R.s they had at the SGC, which Hammond had made standard equipment for whichever team was in charge of gate room security.

After aiming the T.E.R. all over the room, the Marine turned to Engenbe and said, "Clear, sir."

"Stand down, Captain Engenbe." As the Marines lowered their weapons, Hammond softened his tone. "Captain Patel, I'm sorry about your team. Report to the infirmary. We'll debrief after Dr. Fraiser clears you."

Removing her gloves to reveal clean, unwounded hands, Patel said, "There's nothing to clear, sir, I wasn't hurt."

"That's an order, Captain."

One of the side doors slid open to reveal Fraiser and four other medical staff, two of whom were wheeling a gurney. The diminutive doctor pushed past the Marines to look over the Jaffa.

Hammond looked at O'Neill. "Gather the rest of your team,

Colonel. Once we've debriefed Captain Patel, I may need SG-1 to follow through."

"Understood, sir."

O'Neill went to the phone to call Carter and Daniel, who were doing whatever nerd things they did on their downtime, Carter in her lab surrounded by computers, Daniel in his office surrounded by crumbling pieces of paper. Teal'c he'd have to handle in person, as he was in the midst of *kelnorim*.

After calling the major and Daniel, he wandered through the corridors deep below Cheyenne Mountain toward Teal'c's quarters. He didn't know Patel or the other two subordinate members of SG-7 very well, but he and Lagdamen went back a few years. They'd bumped into each other here and there over their years in the service, and when Lagdamen was assigned to the SGC, they'd bonded over their mutual love of *The Simpsons*.

The memorial service for the members of SG-17, all killed when Zipacna destroyed the Tok'ra base on Revanna, wasn't that long ago, and O'Neill was not at all happy that he was going to have to attend another funeral for lost comrades. For that matter, they'd lost a lot of really good people here on the base the last time they'd tussled with the Reetou three years ago.

O'Neill was damned if anyone else would die on his watch if he could possibly help it. But, to his eternal irritation, he often couldn't possibly help it.

Once the colonel got Teal'c back from the depths of *kel-norim* — and somehow managed not to knock over any of the dozens of candles the Jaffa had all over the place — the pair of them joined Carter, Daniel, Hammond, Fraiser, and Patel in the briefing room adjacent to Hammond's office.

The first thing O'Neill did was go to Patel. She had changed out of the fleece jacket and winter uniform and was now wearing the blue BDUs that were standard base-wear for SGC personnel. O'Neill also saw that she looked more than a little shell-shocked. "How you doin', Captain?"

"Been better, sir," Patel said through clenched teeth.

Sitting across from her, Daniel said, "I'm sorry about your team. Sergeant Castro was an amazing linguist."

"Thank you, Doctor."

Once they were all seated, Patel told the general, the doctor, and SG-1 exactly what happened on P3X-418.

Daniel frowned. "You said the First Prime's name was Thakka?"

"I think so," Patel said. "I only heard the name once."

"Why do you ask, Dr. Jackson?" Hammond prompted.

"Well, when I was infiltrating the Goa'uld summit, Kali mentioned that her First Prime was killed by Anubis's Jaffa. Later, I overheard her and Bastet talking, and she referred to her First Prime as 'the Thakka.' And, actually, that kind of makes sense as a title rather than a name. See, here on Earth, there was a guild of assassins and criminals who served Kali known as the Thuggees. In fact, that's where the word *thug* comes from."

"Really?" That actually surprised and impressed O'Neill, though he spoke his reply with his usual feigned disinterest. When either Daniel or Carter went off on an intellectual rant, O'Neill found it was better to always react with annoyance, regardless of whether or not he was actually annoyed, as showing that he thought any of it was cool would just encourage them to babble *even more*, and then nothing would ever get done.

"Yes, and another word for them is *thakka*. It's not a big stretch to go from what the Thuggees did here and what the Jaffa do for the Goa'uld. It's possible that Thakka is the title she gives to her First Prime."

Now O'Neill's disinterest was not at all feigned. "Fascinating," he deadpanned. Then he turned to Patel. "With all due respect to what you went through out there, Captain, I gotta ask — what the hell were you thinking?"

"Sir?"

"Why did you bring this Thakka back here?"

Patel folded her hands together on the briefing table. "Sir, if it wasn't for Thakka, I'd be dead right now with the rest of my team — and none of you would even be aware that anything was wrong for another five-and-a-half hours when we missed our check-in."

"Yeah, but he's the First Prime for a *Goa'uld*."

Raising her eyebrows, Patel said, "So was Teal'c when you brought *him* back through the gate."

O'Neill blinked. "That was different. He saved our li — " He cut himself off. "Walked *right* into that one."

"Indeed," Teal'c said emphatically.

Thankfully, Hammond turned to Fraiser before O'Neill's foot got any further down his throat. "Doctor, how is this Thakka?"

Fraiser sighed bitterly. "Luckily for him, we have a very comprehensive notion of what Reetou weapons do to a human body."

O'Neill winced, reminded again of the personnel who were killed when the Reetou invaded. Fraiser had been able to examine their bodies, giving her useful intel on how the weapons worked, but it was overall a really lousy way to get that information.

The doctor continued. "We were able to stabilize him, which was necessary because his symbiote was damaged. It seems to be healing itself, and when that's done, it should turn its attention to healing him. But I doubt he'll be conscious for several hours. He's in restraints with two guards armed with zats on either side of his bed, and two more guards at the entrance to the infirmary."

"Good," Patel said.

That surprised O'Neill, and he shot her a look.

Patel smiled. "I'm not an idiot, Colonel — he may have saved my life, but he's still an enemy prisoner and quite dangerous."

"Good for you." And O'Neill meant that. He was worried that losing her team had clouded her judgment, but from the sounds of it, the captain had her head on straight.

Hammond said, "Captain, you said that the Jaffa referred to the world as Imphal?"

Patel nodded.

"Teal'c, do you know anything about the world?"

"Very little. Apophis and Kali did not come into conflict very often. However, this particular world is administrated by a Goa'uld in Kali's service named Ramprasad."

Carter finally spoke up. "Sir, I think we should send a UAV through to P3X-418 to do a recon, see the lay of the land."

"Thakka seemed to think the Reetou who shot him was the only one left," Patel said.

Nodding, Carter said, "Best to know for sure."

"Agreed," Hammond said. "If the UAV determines that it's safe to send another team through, then SG-1 and SG-22 will go through the gate. Dr. Fraiser, is Captain Patel well enough to go with them?"

Fraiser shook her head. "I don't want to clear the captain for active duty until she has a session with Dr. MacKenzie."

O'Neill winced. MacKenzie was the SGC's primary shrink, a class of doctor with whom O'Neill had no patience.

"Honestly, Doctor," Patel said, "I'm fine with that. This isn't my first time losing friends in combat, and I've always felt better after speaking with a therapist."

That surprised O'Neill — he'd never found such conversations to be in any way helpful, not when he lost friends or when he lost his son or when his marriage disintegrated — but to each their own, he supposed.

The Unmanned Aerial Vehicle was ready to go in twenty minutes. That impressed O'Neill no end, since the first time they flew a UAV through the Stargate it had taken an hour and a half to prep.

It's almost like we're getting good at this.

In the gate room below, Sergeant Siler gave the UAV a final once-over on its cradle at the base of the ramp. Then he looked up. "All systems are go, Major."

Carter nodded. "Dial it up, Sergeant."

"Starting countdown," Carter said, once the gate was open. "UAV launch in five — four — three — two — one."

She fired the UAV's two jets, released the clamps, and freed the UAV to zoom through the gate.

After a few seconds, Harriman said, "Receiving telemetry now."

O'Neill watched as the monitor next to Carter showed a large body of water crowded with huge chunks of ice, and a very small island housing a Stargate.

Carter flew the UAV over a long stretch of water and ice before they finally found a landmass.

"Can someone explain to me why they put the gate on a teeny tiny little island like that?" O'Neill said.

Carter shrugged. "It's possible the water levels rose after the gate was built. Remember P4X-234?"

O'Neill had to give her that one.

The landmass itself was covered in snow, as the island had been. There were plenty of stone and brick structures, and a giant castle built into the side of a mountain.

And a large number of dead bodies.

The UAV's camera didn't have good enough resolution to make out how many of the corpses had a dark circle tattooed on their foreheads, but enough of them had staff weapons at their sides for O'Neill to figure that they were Jaffa. None of them seemed to wear the big, bulky armor that was common to Jaffa, but O'Neill also knew that not every Goa'uld dressed their Jaffa the same way. Most of these seemed to be wearing robes and sashes.

But the vast majority of the corpses did *not* have staff weapons at their sides. They were just people and the Reetou had wiped them out, too. Jaffa were one thing — they were enemy combatants, and they were soldiers, trained for battle and knowing the risks.

Civilians, though…

A snarl started to build in O'Neill. It pissed him off so much. The Reetou were sworn enemies of the Goa'uld. They should have been fighting by the SGC's side against the snake-heads.

And they might have, if the main government had actually been able to keep any kind of control, but the rebel faction was too powerful, and they'd decided that the best way to stop the Goa'uld was to wipe out every human population they could, thus denying the snake-heads their host pool.

It was, O'Neill had thought then and now, a particularly stupid plan.

The Reetou would have been far better off allying themselves with Earth and the Jaffa resistance and yes, even the Tok'ra against the Goa'uld. But no, they had to go be mass murderers. Worse, invisible mass murderers.

Carter looked up at Hammond. "No sign of the Reetou, General, but the UAV isn't equipped with T.E.R. technology. It's possible that they completed their mission, used the rings to get to the gate, and went home. There was enough time for that between Captain Patel's return and our dialing back."

Hammond seemed to be considering it, so O'Neill put in his two cents. "There may be survivors hiding, General. Only way to be sure is to send a team."

Nodding, Hammond said, "All right. SG-1 you have a go. SG-22 will back you up and also bring the bodies of SG-7 home for burial."

Grateful, O'Neill said, "Thank you, sir." He didn't want Liza Lagdamen and the families of Castro and Johnson not to have anything to bury. "Carter, let's suit up."

CHAPTER TWO

P3X-418

EVERY TIME Teal'c stepped through the *chappa'ai*, it was with the hope that he would be able to prevent a life from ending.

It was the only manner in which he could even begin to make amends for all the lives he himself was responsible for ending as Apophis's First Prime.

He was not always fortunate enough to do so, but it was never due to an unwillingness to make the attempt on his part.

This particular mission would seem to have few opportunities for such, as the Reetou were very thorough. But there might well be others who — like Captain Patel — had survived. It was Teal'c's fervent hope that he and his fellows in SG-1 would find them.

After going through the gate to the island, Teal'c found himself shivering uncontrollably. The temperatures were quite low and Teal'c felt a bitter cold, worse than he'd felt since his days training with Bra'tac on one of Apophis's coldest worlds.

Looking around, he saw that the rest of SG-1 and all of SG-22 were safely through. Seconds later, the wormhole disengaged.

"Carter," O'Neill said, pointing at the snow-covered ring controls.

"Yes, sir." Major Carter knelt down and brushed snow off the controls. As everyone moved to stand in the middle of the rings, Major Carter entered the sequence provided by Captain Patel.

Within seconds, they were transported to a clearing.

Teal'c raised his *ma'tok*, ready to fire the staff weapon at a moment's notice, and reached out with all his senses — not just his eyes, but also his ears and nose, as Master Bra'tac had painstakingly taught him all those years ago.

Bra'tac had actually forced Teal'c to spar with him blindfolded. Teal'c had initially thought the notion to be foolish, more so when Bra'tac was repeatedly able to move to the side or behind him without his noticing and take him down.

When Teal'c had ripped the blindfold off, Bra'tac had shouted at him to put it back on. "You may find yourself fighting in a room with no light. You may be blinded by external means, or by your own sweat or blood getting in your eyes. In those circumstances, you must rely on the other four senses to guide you."

And so Bra'tac had taught him to listen for footfalls, to feel changes in the wind as the breezes touched his body, to identify things by smell and taste as much as by sight and sound.

Now on Imphal, he saw nothing but snow, heard nothing but the wind, and smelled nothing but the telltale stench of burning flesh. In addition, his symbiote larva was placid, which meant that there were no Reetou in the vicinity.

They quickly came upon several corpses: three Tau'ri and many Jaffa.

O'Neill looked at Teal'c. "Junior feeling anything?"

"My symbiote remains unaffected, O'Neill."

"Good." O'Neill turned to Isabelle Mazursky, the commanding officer of SG-22. "Major, get these bodies back to the gate. Send them through, but I want you four guarding the gate just in case. I'll check in with you in an hour — maintain radio silence unless it's an emergency."

"Yes, sir," Major Mazursky said, then she got her people to work.

O'Neill turned to his team. "Let's move."

Teal'c took point due to his symbiote's sensitivity to the Reetou. Major Carter followed close behind with a T.E.R., then Daniel Jackson, with O'Neill defending them from behind.

Systematically, they moved through the snow-covered ground, eventually reaching a settlement. Neither Teal'c's symbiote nor Major Carter's T.E.R. detected any Reetou.

They then went from structure to structure — mostly residences, plus a tavern — but found only corpses.

After confirming that all those inside the tavern were no longer alive, Daniel Jackson said, "Definnitely the Reetou's usual scorched-earth approach. Or scorched Imphal, I guess." He then moved behind the bar. "Hang on, there's someone back here—I think he's still breathing!"

Teal'c and Major Carter both moved to the area behind the bar to see Daniel Jackson kneeling over a man lying on the floor, broken bottles at his side. Teal'c noticed first that his raiments were finer than those of the other civilians they'd encountered in their search.

And then he felt something else. Hosting a Goa'uld symbiote larve meant that Teal'c could sense other symbiotes. Since this person did not have the mark of a Jaffa, it meant that he was a Goa'uld, likely one of Kali's servants.

Major Carter glanced over at him. "You feel it too, Teal'c?"

"Indeed."

The Goa'uld's eyes fluttered open. "Please, help me." He spoke without the distortion that accompanied most Goa'uld's speech. "I am Ramprasad."

Immediately, Teal'c pointed his *ma'tok* at the man and set it to the ready position, the sides of the muzzle separating with an electric sizzle. O'Neill and Major Carter also raised their P90s.

"Please," Ramprasad said haltingly, "I am not who you think I am."

"He thinks you're Kali's chief flunky on this rock," O'Neill said. "So do I."

"I am that, yes—but I am also of the Tok'ra." His eyes glowed briefly, and then his voice *was* distorted. "My host speaks true. *Shree talak mar shaba.*"

Teal'c knew the phrase—it was nonsense, random words strung together, but the Tok'ra used it as a recognition code.

Major Carter and Colonel O'Neill lowered their P90s, but Teal'c did not entirely trust that this wasn't a Goa'uld who had learned the code phrase.

"What happened here?" O'Neill asked.

"The Reetou. They attacked without warning, without mercy.

And it was *not* their usual mode of attack. There were *dozens* of them."

Major Carter looked at O'Neill. "That matches what Captain Patel reported, sir."

"You are of the Tau'ri, yes? In fact, since this Jaffa is with you, you must be their team number one, led by Colonel Jack O'Neill." Ramprasad looked at Daniel Jackson. "Colonel, by the terms —"

"Hey!" O'Neill cried out. "*I'm* O'Neill!"

Ramprasad bowed his head. "My apologies, Colonel. By the terms of your agreement with the Tok'ra, I ask that you bring me to your base. This massacre will allow me cover to return to the Tok'ra."

"Gee, how lucky for you," Daniel Jackson muttered.

O'Neill snorted and spoke in a sarcastic tone. "The 'colonel' has a point. These people got *slaughtered*."

"I am fully aware of what has transpired here, Colonel. Unlike you, I *lived* among these people. I tried to ameliorate their suffering while living under Kali as best I could, while maintaining my cover. I grieve for them. But I have been undercover for a decade now. The deaths of these people will haunt me for the rest of my days, however it does not change the opportunity it presents."

O'Neill shook his head. "Fine, whatever. We'll get you back to Revanna."

Teal'c bridled, then realized what O'Neill was doing. Zipacna had destroyed the Tok'ra's base on Revanna. If Ramprasad was unaware of that event, then it called his true loyalty into question.

Ramprasad sighed. "I appreciate your desire to test me, Colonel, but I am fully aware that the Tok'ra have a temporary base on Kahsban since the base on Revanna was destroyed."

Now, finally, Teal'c lowered his staff weapon. While Ramprasad could easily have learned of Revanna's destruction from Kali — Osiris had gloated over it to the entirety of the summit that Daniel Jackson had infiltrated, after all — he could not know of the new temporary base on Kahsban. If the

Goa'uld knew of the base, they would have attacked it, and Major Carter had visited her father on that world just one day ago.

Teal'c placed his *ma'tok* on the bar and then reached down to help Ramprasad to his feet.

"Thank you," Ramprasad said, his voice now that of his human host.

"All right." O'Neill moved toward the tavern door. "Daniel, stay with Rampart, here."

The Tok'ra felt the need to correct O'Neill. "It's Ramprasad."

"Whatever. Carter, Teal'c, with me — let's see if there are any more survivors." As O'Neill opened the door, he added, "India's in the tropics. Anyone wanna explain why Kali didn't go to a world that's more like *that*?"

As Teal'c guided Ramprasad onto one of the tavern chairs, the Tok'ra agent said, "Kali's homeworld has a much more temperate climate, Colonel. She colonized Imphal because of its naquadah and trinium deposits. Those mines have long since been emptied, but this world also produces several plants that are useful trade items."

O'Neill just stared at Ramprasad, and then Major Carter spoke. "Sir, you *did* ask."

"I did, didn't I? Remind me not to do that ever again."

"Yes, sir."

"Let's go."

Teal'c left Ramprasad to Daniel Jackson's care and followed O'Neill and Major Carter back into the cold. They searched for another quarter of an hour, finding three more survivors. One was a man who had been protected by his wife; the man then hid under the woman's corpse. The other survivors were two adolescents, one male, one female, who hid in Kali's throne room. That room was located in a redoubt that had been constructed inside the face of a mountain. As with most Goa'uld throne rooms, it remained empty and unused as long as Kali was off-world.

They returned to the tavern with their charges in tow. O'Neill grabbed the radio that was clipped to his jacket. "Mazursky, report."

"All's quiet, sir, but —"

After Major Mazursky's hesitation went on for several seconds, O'Neill prompted her. "But *what*, Major?"

"Sir, the wind sounds wrong."

"*Sounds* wrong?"

"I'm from San Francisco, Colonel, and I know what wind shifts sound like, and what they're like when they're obstructed and funneled. And it's been weird here since we ringed back."

"Have you sent the bodies back?"

"No, sir. Given that we're dealing with invisible aliens, I thought it best not to dial home or use the GDOs until we knew for sure the Reetou weren't here watching. It's just a hunch — wasn't worth breaking radio silence — but I — "

"Major!" O'Neill interrupted. "For future reference, don't explain your every move unless I specifically ask you to." Glancing at Ramprasad, he added, "And sometimes not even then. Stay alert, we'll be there in a few." He let go of the radio. "Let's move."

They moved quickly to the rings in the same formation as before, with Ramprasad and the other three survivors between Major Carter and Daniel Jackson.

As soon as the rings placed them on the island, Teal'c felt a stabbing pain in his abdomen. Dimly, he registered Ramprasad react the same way.

"Carter!" O'Neill cried.

Teal'c struggled to straighten and activate his *ma'tok*. Though the pain caused tears to fill his eyes and obscure his vision, he did see Major Carter wield the T.E.R., revealing six Reetou on the island with them — obviously there was another cell on the world in addition to the one who had fired upon the Thakka.

Fighting through the agony, Teal'c raised his weapon and fired it at one of the Reetou. But the effort took all his strength, and he collapsed to the snowy ground even as his target did the same.

Around him, he heard multiple reports of both P90 fire and Reetou energy weapons. Through the tears of pain that welled in his eyes, Teal'c saw Major Mazursky and two other members of SG-22 shoot two of the Reetou—one of whom managed to wound the fourth member of SG-22 before falling to its death. Major Carter was able to kill two of the Reetou with her T.E.R., while O'Neill shot another with his P90.

The moment O'Neill's opponent fell dead, the pain was gone. Teal'c quickly leapt to his feet and surveyed the island.

The man who had survived the attack and one member of SG-22 were both lying on the ground, wounded. One of the SG-7 body bags was also badly ripped and burned, the corpse inside it further damaged.

Teal'c said, "There are no more Reetou, O'Neill."

"Good. What the hell happened to the whole only-five-at-a-time thing?"

Ramprasad stared at O'Neill. "Is this another of your rhetorical queries, Colonel, or would you like an answer?"

O'Neill stared angrily at the Tok'ra for a moment. "Later. Daniel, dial home."

Daniel Jackson, who had tried to protect the civilian survivors during the firefight, got to his feet and did as O'Neill instructed while Major Mazursky performed first aid on her subordinate. Major Carter was doing likewise on the survivor.

After completing the dialing sequence, the wormhole opened—but Teal'c noticed something odd about the way it did so.

"Something's wrong," Major Carter said.

Turning toward her, Teal'c asked, "Did you notice an unusual sound in the opening of the wormhole as well, Major Carter?"

"I did, yes."

Ramprasad added, "As did I."

O'Neill shook his head. "What is it with everything sounding funny today?" He pointed at Ramprasad. "Don't answer that."

"Sir, with your permission…?" Major Carter held up her T.E.R.

Shrugging, O'Neill said, "Sure."

She aimed it at the *chappa'ai*, revealing several devices placed on it that were just as out of phase as the Reetou.

With a tone of some urgency, Ramprasad said, "Those are Reetou explosive devices. We must make haste!"

"Through the gate, now!" O'Neill yelled.

SG-22 and the body bags went through first, followed by the wounded survivors. Teal'c then followed Ramprasad through the *chappa'ai*, expecting the other three to follow right behind him.

But as his booted footfalls echoed on the metal ramp in Stargate Command, the wormhole suddenly deactivated.

From the control room, General Hammond's voice came over the speaker. "Teal'c, where's the rest of SG-1?"

"They were directly behind me, General Hammond."

"Re-dial P3X-418," the general said to Sergeant Harriman.

Teal'c moved down the ramp alongside Ramprasad, SG-22 (carrying the bodies) and the Imphal survivors crowding ahead of him, and waited impatiently for the dialing computer to do its work.

Eventually, Sergeant Harriman announced that the sixth chevron was encoded.

However, the seventh chevron did not lock and the wormhole did not engage.

General Hammond said, "Dial it again," but Teal'c knew that that was a waste of time. The explosives on the *chappa'ai* had obviously gone off after Teal'c had gone through.

At best, O'Neill, Major Carter, and Daniel Jackson were trapped on Imphal.

At worst, they were dead.

CHAPTER THREE

Stargate Command

THE JAFFA once known as Durga had never been more honored than when the Mother Goddess appointed him to be her new First Prime and be given the grand title of the Thakka. There was no greater glory among any Jaffa, and the Thakka intended to prove his worth in the position.

It helped that his predecessor had become an incompetent fool. The last Jaffa to be known as the Thakka was once one of the finest warriors in the galaxy, but he had refused to acknowledge that he was getting too old for the position. He was nearing his two hundredth year when the forces of Anubis attacked the base at Cerador (though they only later learned that the ragtag collection of Jaffa with the marks of many different gods belonged to Anubis), and his stubbornness and growing weakness contributed to their losses. The old man died that day, along with far too many Jaffa.

When he was still merely a Jaffa in Kali's service named Durga, he and another Jaffa — whose name he was now forbidden to even think — had privately wondered why the Mother Goddess had allowed the Thakka to remain in his position. Other gods allowed their First Primes to retire gracefully when age claimed their ability to lead warriors in battle. Yet the Thakka soldiered on, becoming less and less worthy of his title.

But Durga never spoke of this to any but his friend. His friend, however, spoke of it to many other Jaffa, saying that the Thakka was unworthy and that Kali had made a mistake allowing him to remain as First Prime.

His friend was executed, his *prim'ta* crushed in its pouch, his name stricken from all stories and records, never to be spoken or thought of again. None spoke ill of the Mother Goddess and lived to brag about it.

Soon after his friend's death, Anubis attacked, and the old

fool's incompetence caught up to him. Durga was named the new Thakka, the golden circle of Kali etched on his forehead over the black tattoo that had been there.

Not long thereafter, Kali summoned him to her throneworld of Bhopal and informed him that the Reetou — who had already attacked several of the Mother Goddess's worlds — would attack Imphal. Relishing the opportunity to strike a blow at this ancient enemy of the Goa'uld, the Thakka led a garrison through the *chappa'ai* and prepared for the Reetou.

His preparations were for naught. Even though his Jaffa were armed with weapons that could detect and destroy the Reetou, even though the Thakka and Ramprasad, the Mother Goddess's representative on Imphal, had worked out a strategy that should have defeated the enemy, they were slaughtered. Worse, it wasn't just his Jaffa and Ramprasad who were killed; they were Kali's soldiers and servants — their job was to die for her. But the *Kali Kula*, the people who lived under Kali's domain, were the Mother Goddess's chosen, and his job as First Prime was to protect them. In that, he had failed for all of them were massacred.

It was the Reetou themselves who were to blame. They had been dogged strategists, always engaging in guerilla tactics in groups of five.

But a score of them were on Imphal, to the Thakka's surprise. Never had they attacked in such numbers before. To be fair, never had they needed to, either, as the Reetou's victories were many.

The Thakka took only two small moments of satisfaction from the battle. One was that the Reetou were also eliminated, as his Jaffa — with unexpected help from the Tau'ri — were able to kill almost all of the invaders. There was the one who shot at the *Kula*, whom the Thakka had saved, but that was the final one. It was even possible that the Tau'ri woman killed the last Reetou.

The other moment of satisfaction was that he was able to save at least one of the *Kula*. The Tau'ri woman may not have known that she was *Kula*, and the Thakka may have been allowing himself to be guided too much by her appearance, but he had the need to save *someone.*

Perhaps, because he had leaped in front of the Reetou weapon to save Captain Patel, Kali would forgive him. It was a slim hope, but if at least one of the *Kula* was saved then the Thakka may have redeemed himself. He had hoped to die in a state of grace.

So it came as rather a surprise to him to wake up in an unfamiliar place that was filled with people in strange clothing. He lay on a bed, his arms, legs, and neck all held in place by leather straps, rendering him immobile. Wires were attached to parts of his body, tethering him to odd devices that were not Goa'uld in design. His armor and robes had been removed, and he now wore only a flimsy cloth.

There were also other people in beds. He could only make out the features of one, but the Thakka recalled seeing him on Imphal.

"This — this is not the afterlife," he muttered.

"No, it is not," came a voice to his left.

The Thakka was able to turn his head enough to make out the person sitting next to the bed where he lay. He was a large man, and the Thakka could sense that he was Jaffa even before he noted the golden symbol on his forehead identifying him as a First Prime like the Thakka himself.

Then he recognized the symbol as being that of Apophis, which meant there was only one person this could be.

With a snarl, the Thakka said, "*Shol'va*! Why have you brought me here?"

"I have brought you nowhere," the *shol'va* said calmly. "Captain Patel brought you through the *chappa'ai* so that you might receive medical attention." Indicating the rest of the area with a nod, the traitor added, "In addition, we brought the remaining survivors of the Reetou attack here to be treated."

Hope shone in the Thakka's heart. "There were survivors?"

"Only three besides yourself."

The Thakka let out a long breath. "That is good. If three more of the *Kula* survived, then perhaps Kali will forgive my failure."

"How is it you have failed?"

Looking at the *shol'va* as if he were mad, the Thakka said, "Is it not obvious? The Mother Goddess instructed me to fight the Reetou cell that was invading Imphal. But there were at least four cells on the world, and we were overwhelmed."

"Then the Goa'uld you serve was mistaken."

"You speak blasphemy."

"I speak no such thing." The *shol'va* raised one of his eyebrows. "Were Kali truly a goddess as you claim, she would have known the strength of the Reetou. She did not."

The Thakka opened his mouth to reply, and then closed it again when he realized he had no response to that.

The voice of his friend, the one whose name he dared not even think, came back to him. *"If Kali was truly the Mother Goddess, why does she not see that the Thakka is old and senile?"*

And why did she not see that the Reetou had sent more forces than usual? The Mother Goddess had been caught off guard by enemy strategies before, but those were always from other Goa'uld — other gods. The Reetou, for all that they could do harm to symbiotes, were not divine. They should not have been able to fool the Mother Goddess.

He looked around at the place where he was now held prisoner. Humans of all sorts treated the *Kali Kula* of Imphal. Kali had once told him that only the *Kula* could help *Kula*, that those not under the benevolent protection of the Mother Goddess would never come to the aid of those who were.

Yet here were outsiders helping the *Kula*.

Again, the Thakka's friend's voice sounded in his mind, as it always did when doubts crept in. But now it was much harder to dismiss those doubts.

The *shol'va* kept talking. "You were unsuccessful in destroying all the Reetou on Imphal. In addition to the one who injured you, another group of five were present on the world and set explosives on the *chappa'ai*. Those explosives detonated before the rest of SG-1 could enter."

"Then the rest of your team is dead," the Thakka said simply.

"SG-1 has returned from certain death on numerous occasions. I must be sure that they *are* fallen, and if they are not, I must effect a rescue."

"Why are you telling me this, *shol'va*?" the Thakka asked, though he knew the answer.

"You fought alongside Captain Patel against the Reetou. The Tau'ri have a saying: *the enemy of my enemy is my friend*."

The Thakka smiled. "And you wish to be my friend, do you, *shol'va*? You who blaspheme against the Mother Goddess?"

"The Reetou are a threat to Goa'uld, Jaffa, and Tau'ri alike, and they are very difficult to do battle against. It is in all of our best interests to work together."

"Do you wish to fight the Reetou, *shol'va*, or rescue your murderous comrades? Oh yes," he added quickly, "I'm quite aware of the exploits of your precious SG-1."

"Then you are aware that we have killed many Goa'uld: Ra, Apophis, Heru'ur, Seth, Hathor, Cronu—"

"Enough!" The Thakka turned away.

But the *shol'va* kept speaking. "If the Goa'uld are truly gods, how can so many have been killed by mere mortals?"

He turned back. "I said enough! I will assist you in searching for your teammates, in return for your aid in fighting the Reetou. I do not do this to help *you*, but rather in gratitude to Captain Patel. *She* is a true warrior."

"Indeed."

A voice came from the door. "Teal'c."

The Thakka saw a Tau'ri who was as hairless as the *shol'va*. Captain Patel stood next to him.

Rising to speak to the man, the *shol'va* said, "Yes, General Hammond?"

"I'm still not entirely sold on your plan. We've already lost the better part of two SG teams. I don't want to lose more."

"I agree. That is why I believe the strategy of sending a small strike team of two Jaffa is a stronger one than sending in a large force of Tau'ri warriors."

Patel said quickly, "Two Jaffa and at least *one* Tau'ri warrior. General, I'd like to request permission to accompany Teal'c on his mission. Dr. MacKenzie has cleared me to return to active duty — and I owe it to my team."

Hammond looked at the *shol'va*. "Teal'c?"

"I would be honored to have Captain Patel accompany us."

The Thakka finally spoke up. "As would I."

"Your approval is not required, sir," Hammond said tightly before turning back to his subordinates. "There's still the question of how you'll get to P3X-418 with its Stargate out of commission."

"I can get you to Imphal," the Thakka said.

All three of them turned to look at him.

He continued: "I will give you the address to Aizawl, a minor world in the Mother Goddess's empire, but one that is close to Imphal. The two of you will pose as my prisoners. As First Prime, I will easily be able to commandeer a vessel that will take us to Imphal."

Hammond gave him a significant look. The Thakka was impressed, despite himself. Though he was a mere human, this man Hammond was a true warrior. The Thakka rarely saw such outside of his fellow Jaffa. "And how do we know we can trust you?"

The Thakka said gravely, "Were it just me and the *shol'va*, you could not. But Captain Patel and I have fought side by side and she is *Kula*. If she is part of this campaign than you may be assured that I will protect her."

"That's the second time you've called me that," Patel said. "It sounds like something my aunt used to talk about when she took yoga. I meant to ask Dr. Jackson what it means, but he's not really available now, so I'll ask you — what does that word *Kula* mean?"

Though he would have preferred to tell his story while not

restrained at five points on his body, nonetheless the Thakka answered Patel's question. "Long ago, Shiva ruled the land of Bengal in the valley of the Great Mountain, with Kali by his side as his queen. But Kali did not accept her lot to rule in Shiva's shadow, for she was as much a god as he. When he refused to grant her equal power, she slew him and all those who followed him. Those among the people of Bengal who remained loyal to her, she deemed *Kali Kula*, the people of Kali. On that day the Mother Goddess promised that all the *Kula* would remain under her protection. As the Thakka, I am the instrument of that protection, and while my primary duty is to obey the Mother Goddess, my secondary duty is to protect her people. You are of the people who live in the valley of the Great Mountain, are you not, Captain?"

Patel nodded slowly. "My family's from India, yeah — or Bengal, if you prefer — which is, yes, in the valley of the Himalayas."

"Just so. For your sake, Captain, and yours alone, I will fight alongside this Jaffa as if we were allies."

The *shol'va* turned to his commander. "Do not worry, General Hammond. I will be wary of any treachery from the Thakka and will act accordingly should he not live up to his word."

"I don't doubt it, Teal'c. You have a go."

Hammond took his leave, as did Patel. The *shol'va*, however, remained behind and approached a diminutive Tau'ri. "Dr. Fraiser."

The woman turned to face him. "Yes, Teal'c?"

"Is the Thakka well enough to travel?"

The woman called Fraiser looked over the devices to which the Thakka was currently tethered. "I think so. His symbiote has fully healed and is now working on him. He's not a hundred percent, but he should be soon."

"Then may he be discharged?"

She hesitated, then said, "All right."

The *shol'va* — no, Teal'c; if they were to be allies, he had to think of him as a fellow First Prime, not a traitor, at least for the duration of the campaign — bowed his head in acknowledgment, then went to the bed and released the restraints around the Thakka's wrists, ankles, and neck. Meanwhile the doctor removed the other wires from his person, and soon the Thakka could move freely.

To Fraiser, he said, "I am grateful to you for ministering to my health."

"That's my job." She spoke her reply in an oddly wry tone of voice.

As the Thakka gingerly rose from the bed — his legs were sore and had difficulty supporting his weight initially — he said to Teal'c, "I will require a *ma'tok* and some manner of restraints to hold you and Captain Patel." At Teal'c's expression, he quickly added, "The weapon need not be functional, nor must the restraints be anything other than superficial. It is merely so that we might convince the Jaffa who guard the *chappa'ai* on Aizawl."

Teal'c hesitated, then said, "Very well."

"I also require my armor, robes, and sash."

Nodding, Teal'c said, "I will take you to where they are stored."

As they walked through the corridors of the Tau'ri facility, the Thakka said, "I begin to see why you work with the Tau'ri. They are very accepting of outsiders. I would have deemed this a weakness, but they have allied with the Tok'ra and the Asgard and won many successful campaigns against the gods."

"They have also allied with the rebel Jaffa."

The Thakka stopped walking, and laughed. "I did not believe you had a sense of humor, Teal'c."

"My words were not jocular. There *is* a Jaffa rebellion. Many more join our ranks every day as more and more Jaffa realize that the Goa'uld are false gods."

"You may believe that old wives' tale if you wish, Teal'c, but you are the only *shol'va*."

"Indeed, I am not. Perhaps some day you will realize the error of your ways and join us."

"Join *you*, you mean. Unlikely." The Thakka shook his head. Teal'c's delusion that there was a Jaffa rebellion probably explained why he left Apophis's service. Now he was even more grateful for Patel's presence on the mission.

The *shol'va* was very obviously completely mad.

CHAPTER FOUR

Korvale

MASTER Bra'tac stood and watched the two Jaffa as they circled each other.

Armed with practice weapons — lengths of oak that were carved into the shape of a *ma'tok* — they moved slowly around each other, each gauging his opponent.

Both Jaffa bore the mark of Imhotep, as did all the others who came to watch their sparring. One was tall and bald, the other shorter, stockier, and with close-cropped gray hair.

Bra'tac stood in the crowd, the hood of his cloak hiding the mark of Apophis that would make him stand out here among Imhotep's Jaffa.

The tall one swung the staff toward the shorter one's head, but the short one raised his own weapon horizontally to block it, then quickly swung the base end toward the tall one's stomach. The tall one tucked his body inward to dodge it and flailed with the muzzle end.

They clashed a few more times before the tall one attacked aggressively, putting the short one on the defensive. Bra'tac winced as the short one kept moving backwards while the tall one bore down on him.

Shaking his head, Bra'tac watched as the shorter one desperately threw his staff out to block a strike with the muzzle end of the tall one's staff — only for the tall one to then swing the base end hard at the short one's staff, knocking it from his grip.

And then the tall one pressed his advantage by kicking the short one in the stomach, causing him to fall to the ground. The tall one then stood over the short one, pointing the muzzle end right at the short one's throat.

At which point, the short one grabbed the wooden muzzle and yanked the staff out of the surprised taller one's grip, tossing it aside, following it up with a hard kick to the tall one's belly. Bra'tac nodded his approval.

The kick wasn't much, truly, but it distracted the tall one long enough for the short one to leap to his feet.

Now they faced each other without weapons. Bra'tac recognized the flipping double back kick that characterized the art of *mastaba*, a martial art commonly practiced among the Jaffa. Imhotep had forced all his Jaffa to learn this art, and the shorter one used the kick in question on the taller one, though the latter dodged it with ease.

They continued to spar, with several blows struck to the head by both combatants. The short one kept his distance, so he didn't connect often, and the tall one regularly moved in on him.

Finally, another Jaffa stepped forward. "Jaffa, *kree!*" While Bra'tac knew not the combatants, he knew this Jaffa: Sakmal. Like Bra'tac, he was an old warrior, and like Bra'tac, he had retired as First Prime. What few victories Imhotep could claim were due to Sakmal's leadership.

The two Jaffa stopped their fight and then clasped each others' forearms in a warrior's handshake.

"You fought well," Sakmal said. "I am pleased, and I'm sure Imhotep will be as well."

That was Bra'tac's opening. He stepped forward and threw back his hood. "If this is what you deem fighting well, Sakmal, then it is no wonder that Imhotep's holdings are so few."

Several of the Jaffa moved to a ready fighting position.

He held out both arms, palms-up. "I am unarmed. I have come only to talk."

"Jaffa, *kree hol mel!*" Sakmal cried.

The Jaffa all relaxed slightly, but the ones closest to Bra'tac maintained a defensive posture.

"Very well, Bra'tac. One former First Prime to another — talk. Start by telling me why you dishonor me."

Bowing his head slightly, Bra'tac said, "I meant no dishonor, Sakmal. I only offer constructive criticism of your Jaffa's techniques."

Sakmal pointed at the shorter Jaffa. "Kyylar recently came of age and is now a warrior, and Just'lac has fought beside me for many years. I had nominated him to replace me as First Prime, but Imhotep, in his wisdom, chose Kytano instead."

Bra'tac refrained from commenting—he had plenty to say about Imhotep and Kytano, but not just yet—instead saying, "Just'lac is not a poor warrior, though his overconfidence will be the death of him. He had Kyylar prone and lost the advantage."

Shrugging, Sakmal said, "Had they been fighting with actual *ma'tok*s, Just'lac would have activated the weapon."

"A process that takes a full second and a half, an interval which had not yet passed when Kyylar disarmed him. The *ma'tok* is a weapon of distance—it does no good to be as close as Just'lac was and risk the very outcome that resulted."

Just'lac stepped forward. "Do you take me for a fool, old man?"

"Not at all, unless you ignore my words. A true warrior stops learning ten minutes after he is dead. Sakmal called you a true warrior, so will you heed my words?"

That brought Just'lac up short.

Sakmal was smiling. "Well played, Bra'tac. What other advice would you give my Jaffa?"

Bra'tac started to pace around the circle where the training had taken place. He felt the eyes of Imhotep's Jaffa on him. "When you fought with the *ma'tok*s, Just'lac pressed his advantage by moving forward. Kyylar moved backward."

Now Kyylar laughed. "What would you have me do, old man, move forward as well and let him kill me?"

"No, you should move to the side."

Kyylar's laugh died on his lips.

Bra'tac continued. "When a foe bears down on you and you retreat in a straight line, then the foe will continue to strike until there is no more ground on which to retreat and you are trapped. But by moving to one side or the other, you force your foe to *also* change position. It is but a moment's hesitation for your opponent to shift his footing, but that moment can be an eternity in battle."

Nodding, Kyylar said, "The *shol'va* gives good advice."

"Here now," Sakmal said, "it was Apophis who called Bra'tac *shol'va*, and we've no reason to hew to Apophis's words now, do we? Is there anything else, Bra'tac?"

"Yes." He walked to Kyylar. "Your response to Just'lac's greater reach was to keep your distance."

"Should I have moved to the side more?" Kyylar asked snidely.

Bra'tac actually smiled at that. "No. But Just'lac's longer reach due to his height is an advantage that you facilitate by staying so far. When facing a foe who is larger than yourself, it is better to fight in close quarters, thus negating the advantage."

Kyylar scoffed. "That is absurd."

"Is it?" Bra'tac walked over to Just'lac. "Face me."

Smirking, Just'lac said, "I hope your symbiote is robust."

They stood facing each other in the same circle where Just'lac had fought Kyylar. Bra'tac inclined his head as a mark of respect, and Just'lac did likewise.

And then they both got into a ready position. Just'lac circled Bra'tac, which allowed the latter to simply pivot, holding his ground, waiting for the impatience of youth to take hold, forcing Just'lac to make the first move. This enabled Bra'tac to take Just'lac's measure, noting that he kept his hands low, no doubt to make it easier for him to go into the signature kick of their style.

Eventually, as Bra'tac predicted, Just'lac made the first move. A hundred and thirty years of life had taught Bra'tac the value of patience. Bra'tac easily deflected the punches and strikes Just'lac threw at him and then Bra'tac faked a kick to his knee before striking him on the side of the head.

Just'lac stumbled, and then Bra'tac again pressed the attack. He maintained the general pattern of a fake — sometimes a kick, sometimes a strike — to the middle or lower part of Just'lac's body, then striking his head. Almost every time, he struck.

Then Just'lac rolled around to attempt the *mastaba* double kick. But to Bra'tac it was as if he was moving in slow motion, and he ducked the first kick, raising his hand to grab the ankle of the leg making the second kick. With a simple flick of Bra'tac's wrist, Just'lac was flipped onto his back.

Bra'tac knelt on the youth's chest.

And then he smiled and got to his feet, offering the Jaffa a hand up.

Nodding with newfound respect, Just'lac said, "Impressive."

Turning to face the Jaffa gathered 'round, Bra'tac said, "Always keep your arms where they may protect your head."

One of the Jaffa cried, "We wear helmets!" while another yelled, "Our symbiotes will heal us!"

"When the battle is over, yes, your *prim'ta* will heal you, but in the heat of battle there is no time. As for helmets, they may fall off or become damaged. And wounds to the head bleed greatly. The symbiote will heal a wound and cure an illness, but it will not stop blood from falling into your eyes and blinding you."

"Impressive," Kyylar said bitterly, "that you give advice to those you will *face* in battle."

Taking the cue, Bra'tac answered Kyylar by raising his voice to address all the Jaffa present. "I give you this advice because I do not wish to face you in battle in the service of false gods, but rather fight side by side against them!"

The expected cries came in reply. "Blasphemy!" "*Shol'va!*" "Imhotep will strike you down!"

Staring at the Jaffa who spoke that last interjection, Bra'tac said, "Imhotep will do no such thing, for he is dead! I saw him slain with my own eyes on Cal Mah. And he is not the only Goa'uld to fall."

Kyylar had grabbed a staff weapon and activated it. "You lie, *shol'va!*"

Bra'tac stared at the youth.

Sakmal moved to stand behind Kyylar and spoke a warning. "Jaffa!"

But Bra'tac held up a hand. "Kyylar speaks with the impetuousness of youth — and the brashness of faith. But faith must be earned. Devotion and loyalty must also be earned, not commanded from a parasite who uses a human form to pretend to rule! For years Apophis demanded my fealty as Imhotep demanded yours, both insisting it was theirs by divine right. Yet could any god truly be slain by a mortal?"

"The gods *cannot* die!" Kyylar cried.

Sakmal said, "Bra'tac speaks the truth, my friends. Imhotep himself spoke to me of the death of Ra. I could not believe my ears, and then later I was told of Heru'ur's demise. Imhotep himself told me of this madness! On that day, I began to question what I had always believed."

"Your god is dead, my friends. Join us in liberating *all* Jaffa from the tyranny of the Goa'uld! Join us in—"

Bra'tac cut off his own words as he felt as if a knife sliced through his belly. His *prim'ta* had become agitated to the point of pain.

Struggling to straighten and observe his surroundings, Bra'tac saw that the other Jaffa around him were similarly afflicted.

Once before, fifty years earlier, Bra'tac had felt this type of pain, when Apophis had sent him to a world that had been overrun by the Reetou.

A bolt of energy flew through the air and struck Sakmal in the belly. The old Jaffa fell to the ground and Bra'tac knew that he was dead, as his symbiote pouch had been destroyed by the blast.

The type of weapon used also confirmed Bra'tac's supposition that it was the Reetou, as the blast matched that of the weapons he'd encountered five decades ago.

More blasts came from all around. Just'lac cried, "Jaffa, *kree!*"

Bra'tac heard the report of Kyylar's *ma'tok*, soon followed by several more intermixed with the Reetou blasters. He struggled to pull his own *zat'ni'katel* from where he had concealed it on his armor.

The screams of dozens of Jaffa echoed in his ears as one by one they fell to the invisible foes. Bra'tac closed his eyes. The Reetou were invisible, so sight was of no use to him. He tried to focus past the pain of the Reetou's effect on Goa'uld, past the screams of his fellow Jaffa and the sound of energy weapons discharging.

Then he heard the blast coming straight for him, and he leapt to the ground, the Reetou bolt sizzling overhead.

Even as he dove, Bra'tac aimed the *zat'ni'katel* at the place where the bolt had come from and squeezed the base of the weapon.

But he could not tell if the weapon struck. The Reetou were vicious foes, and Bra'tac did not have the eradication rods that could destroy them.

Opening his eyes, he saw that most of the Jaffa around him had fallen. Just'lac was among them, but Kyylar was still firing randomly.

Bra'tac was about to admonish the youth to fire less blindly when he heard another bolt from behind him. Again he dove, but this time the bolt struck him square on.

The world went dark…

CHAPTER FIVE

P3X-418

THERE WAS no sound, except for a ringing in his ears.

Dozens of images flew through Daniel Jackson's muddled brain at once.

He saw Sha're standing next to Apophis with her eyes glowing.

He saw a room full of people get up and walk out of his lecture.

He saw the Stargate for the first time.

He saw Jack, Sam, Kawalsky and Ferretti step through the Stargate on Abydos.

He saw Sha're attacking him with a hand device.

And then he let out a massive sneeze, which only added to the ringing in his ears. A moment later, mucus-covered snow went into his mouth and up his nose — it felt as if he was being suffocated by a cold towel.

But the sneeze focused him. There had been a strangely muffled explosion — that was why his ears were ringing — just after Teal'c had gone through the Stargate. Now he was buried deeply in a drift of snow.

Desperately, he started digging his way out.

Luckily, the snow itself was soft and fluffy and easily pushed out of the way, so he soon was out of the pile, yanking a handkerchief out of his pocket. Staring down at it, he saw that it was soaking wet and therefore useless.

He had never liked the cold, as winter always kicked up his allergies. There were times when he thought that he pursued Egyptian studies in part because travelling to a hot desert land would be a palliative after growing up in New York, Chicago, and other areas that had significant winter weather.

Sighing, he wiped his nose and mouth with the sleeve of his thermal jacket and took a quick look around the island, only to find that it was incredibly blurry.

Of *course* his glasses had come off when he was snow covered. Squinting, he felt around before he finally located his wireframes, half buried. Brushing the snow off, he slid them on. The right arm was a bit bent, so they were at an angle on his head, but otherwise they were actually in decent shape. *Thank heaven for small favors.*

Now that he could see, he regarded his surroundings.

He saw Sam helping Jack to his feet. He saw the DHD. He saw snow falling from the sky.

He did *not* see the Stargate.

"Oh, this isn't good."

Sam looked up at his voice as she assisted Jack. "Daniel, you okay?"

"I've been better. What happened?"

"We think the Reetou explosive must have knocked the Stargate into the water."

Daniel frowned. "That would be the *icy* water."

Sam nodded.

Jack got to his feet, let out a yelp, and then sat back down on the snow. "Yeah, that ankle's sprained."

"Let me take a look, sir." Sam knelt down beside him and rolled up Jack's left pant leg.

"Carter, trust me, I know sprained ankles and what the difference is between it and a broken one." Jack winced as Sam touched his ankle.

"Doesn't feel broken, sir."

"What did I just say?" He sighed and rubbed the bridge of his nose with his thumb and forefinger. "So this is bad, right?"

"Yes, sir," Sam said. "The wormhole would have absorbed some of the explosion, which is why we were able to survive the blast, but it was obviously still enough to knock the Stargate into the water. There's no way we can retrieve the gate, and there may be no way for anyone to dial in."

"The gate's worked in water, before," Daniel said.

But Sam shook her head. "Given that the SGC hasn't dialed

in, it's a good bet the gate hit the bottom facing down, which is just like it being buried. And even if it's facing upward and the DHD is still close enough to dial out, how would we get to it? We have no idea how deep the ocean is, or even if it's swimmable, and anyway, by the time we got down there we'd probably freeze to —"

Jack held up his hands. "All right, all right, the gate's not an option. What about the rings?"

The ring controls were also buried in snow, so Daniel and Sam brushed them off — Daniel pausing twice more to sneeze — revealing that the controls were intact. But when Daniel entered the code Patel had given them, none of the controls lit up or made a sound.

"Let me guess," Jack said with a sigh.

"The console's dead, sir, yes." Sam pulled out a multitool in order to pry open the casing.

Daniel sneezed again, then looked over at the collection of rafts moored on the small island. To his dismay, they were all damaged, some of them broken right in two. He couldn't tell if it was from the exchange of fire with the Reetou or from the explosives on the gate — not that it really mattered all that much. "I don't think *these* are an option."

"Good news, sir," Sam said. "I think I can fix this. The console didn't take any physical damage, but the blast shook loose a lot of the crystals. I think I can get them all back in place."

"Get to it, Major," Jack said. "There was a whole village back there complete with food and shelter. And I'm betting Ramprasad has some Tok'ra goodies lying around that can help us get out of here."

Daniel looked over at Jack. "Like what, exactly?"

"Any good covert op has an exit strategy, Daniel. And his wasn't to let everyone get massacred by Reetou and go to the SGC, which means it might still be in place." He sighed again. "Of course, that assumes that the Tok'ra *can* run a *good* covert op..."

Before Daniel could reply to that, Sam said, "We've got a bit of a problem, sir." She had moved to the rear of the ring controls and was staring at the lower part of the back of the console. Daniel recalled that that was where spare parts were generally stored.

Jack rolled his eyes. "Of *course* we do."

"There's a hairline fracture in one of the crystals. Unfortunately, it turns out there *was* a part of the console that was damaged."

Holding up both hands, Jack said, "Wait, don't tell me, let me guess — the spot where they keep the backups?"

Sam nodded. "Yes, sir."

"Well, this sucks." Jack sighed and looked around. "Any chance of repairing the rafts?"

Standing up, Sam said, "Maybe, sir. Certainly a better chance than we have of fixing the rings."

As she went over to inspect the rafts, Daniel looked at Jack. "Teal'c went through the gate, right?"

"Right before the earth-shattering ka-boom, yeah." Jack shook his head. "Carter?"

"It's iffy, sir," Sam said from where she was crouching by the rafts. "Based on the UAV's flyover, it's about a hundred miles from here to the coastline nearest to the Imphal settlement. Rowing by hand, it'd take us at least thirty-six hours to get there. I'm not entirely sure we can make any of these raft fragments seaworthy enough to last a day and a half."

"Maybe not, but I'm *completely* sure that if we stay here with no rings, no Stargate, and best of all, no food, water, or bathrooms, we're toast. Get to work. Daniel, give her a hand."

"Uhm, sure," Daniel said. He went back to the rafts, sneezed two more times, and then crouched down next to Sam. "So, uh, how do we do this?"

Sam smiled. "What, you weren't a boy scout?"

Daniel just shot her a look, which was about all that the question deserved in response. "I couldn't even do arts and crafts in summer camp. I just kept drawing hieroglyphics on construction paper and getting yelled at for not making an ashtray like all the other kids."

"I drew constellations on mine." Sam grinned for a moment, then got serious again. "All right, this piece here is almost big enough to fit all three of us, so what we need to do is attach a few smaller pieces to the perimeter."

"Attach how, exactly?"

Sam blew out a breath. "Good question. Not in any way that would really be water tight."

"So we'd be spending a day and a half sitting on the wet spot?"

"Water that's literally freezing." She stood up and turned to Jack. "Sir, I'm not sure that with the tools available we can do this. Unless…"

"Unless what, Major?" Jack prompted.

Daniel stared at Sam, waiting for her to pull a rabbit out of her hat.

"Well, sir, we might be able to cram into the biggest piece left, but we will have to attach a rudder — that won't need to be water tight. But sir, it'll be a *really* tight fit, and with your sprained ankle — "

"I'm willing to take the risk, Carter. Get to it before night falls."

"Yes, sir. Come on, Daniel, we can cannibalize the ring controller for parts."

Daniel had just been about to ask again what Sam would use to attach the rudder, but as usual, she was three steps ahead. "Good thing you're here to think of this stuff."

"Hey, the only reason why I know *how* to mess with a ring controller is because of you, Daniel. And look at all the other skills you've picked up over the past five years."

"True. If I met the me that first went through the Stargate with Jack, I don't think I'd recognize myself. I didn't even know how to load a gun, much less shoot one. Although I did have to — shoot one, that is."

"All right, let's — " Sam interrupted herself and looked up.

"What's that noise?"

Before Daniel could even say "What noise?" he heard it too. A low hum that sounded a lot like a ring transporter activating. But this one was inactive…

Looking up, Daniel saw four rings falling through the snow-filled sky right toward the pair of them. Before he could even think about moving, the rings dropped around him and Sam. There was a blinding flash, and then the rings rose back up.

From Daniel's perspective, it didn't feel as if anything had happened. But when the light dimmed, he found himself aboard a Goa'uld ship — probably a *ha'tak* — surrounded by a dozen Jaffa, who all had the same circular mark as the Thakka on their foreheads, albeit in black. Instead of the usual Jaffa armor, they wore robes in various light colors, similar to those worn by the Thuggees of India, complete with brightly colored sashes which held their *zat'ni'katel*s. The main difference between these Jaffa and the Thuggees were the lack of turbans and the fact that they did wear metal armor underneath the robes. Said armor wasn't as all-encompassing as the Horus Guard or Serpent Guard armor, but it still provided significant protection.

The dozen Jaffa were all pointing staff weapons at him and Sam. "Step out of the rings," one of them said. "Move!"

Daniel shot Sam a quick glance. She gave a curt nod and moved toward the door, since the Jaffa gave no specific direction. Daniel followed her, figuring it was better to be near the exit.

A moment later the rings activated again, revealing Jack kneeling on the deck, P90 raised. But when he saw how many Jaffa surrounded him, he lowered his weapon; twelve against one were bad odds, even for Jack.

"On your feet!" the Jaffa barked.

"Kind of a problem, there."

"His ankle's sprained," Daniel said quickly before the Jaffa could respond. "He can't walk."

With a laugh, the Jaffa spoke in Goa'uld: "The human is weak." Then back in English, "Pick him up, then. Your presence is requested by the Mother Goddess."

"Kali is *here*?" That surprised Daniel, since Patel's report had indicated that Kali was leaving the mission to her First Prime. Then again, it wouldn't be out of character for a Goa'uld to send a force of Jaffa through the Stargate to engage in a campaign and then come by ship to arrive in time to either bask in the glory of victory or punish any surviving Jaffa for failure.

Both Sam and Daniel helped Jack to his feet. Jack rested his arms on the backs of their respective necks and hopped along between them as they walked out of the ring transport room, led by six Jaffa and trailed by the other six.

"You are fortunate," the lead Jaffa said. "Few are graced by the Mother Goddess's presence."

"I could've lived without the grace," Jack muttered.

As they trudged through the corridors, Daniel noted that, while the basic design was the same as every other *ha'tak* they'd been on, there were subtle differences in decoration. The basic décor screamed "Egyptian," for the most part, but Kali had taken on the persona of an Indian deity. Of course, Goa'uld technology mostly looked Egyptian in design, mainly because the most powerful of the System Lords were all of that region: Ra, Anubis, Apophis, Hathor, Bastet — they were all posing as gods from northeast Africa, so the primary design take, as it were, was also similar to artifacts found in that region.

One not-so-subtle difference was that the corridors of Kali's ship were all lined with rugs decorated with intricate patterns that looked to Daniel like they'd been pilfered from the Taj Mahal. It had the dual effect of making the corridors more pleasant and also softening the sound of the Jaffa stomping through them. Daniel had to admire the sense in placing the carpets, since he'd lost track of the number of times they'd been able to hide from approaching Jaffa while in a Goa'uld stronghold simply because they could hear them coming a mile off.

Then again, as Jack had so astutely pointed out to the rebel Jaffa on Cal Mah, the Jaffa weren't so much trained in warfare as they were in terror. Their job was to intimidate the masses into obeying. Using their stompy feet to pound through a corridor may have served as a warning to a trained Air Force team, but it'd be scary as hell to unarmed civilians who'd lived under a totalitarian state their whole lives.

As they walked, the deck seemed to shift and all three of them almost lost their footing.

Sam looked over at Jack and Daniel. "Hyperdrive."

"Yeah, well," Daniel muttered, "not much left for Kali on Imphal."

Soon they were brought to the *pel'tak* and here all pretense of Egyptian décor was out the window. The ship's bridge was covered in red and gold beaded curtains, more of the ornate carpets lined the floor, and translucent silk drapes covered all the available wall space. Kali's throne was a flared chair of red velvet and gold lining. The woman herself, whom Daniel had last seen during the System Lord summit he'd infiltrated, wore the same lavish silk finery she wore at the summit, complete with headpiece, though she was not wearing the beaded face covering that she had favored during the meeting.

The throne itself had ornate writing at the base of it that looked to Daniel's practiced eye like the Devanagari alphabet used to write Hindi, Sanskrit, and many other languages of central Asia. He was pretty certain that the inscription read, 'the Mother Goddess protects.'

As they were turned to face Kali, the Goa'uld herself rested her hands on the flared arms of her throne and leaned forward, eyes glowing.

Like we need reminding of what she is, Daniel thought bitterly.

She looked at him first. "Daniel Jackson. When last we met, I thought you to be a slave of Lord Yu's. You are to be commended on your ability to infiltrate a Goa'uld summit. Few would have dared to even consider such a course of action, and fewer still could do so and live. Well done."

"Uhm, okay." To anyone else, Daniel would have responded

with gratitude, but he was damned if he'd thank a Goa'uld for anything. "Is that why we're here?"

"Hardly. No, I have need of the services of the famous SG-1."

Jack's eyes went wide. "If we're *that* famous, then you probably know that serving you snake-heads isn't exactly something that we do."

Kali turned to face Jack. "Perhaps not, but I believe you may find my terms — acceptable."

"I doubt it."

"We shall see." Kali rose from her throne. "This attack on Imphal is but the latest indignity that the Reetou have visited upon my holdings. I had several scientists working on a method of detecting the Reetou that is more permanent than the transphasic eradication rods. The work was being performed on Anjar. Unfortunately, the base on Anjar was attacked by the Reetou, and both the work and the scientists doing the work were destroyed."

Sam asked, "Did any of the work survive — was it backed up anywhere?"

"No," Kali said with more reluctance than Daniel ever expected to hear from a Goa'uld. "For security reasons, the information was kept in that single secure location. Or at least, what I was *told* was a secure location."

"Well, *that* was bad planning," Jack said.

Kali whirled on him, holding up her left arm. The hand device glowed, and a yellow light went from it to Jack's head. To his credit, Jack didn't flinch or cry out, though he did go rigid as sweat beaded on his brow.

Daniel tensed, and so did Sam, but the Jaffa behind them all activated their staff weapons at once, preventing them from helping Jack.

After only two seconds, Kali lowered her arm. Jack let out a long breath and closed his eyes. "*God*, I hate that..."

Ignoring him, Kali said, "What I wish from you is simple. I referred to you as famous, and one of the reasons for that fame is Major Samantha Carter. I have faith in your ability to come up with a manner of detecting the Reetou."

Sam said nothing, but Daniel could see revulsion warring with flattery at being complimented by a Goa'uld. They usually went the 'puny primitive humans' route.

"In addition, Dr. Jackson, I require your assistance. I desire to negotiate a peace with the Reetou, but actual talks are impossible for me or any Goa'uld or Jaffa in my service due to the adverse effect the Reetou have on us. Therefore I wish you to be my voice."

"Even if I was willing to do this — and I'm really, really not — why me?"

"You negotiated your world's treaties with the Asgard and the Tok'ra, and you assisted in the negotiations with my fellow System Lords to make your world a planet protected by the Asgard."

Jack said, "Never gonna happen. You might as well go ahead and kill us."

Kali smiled in the manner of a predator about to eat its prey. "Oh, I will happily kill *you*, Colonel O'Neill. You see, while your subordinates are of great use to me, you are of absolutely none except as leverage. We are currently en route to Bangalore, one of my subject worlds. If your military training permits your team to allow their commanding officer to be killed, then when we arrive at Bangalore I will simply instruct my *ha'tak* to fire upon the surface and kill the *Kali Kula* who reside there."

"I thought your duty was to protect the *Kula*," Daniel said tightly.

"And I am doing so, Dr. Jackson, by enlisting your aid. But without that aid, the Reetou will kill them just as readily as they slaughtered the people of Imphal, as well as two other worlds of mine, Chennai and Jaipur. It matters not to me by whose hand they are killed — but the thousands of innocents on Bangalore will die, one way or the other, unless you aid me."

"Sounds to me," Jack said slowly, "that you're pretty desperate."

"My forces were already weakened by what I now know to be strikes by Anubis, and no sooner did he cease his attacks after rejoining the System Lords than the Reetou began theirs. I have lost two First Primes in less than a year, and it must stop."

"So you want to have Daniel negotiate for peace while the major gives you a weapon to stop them."

Kali half-smiled. "I already have a weapon to stop them, what I need is to have a more readily available means to target them with it. And I will, of course, allow you to use whatever breakthroughs you achieve for yourselves as well."

Jack rolled his eyes. "I guess we have your word on that?"

"I will offer my word, but I doubt you would accept it. That is why I have had to resort to kidnapping and threats in the first place, Colonel. Nonetheless, in the Reetou we share a common enemy. Does it not make sense to pool our resources against them?"

Daniel felt the need to correct her. "The Reetou aren't our enemy — the Reetou rebels are. In fact, the Reetou government enlisted our help and warned us of a rebel attack on our planet."

"Indeed, doctor, I am aware of your previous encounter with the Reetou. And it does not alter what I said. Yes, not *all* Reetou are your enemy, but the rebels still are. Your alliance with the Tok'ra has not changed your desire to fight the Goa'uld, so you should be equally willing to do whatever is necessary to win your own battle against the rebels." She sat back down on her throne. "I have the technology, and you have the ability to bend it to your will, Major. And Dr. Jackson is uniquely qualified to speak on behalf of *all* those who have been attacked by the Reetou."

"Forget it," Jack said.

"Jack, she'll kill innocent people!" Daniel blurted out.

"Yeah, 'cause *that's* out of character for a snake-head."

"I promise, Colonel," Kali said, "that you will be permitted to return to your homeworld when the negotiations are finished. I have no particular animus for your world or its people. The

Tau'ri have removed many rival Goa'uld from the field of play, and that has only served to improve my own position. Killing the mighty SG-1 would not aid me. I would much rather you were out there, targeting Ba'al and Anubis and the other System Lords who might try to conquer me."

Jack lifted an eyebrow. "So let us go now, then."

"Once you have finished aiding me more directly, I shall. Since you asked, Colonel, I give you my word."

"Like you said, I'm not about to buy the word of a snake-head."

"Very well. Jaffa, *kree!*"

Everything happened very quickly after that: one of the Jaffa activated his staff weapon, Daniel cried, "Wait!" the Jaffa fired his staff weapon, and Jack screamed as the blast from the weapon struck his good foot.

"Take them to a cell. When we arrive at Bangalore, bring them back so that they may witness the carnage for which they will be responsible."

Jack held up a hand and cried out in a strained voice, "Hold it!" Through gritted teeth, he said, "Fine, we'll do it your way."

"On one condition," Daniel added quickly.

"You are in no position to dictate terms, Dr. Jackson," Kali said.

"Very well, then." He spoke in Goa'uld. "It is with great humility and respect that I request that the Mother Goddess please show mercy and heal Colonel O'Neill of his wounds."

Jack stared at him. "Daniel, what was that? Only words I understood were 'colonel' and 'O'Neill.' I'm gonna go out on a limb and say you were talkin' about me."

Daniel nodded. "I asked that Kali heal you."

"And he did so with respect." Kali nodded. "Very well. Jaffa — take Colonel O'Neill to the healing room."

"Daniel," Jack said quickly, "*tell* me I'm not gonna get put in a sarcophagus!"

Disdainfully, Kali said, "Do not worry, Colonel, such as you are not worthy of being placed in a sarcophagus. However, we have more mundane ways to heal your wounds. Take him, and set course back to Imphal. There, Dr. Jackson, you will be able to do your work. I will also provide several of the *Kula* to assist you during the negotiations."

"I'm sorry?" Daniel asked, legitimately confused.

"Since neither I, nor any of the Goa'uld who serve me, nor any of my Jaffa may be present, your assistance will have to come from among the *Kula*."

"O-okay." Daniel wasn't really expecting any kind of help, and he wasn't sure what good the other human slaves would be—except maybe target practice if the Reetou decided not to bother talking.

Two Jaffa took Jack from Sam and Daniel's side. Daniel did not like the idea of letting Jack out of his sight, but they weren't overburdened with choices. Going back to Imphal at least meant that the threat of a mass extermination of the population of Bangalore wasn't as immediate. On the other hand, Kali probably had plenty of Jaffa who could carry out that order over a distance.

Sam blew out a breath. "If nothing else, this means that we'll get a chance to learn more about the Reetou."

"Yeah." Daniel, however, wasn't at all sure that it would do them any good in the end. Kali seemed to be more reasonable than the average Goa'uld, but that just meant it would be easier to let their guard down around her. This was the same System Lord who allied with Bastet and Sobek, only to turn around and kill Sobek during the feast celebrating their alliance. For that matter, she voted to allow Anubis back into the System Lords, even after taking heavy losses from him, though that was more semi-enlightened self-interest than it was a change of heart.

He would have preferred to say all this out loud, but it wasn't a conversation he dared have with the so-called Mother Goddess herself in earshot.

Daniel just hoped that Teal'c had survived the Stargate's explosion. He knew the Jaffa well enough at this point to know that there was no way he'd rest until he tried to effect a rescue of his teammates.

If he was still alive…

CHAPTER SIX

Kahsban

RAMPRASAD had to admit that he had wondered if he would ever see the crystal tunnels of a Tok'ra base again.

A Tok'ra never truly had a home, but the tunnels that they created in their bases gave the familiarity of one. It brought consistency to their lives.

Of course, if you asked the members of the High Council, they would all say that it was for practicality. They lived in the shadows and constantly on the run. The sameness of the tunnels made it easier to set them up quickly and put them to use.

But to both Ramprasad and the symbiote he shared his life with, Maireth, they were home.

The last time he'd set foot in the tunnels, the Tok'ra's primary base was on Telnek. Based on the contact he'd had with his fellow Tok'ra since then, they'd gone to half a dozen different bases over the years he'd been embedded in Kali's service. With the help of the Tau'ri, the Tok'ra had most recently relocated to Kahsban.

He arrived there now, walking through the *chappa'ai* into a dense forest. Within moments he was met by Kelmaa, who emerged from behind one of the larger trees and favored him with her wonderfully wide smile. "It is good to see you, Ramprasad. Far too long has it been since you were among your fellow Tok'ra."

"It is good to be with our people once again, but I'm afraid that this is more than a simple extraction. My time in Kali's service must end — she believes me dead — but there is a greater threat."

Kelmaa nodded. "Come. Several members of the High Council are waiting to see you."

Ramprasad followed Kelmaa to the rings, which were hidden in a small clearing.

Once the ring's lights dimmed and the rings themselves fell, Ramprasad saw the interlocking gray-blue ovals that made up the Tok'ra tunnels, and he felt as though he was releasing a breath he'd been holding for years.

It has definitely been too long, Maireth said into his mind.

Indeed, Ramprasad replied. *After ten long years…*

He wished he could have had a meal and gotten a good night's sleep in the comforting confines of the crystal walls, but alas, that would have to wait. Even if his need to report to the council wasn't urgent — and it most assuredly was — Kelmaa had said that they were already waiting for him. It would be bad form to keep them waiting. Besides which, he had rested and eaten on the Tau'ri base. The food was pedestrian, but nutritional, and the life of a covert operative meant having to take nourishment where one could get it. A Tok'ra could not afford to be a gourmet.

Kelmaa showed him first to where his quarters would be, a section she informed him was carved out for his use right after he contacted them from the Tau'ri base. She then led him to a chamber with a long table that grew out of the floor. Seated around it were Garshaw of Belote, Selmak (who was now in a male host), Malek, Corvina, and Delek. He knew this was not the entirety of the Council, but it was enough of them for a quorum.

Garshaw rose to her feet with her usual grace and elegance. "It is good to have you and Maireth back among us, Ramprasad."

"I wish, Councillors, it was under better circumstances. I'm afraid that the threat posed by the Reetou has increased. They are attacking larger targets — and in larger numbers."

As Ramprasad had expected, it was the latter part that got their attention.

Retaking her seat, Garshaw said, "The Reetou have always been dogged strategists."

"No longer. Perhaps the rebels have improved their position in Reetou society, enabling them to make more frontal assaults like the one on Imphal." He then bowed his head and let Maireth describe the full details of what happened on Imphal.

Selmak's host said, "So they're still targeting civilians, just like they did at the SGC. Trying to deny the Goa'uld hosts."

Malek shook his head. "It is a foolish strategy. The human population of the galaxy is far too scattered for that to be effective."

Maireth remained dominant for the moment. "They are truly indiscriminate. They not only slaughtered all the people of Imphal and the Jaffa Kali sent to defend the world, but also the team of Tau'ri soldiers who happened to come through the *chappa'ai*."

That got Selmak's host's attention, as he leaned forward. "Which SG team was it?"

"I beg your pardon?"

"Which SG team?" The host was surprisingly anxious. Ramprasad knew that the Tok'ra had allied with the Tau'ri, but he'd assumed it to be a political alliance, not one that would engender personal concern on the level being shown by Selmak's host.

Recalling the patch on the sleeves of the bodies that were brought back to Earth, Ramprasad said, "I believe it was team number seven. Three of the four team members were killed by the Reetou."

Relief spread across Selmak's host's face.

Corvina's host Dahla came to his rescue. "Jacob's daughter is a member of SG-1."

Ramprasad blinked. There were obviously significant details of the Tok'ra/Tau'ri alliance he was not made aware of. "It was team number one that rescued me after the attack. Your daughter is a woman with straw-colored hair?"

Jacob — which was apparently the name of Selmak's new host — nodded.

Dahla lowered her head, and then Corvina spoke. "Our latest intelligence reports indicate that the Reetou are now using the planet Anzarra as their new staging area. It is eight months away via ship—the *chappa'ai* is too well guarded to risk travelling by that means."

"We have a *tel'tak* on Gardosh," Delek said. "Anzarra is only two days distant from that world, and it is currently uninhabited."

Ramprasad recalled that that world had belonged to the Goa'uld Apophis, and then was taken by Cronus by force. Cronus then wiped out the population of the world out of spite, as he was apparently only interested in taking the world away from his rival Goa'uld, not actually going to the trouble of administering it once he had it. Apophis never bothered to reconquer it, and the abandoned world soon became a Tok'ra bolt-hole.

Garshaw looked at Selmak's host. "Jacob, you will gate to Gardosh and take the *tel'tak* to Anzarra. You are to perform reconnaissance only. Try to determine the Reetou's plan of attack and where they might strike next."

Jacob said, "You bet."

Turning back to Ramprasad, Garshaw rose to her feet once more. "Ramprasad, the Tok'ra High Council congratulates you on a successful mission, and thanks you and Maireth for your excellent service. Many lives were saved due to your good work. Get some rest, and when you are ready, please make a full report on everything you know about Kali. Now that you may report at your leisure instead of in brief, please include every detail, no matter how insignificant. It will no doubt prove useful in future campaigns against the Goa'uld."

Ramprasad bowed his head. "No doubt. Thank you—thank *all* of you." He smiled. "It is good to be home."

The council all rose and they went their separate ways. Ramprasad moved to catch up to Jacob.

"Selmak?"

Turning, Selmak said, "Ramprasad. It is very good to see you and Maireth again."

"Thank you, we both feel the same. I did not know that we had lost Saroosh."

"She perished shortly before we moved our base to Vorash." He sighed. "I still miss her. She had a superlative sense of humor."

"Your current host is of the Tau'ri?"

"Yes."

Ramprasad chuckled. "That explains his odd mode of speaking. I encountered it when I arrived at the Tau'ri base."

"Jacob agreeing to be my host was the cornerstone of the Tok'ra/Tau'ri alliance. And it has proven to be quite interesting so far."

"Selmak, you and your host should know that, when I departed the Tau'ri base, your daughter and two of her teammates were trapped on Imphal." He quickly told Selmak about the explosives the Reetou had left behind on the *chappa'ai*.

Selmak's host lowered his head, and then it was Jacob who spoke. "Figures that SG-1'd be the last ones through. Did they mount a rescue mission?"

"The commander of the Tau'ri forces — I believe his name is Hammond? — was discussing such a mission with the Jaffa renegade when I departed."

"Yeah, Teal'c wouldn't just sit on his thumbs." He nodded. "Thanks, Ramprasad. It's, ah — it's good to meet you. Selmak thinks very highly of you."

"That is a great honor, indeed."

Ramprasad took his leave of Selmak and Jacob and proceeded to his quarters. He was looking forward to the simple pleasure of sleeping surrounded by the wonderfully familiar ovals that made up the walls and furnishings of the Tok'ra base. The actual location in the galaxy always changed, but the sameness of the walls was a huge comfort after so long undercover.

CHAPTER SEVEN

Anzarra

THE THING that amazed Jacob Carter the most was that he *could* climb a tree.

He'd been sharing his life with Selmak for three years now, and still every morning he got out of bed expecting the snap-crackle-pop of bones and tightness of muscles. Those had been his constant companion as he barreled forward into middle age, but since becoming a Tok'ra there had been no pain.

Well, no internal pain, anyhow. He still had nightmares (and occasional bits of phantom agony) from their imprisonment by Sokar on Netu, during which the torture was incessant.

However, he had recovered from that — and it was a quick, full recovery, as opposed to the half-assed recovery from the accidental knife wound he'd received during training at the Air Force Academy. It took months of physical therapy just to be able to raise his left arm again, and even then it was only about halfway up and there was a scar.

As a Tok'ra, though, he could raise his arm as high as he wanted and the scar was long gone.

Right now, he sat on a thick branch on a tree in a deep forest in Anzarra. Intelligence from a Tok'ra embedded on Bastet's mothership had indicated that the Reetou were using a nearby clearing proximate to the Stargate as their new staging area.

Jacob had gated to Gardosh, and the cargo ship Delek had mentioned was not only there, but intact. Selmak had feared that the *tel'tak* would be damaged, and that they would lose valuable time repairing it, but the only 'damage' was a control crystal that had been deliberately removed to prevent it being taken. Jacob had, at Delek's instruction, taken a replacement crystal along.

From there, it was easy enough to fly under cloak to Anzarra, leave the vessel many miles from the clearing, and go on foot. Between his own Air Force training and Selmak's covert skills, Jacob was able to move swiftly and silently through the forest.

I was never this good when I was a young officer, much less now that I'm an old fart, he had thought with amusement as he'd moved through the trees.

In truth, Selmak had replied, *none of my prior hosts were able to integrate the skills we as Tok'ra have learned for stealth as well as you.*

Jacob had chuckled to himself, as that was amazingly sentimental by Selmak's standards.

Once he had arrived at the clearing he placed several listening devices near the gate, then found a good tree to climb and waited. Patience had never been one of Jacob Carter's virtues, but Selmak had it in spades. Which was good, because Jacob knew that, before the blending, he would've gone bonkers sitting on his butt this long.

Climbing atop vegetation is a common trait among human children, yet I find no memory of you doing so, Selmak said.

Smiling, Jacob recognized that the symbiote was acknowledging his host's impatience by conversing to pass the time. *I was never any good at it. And we didn't have any decent climbing trees around when I grew up. That's why I always tried to find houses that had trees in the yard that you could actually clamber up. Didn't always work, but I tried.*

Your son did not indulge, but Major Carter did.

Jacob's smile widened. *Yeah, Sam was like a monkey in the maple we had in Dover. But she mostly used it to get a better look at the stars.*

Their reminiscence was interrupted by the Stargate activating and a Goa'uld walking through. Neither Selmak nor Jacob recognized the Goa'uld from this distance — he was wearing a hood — but he wore a hand device on his left hand.

It is possible that he is a Tok'ra who is working undercover. Several operatives are under deep cover and could have need to come to this location.

Yeah, but I still don't like it. Best stay put and see how it plays out.

Agreed.

The gate deactivated, and the Goa'uld just *stood* there. Jacob had to admire his discipline. He had a satchel over his shoulder, but he didn't drop it, and remained standing around, just letting it all hang out for whatever reason.

A few minutes later, the gate activated again, there was a pause—

—and then Jacob winced and clutched his belly. They were far enough away that the effect was mitigated, but the rumbling in his abdomen meant that some Reetou had come through the gate.

The Goa'uld held up his hand device, and it glowed. A moment later, five Reetou became visible near the gate. He also dropped his satchel and removed a small globe that neither Jacob nor Selmak recognized.

Oh, this is very not good.

Agreed.

"Welcome, my new allies," the person's symbiote said in Goa'uld. The globe then 'spoke' in the Reetou language. "I received your message that Kali has requested a negotiation?"

One of the Reetou replied, and then the globe rendered its words into Goa'uld in a mechanical tone: "Yes. She wishes the talks to take place on Imphal, the world we recently purged of all potential hosts."

That prompted a laugh from the symbiote. "How the mighty have fallen. There was a time when no Goa'uld would ever negotiate with any but another Goa'uld. But all the truly strong gods are dead, and those that remain are small and foolish. And weak. Kali now claims a seat amongst the senior most of the System Lords, but it was not long ago that she was Shiva's lapdog—when Shiva himself was the most minor of Goa'uld."

Then the Goa'uld threw his hood back, and now Selmak recognized him. *That is Belos. It is no surprise that he is an expert on who might be considered a 'minor' Goa'uld, as he is very minor indeed.*

Jacob frowned. Thanks to Selmak, he knew that Belos had been directly in the service of Ra, assigned to rule a minor world known as Oannes. However, the planet's native population rebelled and Ra demoted Belos to ruling just the city of Babylon — a big step down. And then one of his Oannes slaves, Omaroka, helped foment the uprising that overthrew Ra and forced him and the other Goa'uld to leave Earth.

He had been a minor servant in Ra's retinue since then, never permitted to rule again. However, by all accounts, he remained fiercely loyal to Ra. This is the first intelligence we have had of him since Ra's death on Abydos.

Yeah. I'm guessing he sees the Reetou as his road back to glory.

I believe you are correct, Jacob.

Though if he's so minor how come he *doesn't look like someone stuck a knife in his gut?*

An excellent question — if Belos has found a means of negating the deleterious effect of proximity to the Reetou, we must learn what it is.

"Still," Belos was saying, "Kali's territories are not inconsiderable, and her Jaffa are fiercely loyal. Without her, Bastet's position will be greatly weakened, and she will also be easily eliminated."

The Reetou said, "Negotiation serves no purpose. Your people are a plague that must be eliminated. We care not for the politics, only to eliminate more of the foul creatures and the beings who might serve as their hosts."

"Nonetheless, the negotiations will serve as an effective cover for the final strike against her. Your last campaign was a success, but too many of your own lives were lost."

"We are fully aware of the situation, and do not need you to remind us of our dead. No more Reetou lives shall be lost to your foul kind or to the creatures you take as hosts."

"And no one shall be happier than I when you rid the universe of the Goa'uld," Belos said emphatically. "Once we were great, ruling the entire galaxy as was our birthright, but that might has been systematically destroyed by the Tau'ri. They almost destroyed us when we tried to rule Earth, and it was only after we departed that foul planet that we became great again. Now, since once again dealing with the Tau'ri, we have become weak, fit only to be exterminated by a superior race. Like yourselves."

Jacob shook his head. *What does he wanna do, go back to the good old days when the Goa'uld had Unas hosts?*

Selmak said nothing, recognizing the question as rhetorical.

The Reetou's voice was still rendered mechanically, but Jacob imagined he could hear a tinge of annoyance even in the computerized translation. "We do not wish to be flattered by the likes of you. Your continued existence has only been due to your usefulness. Be careful that it does not end."

"Then behold my latest piece of usefulness." Belos shrugged the satchel off his shoulder. "This is an explosive that, when armed, moves into the same dimensional plane as you. It remains there until it explodes, when it transitions back to our space. But the explosion will only affect our space. You could be right at the explosion's epicenter and it will not harm you in the least."

Crap.

As usual, Jacob, you sum up the situation succinctly.

"Yes. We find this useful. Continue to aid us and you will continue to live."

"Continue to harm the Goa'uld," Belos said with a wry smile, "and I will continue to aid you." Then Belos walked over to the DHD and dialed out. He had to lower his hand to do so, which meant that the hand device wasn't keeping the Reetou visible anymore. But the roiling in Jacob's gut told him that they were definitely still around. That it was only discomfort meant that, at least, they weren't getting any closer.

The gate opened, stayed active for several seconds, and then deactivated. Belos stayed at the DHD the entire time, but Jacob stopped feeling like he was being stabbed.

Thank God, the overgrown insects have vamoosed.

We should attempt to capture Belos and interrogate him.

Jacob nodded, even though he hardly needed to do that for Selmak's benefit, and started to hop down from the tree even as Belos waited for the gate to deactivate and then began dialing another address.

When he was halfway down one branch, Jacob heard the distinctive sound of a staff weapon activating.

"Do not move," came a very familiar voice from the other side of the clearing that held the Stargate.

A moment later, Bra'tac came out from behind a tree with his staff weapon aimed at Belos. To his credit, the Goa'uld stopped dialing and held up both hands.

Since blending with Selmak, Jacob had had very few causes to gape, as the Tok'ra had such a vast store of knowledge that very little surprised him anymore. This was, of course, in direct contrast to the twenty-four hours or so before he blended, when he learned of Stargate Command, that there was life on other planets, that there were megalomaniacal beings out to rule the galaxy, and that his daughter was embroiled in all of it. That was more surprises than anyone should have in a lifetime, much less a day, and he was grateful that sharing his life with an old, wise Tok'ra enabled him to be mostly shock-free.

But Jacob and Selmak had made a thorough investigation of the area near the Stargate before planting the listening devices, and neither he nor the devices he placed had detected any sign of Apophis's former First Prime.

Yet there he was, holding a staff weapon on Belos.

The Goa'uld scoffed. "You cannot harm me with your mortal weapon, Jaffa."

"The crystal that activates your force field has been removed, no doubt replaced with whatever you used to safeguard yourself from the Reetou's effects on your symbiote. Shall I test my theory?"

Jacob shook his head. *He's good.*

He would have to be to stay alive as long as he did after betraying Apophis.

Bra'tac then called out toward Jacob himself. "You may as well come out, Tok'ra! I have this one well under control."

This surprised Jacob less. Just because he didn't see Bra'tac didn't mean the Jaffa didn't see him.

"Nice job," Jacob said after hopping out of the tree and approaching the clearing. "I'm guessing you heard their conversation, too?"

Bra'tac simply nodded. Now that he was close enough, Jacob could see that Bra'tac's armor was dented and scorched, and he had several wounds that were in the early stages of healing.

Selmak nudged him, and Jacob allowed him to come to the fore. "What is it you wish to accomplish by allying yourself with the Reetou rebels, Belos?"

Bra'tac's eyes widened for a moment, and Jacob felt a tiny bit of mock triumph. The Jaffa hadn't recognized the Goa'uld in question.

Good to have something over on him, for a change.

Belos chuckled. "As usual, you Tok'ra have faulty intelligence — which is why you continue to fail. The Reetou with whom I just met are rebels no longer — they have overthrown their pitiful ruling council."

Dammit. This is a helluva lot worse than we thought.

Yes. Aloud, Selmak asked, "Do you truly believe helping them will improve your position with the System Lords?"

But Belos just shook his head. "You are a fool, Tok'ra. I have no interest in currying favor with the preening, posing imbeciles who call themselves 'System Lords'. My loyalty was to Ra, and those who swore fealty to him. Those Goa'uld are dead, and the pretenders who now rule are pale shadows of Ra. None of them are worthy of the title System Lord, nor are they worthy of continuing to draw breath. They should all perish — and when the bomb I gave the Reetou destroys Kali, her Jaffa, and her Tau'ri negotiator, it will be — "

At the word *Tau'ri*, Jacob all but forced himself back to the fore and grabbed Belos by his cloak. "Tau'ri? What're you talking about?"

"Neither Kali nor her Jaffa may be in the Reetou's presence without suffering — as you both do, as you did not reveal yourselves until they departed — so she has conscripted one of the Tau'ri to speak for her."

Kali has had no dealings with your homeworld, Jacob.

I know, but Ramprasad said that Sam, Jack, and Daniel were left behind on Imphal. "Which human has she — she 'conscripted'?"

"What does it matter?" Belos asked dismissively. "He'll die."

If it is a male, Jacob, then Major Carter is not the representative.

Yeah, but I got me a gut feeling that it's the one human Kali has met, *thanks to us.* Jacob pulled on the cloak, yanking Belos closer to him. "*Tell* me."

"I do not know his name, but he is one of the humans who killed Ra."

It would appear you are correct, and it is Dr. Jackson.

Yeah.

Jacob tossed Belos to the ground. "You cannot stop the Reetou, Tok'ra. Both of you would do well to — AAAARRRRRRRR!"

Whatever it was Belos thought it would be well for them to do was cut short by Bra'tac wounding him with the staff weapon.

Shooting Bra'tac a look, Jacob said, "What, you didn't wanna hear him rant and rave?"

The look on Bra'tac's face spoke volumes as he lowered his staff weapon. "He had provided all the intelligence we would receive from him."

Selmak came back to the fore. "That is true. And we now know a great deal more." He reached for Belos's left hand to remove the *kara kesh*. "This will prove useful."

Then Selmak let Jacob take the wheel again. "What the hell happened to you?" he asked Bra'tac.

"The Reetou. They attacked the world on which the last of

Imhotep's Jaffa were training. I was attempting to recruit them for the rebellion now that their false god is dead by Teal'c's hand."

Jacob nodded. When she visited him a few days ago, Sam had told him about Imhotep posing as his own First Prime in an attempt to destroy the Jaffa rebellion.

Bra'tac continued. "My fellow Jaffa were killed, but I managed to escape. I was able to determine that this location was a Reetou staging area, and came here in a *tel'tak*."

"I came in one of those, too. So we'd better beat feet to Imphal and save SG-1's butts."

"We will take your ship," Bra'tac said definitively.

Jacob frowned. "Okay."

Bra'tac then looked away. "I was forced to — *borrow* a vessel that was under repair at the time. My landing was far from optimal."

Shaking his head, Jacob said, "Fine, let's move. It's three days to Imphal, and then only if we floor it."

CHAPTER EIGHT

P3X-418

SAMANTHA Carter was like a kid in a candy shop.

Kali had installed her in a laboratory on Imphal. She had been hoping that the lab would be on the mothership, but the Goa'uld was smart enough to put her instead on the planet, which had nobody left alive on it, a sunken Stargate, and a busted ring transporter.

"This," Kali had told her after they'd ringed down to the surface, "is what is left of the laboratory on Anjar. Much of the equipment was damaged. The only intact items are from a backup storage locker that was left untouched by the Reetou assault."

"I'm gonna need some help."

That had prompted a glare from Kali. "I beg your pardon?"

"I need a — a lab assistant. Just to organize all this stuff, I'll need an extra pair of hands. Either Colonel O'Neill or Daniel. Unless you want to assign one of your Jaffa."

Sam had feared that Kali would go for the latter option, but she agreed to send the colonel down. "Dr. Jackson," she had said, "is readying himself for negotiations with the Reetou."

After Kali had taken her leave, Sam started organizing the equipment. Initially, it was a matter of separating what was intact from what wasn't, which was simple enough. Quite a bit had been damaged by weapons fire. Based on the burn marks and patterns, both Reetou blasters *and* staff weapons had been used, which meant, at least, that the scientists — or, more likely, the Jaffa guarding them — didn't go down without a fight.

After that, it was a question of figuring out what each item was.

As she studied one oval piece with a jewel at its center, a Jaffa appeared at the door, gripping the colonel with his right hand, staff weapon in his left. To her delight, O'Neill was standing on his own two feet.

Or, rather, stumbling, since the Jaffa literally threw the colonel into the room. O'Neill managed to keep himself from falling completely to the floor, and got himself upright in a second before Sam could even offer him a hand.

Brushing off his shirt and pants with his hands, he said, "That's the last time I use your cab service. And forget getting a tip!"

Unable to help herself, Sam smiled.

The Jaffa said nothing, simply turning to leave after nodding to the Jaffa who guarded that same entryway.

"Carter." The colonel nodded to her. "Not that I'm not happy to be out of the cell, but what am I doing here?"

"I needed an extra pair of hands, sir. And I figured better for you to be here with me than sitting in that cell."

"Yeah, this is a *huge* improvement."

Glancing around, Sam shrugged. "Well, that door you just got tossed through — "

"Literally," O'Neill muttered with annoyance.

" — is the only way in or out. No windows, no air vents bigger than a penny, plenty of places to put cameras. Though the Goa'uld don't usually go in for that sort of thing."

The colonel nodded. For whatever reason, the notion of surveillance in cells had never occurred to the Goa'uld. That lack had saved SG-1 on more than one occasion.

Carter glanced down at O'Neill's legs. His pants were still torn where the staff weapon struck him, but the leg underneath it was perfectly normal and unscarred. "Healing device?"

O'Neill nodded. A Goa'uld healing device wasn't as all-encompassing as the sarcophagus, but it could take care of a lot of wounds. "They threw me into a room, some snake-head stared at me like I was the fly that got in his soup, he ran the thingie over my leg, and suddenly I could walk again. Never even said a word the whole time." He tilted his head thoughtfully. "Actually, it was kinda nice, meeting a Goa'uld who *didn't* love the sound of his own voice."

"I can imagine, sir."

The colonel walked over to the table where Sam was sorting stuff. "Have any idea what this crap *is*?"

"Some of it." She smiled. "Four years ago, I'd probably be giving it the same blank stare you're giving it now, sir."

O'Neill looked up. "It isn't so much a blank stare as a poker face."

"Of course, sir," she replied politely. "In any case, I've spent enough time with alien technology that I believe I can determine what they all do — and how they can help us fight the Reetou."

"You mean help a snake-head fight the Reetou. This isn't exactly furthering our cause."

"Yes, sir, I know, I just — "

O'Neill shot her a look. "You're not buying her line about sharing this with us when it's all done, are you?"

"Of course not, sir, I just — I prefer to think of it as doing it for us. As it is, working for a Goa'uld is…"

She trailed off, but O'Neill just nodded. "Right there with you, Major, believe me."

"It's not just that, it's…"

Again, she trailed off, and the colonel said, "Major, is there something you want to say?"

"There — there isn't. Let's just get this done?"

O'Neill shrugged. "Sure."

Sam was grateful that the colonel didn't push, since if he did ask what was bothering her, she would have been duty bound to tell him.

They worked in companionable silence for a while as Sam finished organizing what they had.

The colonel found one piece that was a bit damaged: an elongated crystal embedded in what looked like a brass ball. "This looks like something Colonel Mustard used to kill someone with in the parlor."

"Wait a second." Sam rummaged through the pile of intact

items and found what she had seen at the beginning of the process: a brass box that had a circular indentation that was the same size as the ball at the end of the crystal.

Holding out her hand, Sam asked, "May I?"

"Don't let me stop you," O'Neill said as he handed the crystal over. "The crystal with the ball — or, dare I say it, crystal ball — is all yours."

Sam sighed. There was no way she was going to be able to think of this as anything other than a 'crystal ball' now.

Sure enough, the brass ball fit perfectly into the indentation in the box, and as soon as she placed the former into the latter, the crystal glowed and a holographic display appeared next to it.

While Sam didn't have any kind of fluency in Goa'uld, written or spoken — that was Daniel's bailiwick — she did know the number system they used, since that was critical to understanding their technology.

And what she saw now were *lots* of Goa'uld numbers, as part of formulae.

"Please tell me this makes something like sense, Major," O'Neill said plaintively.

"Yes, sir. It looks like Kali was wrong about there not being a backup. If I'm reading these numbers right, then these equations apply to the fabric of space. It looks like her scientists were trying to find a way to bring the Reetou completely into phase with normal space."

"And that's good, right?"

Sam smiled. "Yes, sir. I think they were trying to find a way to make it permanent, so the Reetou would always be visible and tangible." She peered at the formulae at the bottom, and then her face fell. "Unfortunately, from the look of things, it requires a warping of space that would cause a cataclysmic explosion. I'll need to look into it some more."

"Knock yourself out, Carter."

"Yes, sir." Sam hesitated. "Sir, what if this does work?"

The colonel frowned. "Whaddaya mean?"

Sam took a deep breath and then exhaled. "If I make this work and make the Reetou permanently in phase with us, the Goa'uld can use it to wipe them all out. And you know they won't just target the rebels — they'll be indiscriminate. For that matter, what if by some miracle Kali *does* keep her word and lets us take this tech back with us? If the NID gets their hands on it…"

"One thing at a time, Major. Get it to work, first."

Sam nodded. "If I can, sir. I just don't like the idea of doing it for the Goa'uld — or the NID, for that matter."

"Forget about the NID. We took care of Maybourne and we took care of Simmons."

"Yes, sir." Sam wasn't as sanguine, though it was the colonel himself who had exposed both Maybourne's covert Stargate operation and Simmons keeping a Goa'uld prisoner. The former was a fugitive and the latter was in prison, both charged with treason. Still, Maybourne's ousting had just led to Simmons rising to power, and with the NID, the crap seemed to always rise to the top.

A few hours passed, and she managed to figure out how far Kali's scientists had gotten before the Reetou hit them. She had the equipment to build another phase-shifter — the one they'd constructed was so much slag after the attack — but it would take time.

Before she could start, however, a Jaffa came in with a tray. "Here is your meal." He dropped the tray on a table and took his leave.

O'Neill called after him. "Keep up that attitude, it'll come out of your tip!" He went to the tray and popped what looked like some kind of purple vegetable into his mouth. "Well, this is awful. Crappy food *and* crappy service. Definitely not coming to this restaurant again."

They still sat down to eat. The colonel had been correct, the food was horrible, but they had to eat *something*. She managed to choke it down. The tray also had a pitcher of what turned out to be some kind of fruit juice that managed to be too sweet *and* with a bitter aftertaste all at the same time.

After swallowing the last bite of the purple vegetable, O'Neill said, "This really sticks in my craw."

Sam smiled. "I'm guessing you don't mean the food, sir?"

"I mean working for the snakeheads. I don't buy this I'll-let-you-go-when-it's-done act for a second."

Sam sighed. "Neither do I. But we don't have a choice. Besides, this is some really interesting technology Kali is letting me look at here."

The colonel waggled a finger at her. "Watch it, Major — don't get sucked in."

"Oh, I won't, sir. I learned that lesson a long time ago."

"What do you mean?"

Smiling, Sam asked, "Remember that time I hustled those guys at pool?"

"Those would be the guys we beat the crap out of at O'Malleys?" O'Neill asked with a grin.

"Right."

"I thought that your pool mastery was from the Tok'ra's hinky bracelets."

Grinning, Sam said, "No, that was all me." Then the grin fell away and she covered her hesitation, and the reawakening of awful memories, by taking another bite of food. "After my mother died, my father and I — we didn't talk much. Neither did my brother and I."

Unbidden, the memories all came back — the day her father told her that Mom had died. The day everything changed between them.

She went on. "So I spent a lot of time on my own. I taught myself how to play pool — it was fun, like geometry."

"For the record? Your definition of 'fun' differs from mine."

Were he not her commanding officer, Sam might have pointed out that the colonel's ideas of fun didn't intersect all that much with hers, either, but he was, so she just said, "Yes, sir. Anyhow, pool tables tend to be in places that — well, they don't have the nicest people around. It would've been really easy to fall in with a bad crowd. And I did hang out with some of them for a while. That's where I first learned about motorcycles."

O'Neill was grinning.

"Sir?"

"Always wondered where the bike love came from. Also, I'm trying to imagine you as a biker chick. Image isn't really taking. So what happened?"

"Nothing, really." Sam shrugged. "I mean, I was tempted by that life, but I realized that it was a bad path and I needed to stay away from it. And then I enrolled in the Academy."

"Set you on the straight and narrow, did it?"

Sam looked away. "Well, eventually. Let's just say there's a reason why I wanted to mentor Lieutenant Hailey."

The colonel nodded. Jennifer Hailey had been a troubled cadet whom Sam had all but rescued from being expelled from the Academy. She'd graduated with honors and had been, at the recommendations of both Sam and O'Neill, fast-tracked to the SGC.

"That first year, I still had some resentment toward Dad. Mostly because I was a legacy, and half the people who taught me knew Dad and kept comparing me to him — the same way all of Hailey's professors compared her to me. But by second year, I'd settled down, especially with everything I was learning there." She didn't tell the colonel the other part — that she got into a couple of fights that first year, too. They were never reported, thankfully, as they might have gotten her expelled. Of course, that was mainly because she won all of them, and the boys she fought were too embarrassed to say they got their asses kicked by a girl. But that stopped by her second year.

Out loud, she continued: "One of the reasons why I got so interested in math was because numbers actually made *sense*. Mom dying, Dad and Mark fighting — I couldn't explain any of that, but I could explain numbers. I could *understand* them.

But then at the Academy we started learning about astrophysics and the Uncertainty Principle and Schroedinger's Cat and the double-slit experiment — it was amazing. Math was just as crazy and complicated and variable as real life."

O'Neill frowned. "And that made things *better*?"

"I guess?" Sam shook her head. "It helped that I was in a more structured atmosphere, and that I was older, and that I'd finally started to forgive Dad."

O'Neill swallowed the last of the food they had on their plates. "Well, much as I'd love to hear more about wacky teenaged Carter, you'd best get back to that crazy and complicated and variable math so we can get the hell out of here."

Sam smiled and drank the last of her fruit juice. "Yes, sir."

As they rose from the table where they'd been eating, the Jaffa who'd brought their food returned with two other Jaffa who were carrying a pallet bearing something wrapped in a sheet. They set it down and one of the Jaffa unholstered a T.E.R.

The first Jaffa silently cleared the table of the remains of their lunch, and then nodded for one of the others to remove the sheet, revealing a Reetou corpse.

O'Neill looked up at the first Jaffa. "Dessert?"

"The Mother Goddess thought you would desire a test subject."

Sam nodded. "Useful."

The third Jaffa lowered the T.E.R. and handed it barrel-first to the colonel. "You will need this."

To prove the Jaffa's point, Sam could no longer see the Reetou.

"Be advised," the first Jaffa said, "that the weapon's function has been neutralized."

"Really?" O'Neill took the T.E.R., pointed it at the Jaffa and pressed the activator.

Nothing happened.

The Jaffa smiled. "Did you truly think we would simply hand you a weapon?"

The colonel shrugged. "Worth a shot. Or a lack of one, as the case may be."

"Even if the weapon had been active, you would have been struck down by my fellow Jaffa the moment you fired."

O'Neill smiled. "*Still* worth a shot."

The Jaffa snorted, muttered words in Goa'uld that Sam was pretty sure translated to something along the lines of, 'Humans are morons,' and then the three of them left.

Sam looked at the seemingly empty table. Obligingly, O'Neill activated the T.E.R., making the Reetou corpse visible.

"Now," O'Neill said, "it's a party."

Raising her eyebrows and blowing out a breath, Sam said, "Yeah. I better get to work on scanning it."

CHAPTER NINE

A Tok'ra *tel'tak* in hyperspace

MEMORIES swam into the mind's eye of Master Bra'tac as he slowly awakened from *kelnorim*.

The meditation itself was a state of blissful nothingness. Jaffa who achieved *kelnorim* emptied their minds, thus cleansing their spirits and renewing their bodies. It enabled warriors to face their next trials fresh.

However, the intermediate state, both when one first went into the trance and particularly when one came out of it, was fraught with memory and distraction.

The memories came and went like quicksilver, flitting to the fore of his conscious mind and then receding just as fast.

…the day his father told him that the Goa'uld were false gods and that one day the Jaffa who threw off the shackles of servitude would find their way to the paradise of Kheb.

…the day he met Mowren.

…the day Apophis named him First Prime, which was a proud day — not because he was serving a god, for he knew better, but because he was in a better position to aid those oppressed by Apophis's madness.

…the day he took on Moac as an apprentice, thinking him to be a strong warrior and a noble soul.

…the day he met young Teal'c on Chulak, the boy filled with thoughts of vengeance against Cronus for the death of his father.

…the day Apophis made Teal'c his new First Prime following Bra'tac's own retirement from that position.

…the day Mowren died.

All those memories and more assaulted Bra'tac in an instant, and then he was awake.

Blinking, he took in his surroundings. The Tok'ra had allowed Bra'tac to use the cargo compartment for *kelnorim*, saying he himself could, as he put it, "sack out up front."

Bra'tac had only brought a few candles with him, which was probably why the memories were so much more intense than usual. The smell of the melting wax and the burning wicks always helped calm his mind.

Based on how far down his *salvak* candle had burned, he had been in *kelnorim* for three hours. Based on how readily he rose to his feet, it was more than enough time to refresh him. A quick check of his face with his fingers revealed that his *prim'ta* had healed all his wounds suffered at the hands of the Reetou.

After blowing out the candles and storing them in his satchel, Bra'tac went to the forward compartment.

Jacob Carter turned and smiled at Bra'tac as he entered. "Good, you're awake. We should arrive at Imphal in two hours."

Bra'tac frowned. "I was only in *kelnorim* for three hours." It was not a question — his *salvak* had never been wrong before.

"Yeah," Jacob Carter said with a small smile. "I've been flooring it — running the engines at a hundred twenty-five percent." The smile fell. "That's my daughter on Imphal."

Bra'tac nodded and took the co-pilot's seat. "You will not have the opportunity to rest."

Jacob Carter shrugged. "I may catch a quick nap now that you're up, but I'll be fine. I slept on the trip to Anzarra." He glanced over at Bra'tac. "Good dreams?"

"Jaffa do not dream as humans do. Sleep is unnecessary and *kelnorim* is a deep, dreamless state." Bra'tac hesitated. "Although we do often see memories upon awakening."

"Good ones?"

"A few." Bra'tac allowed himself a small smile of his own. "I was reminded of Mowren. It has been some time since I last thought of her."

"Old girlfriend?"

"Not as you would define it." Bra'tac shook his head. "I was very young — I had only just finished my training and was on my first campaign in the service of Apophis. We had been sent to defend a naquadah mine against Cronus. The world had originally belonged to Cronus until the naquadah ran out, at which point he loosened his hold on it sufficiently that Apophis was able to take it from him. When Apophis discovered a fresh vein of the mineral, he created a mine — and sent his Jaffa to defend it in case Cronus decided to take the world back."

"And did he?" Jacob Carter asked.

Bra'tac nodded slowly. "On the evening of our arrival, I went off duty and reported to the inn where we were to be fed. There was a woman serving the food that day. She was magnificent — skin the color of dark wood and a smile radiant as the sun." Bra'tac shook his head ruefully. "I fell in love with her instantly."

"So did you talk to her?"

Shaking his head, Bra'tac said, "Not for many days — except to express my gratitude for the food she served, of course. Finally, on the fifth day, I asked her what her name was. 'I am Mowren,' she said, 'and you are Bra'tac of Chulak.' I was surprised that she knew my name, for I was but a lowly Jaffa among many whom she served, and told her as much. She said to me, 'Of all the Jaffa, you are the only one who thanks me. So I asked who you were, and your First Prime told me.'"

Jacob Carter grinned. "A match made in heaven."

Bra'tac's own face fell. "Sadly not, though her words made me love her even more. I resolved to court her, for all Jaffa are encouraged to have families so that more worshippers — and more potential Jaffa — may be born. But the next day was when Cronus attacked. His Jaffa came through the *chappa'ai*, his gliders strafed the surface, and his *ha'tak* fought in orbit against ours.

"Our forces won the day, driving Cronus from the world and maintaining Apophis's hold on the mine. But the inn was one of the places targeted by the gliders. When the battle was done, the First Prime — knowing of my feelings and of Mowren's — released me to dig through the rubble of the inn for survivors. It was there that I found her broken body, the light of her smile dimmed forever."

Jacob Carter said nothing, simply giving him a look of sympathy.

"In truth, that was the day I realized that Apophis was at the very least a capricious god. For the first time, I questioned him. I had fought well and defeated his enemy. I was loyal to him. Why, then, did he permit Mowren to die when we had only just found each other?" Bra'tac shook his head. "I have lived for over a century since that day, Tok'ra, and never have I loved another as I loved her."

"That why you never started that family you said they encouraged?"

"Indeed." Bra'tac smiled then. "Unless one counts the Jaffa I have apprenticed. They became my children — and I am proud of many of them, especially Teal'c." He shook his head. "It has been years since I told anyone that story. I never even spoke of it to Teal'c."

"Yeah, well, kids don't always get it. They always figure they're smarter than us." He snorted. "'Course in my case, she really *is* smarter than me."

"Major Carter's strength and intellect are renowned. You should be proud."

"I guess. I wish I could take more credit for it. You're lucky, you got to mold Teal'c, train him. With Sam, it all pretty much happened on its own."

Bra'tac stared, confused, at the Tok'ra. "Did Major Carter not also enter the same unit as you?"

"Well, yeah, she joined the Air Force like I did, but it was more despite me than because of me. Honestly, we barely even spoke to each other after her mother died. Not that I blame her. The accident was my fault."

Frowning, Bra'tac asked, "Did you cause the accident?"

"Not exactly." Jacob Carter squirmed a bit in the pilot seat. "I was supposed to pick her up, but something happened at the base that distracted me. She called from a pay phone wondering where I was, and she said she'd just call a cab when I told her I was still on base. The cab got T-boned by a truck on the way to our house."

"Might that still have occurred had you been the one to convey her?"

Jacob Carter shook his head. "Not a chance. I'm allergic to traffic lights," he said with a wry smile. "I always take the back roads. I wouldn't've been anywhere near where that donnybrook happened."

As usual when he spoke to humans, Bra'tac only understood about a quarter of what Jacob Carter said, but he was able to ascertain the meaning even if the specifics were beyond him. "It is a terrible thing to lose the one you love."

"Yeah, well, like you, I haven't talked to too many people about that day. Selmak groks, but he shares my head. The other Tok'ra—I'm not sure they'd really get it, y'know? Especially since I didn't just lose my wife that day—I pretty much lost both my kids, too."

"I am honored that you shared with me, then."

"Yeah, well, I figured you *would* get it." He chuckled bitterly. "It's funny, I can't for the life of me even remember what it was at the base that got me so sidetracked." He sighed. "Anyhow, Sam kept wandering off on her own, hangin' out in places I wasn't too thrilled with. I tried to warn her, but I was pretty much the last guy on Earth she'd listen to at that point. If I told her the sky was blue, she'd convince herself it was green. So I let her make her own mistakes."

"That is," Bra'tac said gently, "sometimes the only alternative."

"Still stinks, though. But she found her way eventually. Kinda nice when your kid outdoes your expectations, ain't it?"

"Indeed. When I trained Teal'c it was to replace me as First Prime and to use his position to work from within, to make life under Apophis at least tolerable. I never believed a true Jaffa rebellion was possible until Teal'c met O'Neill, your daughter, and Dr. Jackson. I thought he was a naïve fool to even consider such an action — but he took it, and we are better for it. The Jaffa Rebellion grows with each passing day, and it is all because of Teal'c. I could not be more proud."

"Hey, if it wasn't for Sam being part of the Stargate program, I'd be dead right now. I was less than a week from cancer killin' me before I blended with Selmak. My entire life's changed 'cause of her."

"That would not have happened but for your guidance. Perhaps that guidance was not as overt as mine with Teal'c, but I have seen your work in this battle we both fight, Jacob Carter, and I see a great deal of you in your daughter. She has your courage, your forthrightness, and your strength."

"Yeah, and somebody else's brains." He grinned. "I've been joking that she gets her smarts from Selmak's side of the family. But seriously, thanks, Bra'tac. I've seen your work, too, and that means a lot."

Bra'tac nodded, and Jacob Carter nodded back.

They continued the rest of the way to Imphal in companionable silence.

CHAPTER TEN

P3X-418

DANIEL Jackson really didn't want to be enjoying himself.

But it was hard to resist the allure of what Kali had given him.

Her Jaffa had led him to an office that had an old oak desk, with everything in easy reach — including the mug of water he'd asked for. The desk itself was in the center of the room, with the large window looking out over the majestic snow-covered mountains just to his left. Daniel appreciated the effect: the magnificent vista was accessible but not a distraction.

Of course, the material Kali had provided was distraction enough. Some of it was recorded on scrolls, amazingly enough, but most was on the tablet readers that they'd found on a number of Goa'uld worlds. Daniel had about a dozen tablets, plus one of those eggs that moved the text from one 'page' to the next.

The scrolls were, like the lettering on Kali's mothership, written in the Devanagari alphabet, and Daniel was able to struggle through enough to recognize them as accounts of the colonization of Imphal. It took a while to muddle through those, partly because the language had evolved in odd directions, partly because the descriptions could charitably be described as flowery. Kali didn't simply travel to the world, instead she was decribed as 'journeying powerfully across the stars in her grand vessel that conveyed her between the stars'. Her Jaffa didn't just construct the settlement, but rather they 'painstakingly crafted the finest shelters from the raw materials on the world, using only their bare hands and their fortitude'.

Curiously, Daniel found no references to the construction of the redoubt that he was currently inside. Then again, he was fairly certain that it was already here when Kali arrived.

The tablets were much easier to get through, written as they were in the standardized Goa'uld language, which Daniel had become fluent in during his year on Abydos.

Daniel had always had a natural facility for languages. When he was a boy in school, he'd always aced his foreign language classes, having mastered French, Italian, and Spanish upon completing the sixth grade. By the time he got his Bachelor's, he knew a dozen, and he was up to twenty-two on that fateful day when Catherine Langford had approached him.

He had hit rock bottom, that day. That morning, he'd awoken to an eviction order, and then the entire crowd walked out of his lecture. In their defense, the eviction notice had caused his speech to be somewhat more histrionic than he'd originally intended.

Either way, though, he kind of wished he could go back in time and tell his younger self not to hesitate when the strange old woman pulled up in a limousine and made him an offer he couldn't refuse. He went from a homeless laughingstock to an Air Force employee who had an apartment in Colorado Springs.

After deciphering the chevrons on the Stargate, he got to go to an alien planet. On Abydos, for the first time in his life, he was home. On Earth, his only family was parents utterly absorbed by their work before their tragic deaths in an accident at a museum in New York, and a crazy grandfather. But on Abydos, he found in Sha're, Skaara, and Kasuf the family that Earth had never been able to give him. Instead of Claire and Melburn Jackson's distraction and Nicholas Ballard's insanity, the Abydonians gave him unconditional affection. They welcomed him without question, gave him food and shelter and, most of all, love.

Sha're gave Daniel many things, including the twenty-third language in his lexicon — which enabled him to sit and read through the tablets Kali had provided for him.

Had he not been able to read them, Kali might have viewed Daniel as equally expendable as Jack.

He was just glad that she had agreed to heal Jack.

As System Lords went, Kali wasn't all that bad. Not that

she was in any way *good*, but as he flipped through the tablets, he noticed that — for a goddess with a reputation as a destroyer — she had surprisingly few conquests. He knew from Tok'ra intelligence that she had been elevated to the ranks of the System Lords mainly by attrition. SG-1 had wiped out so many of the extant System Lords that it created a power vacuum. Kali had been one of those to fill the vacancies.

Her record of conquest, though, was almost paltry by comparison to her fellows. The number of planets under her domain was among the smallest of the current spate of System Lords.

However, her holdings were all fairly strong, and very few of them had changed hands. The tablets included all those records.

Kali had promised Daniel some assistance from among her subjects. That was mostly for the negotiations themselves, but for now Kali did send one young woman up. "My name," she said, "is Aparna, Dr. Jackson. I'm here to give you aid with translating the tablets. I am fluent in the written language of the gods."

"Um, okay, well, so am I."

Aparna's eyes went wide. "I apologize." She bowed her head. "While all the *Kula* speak the gods' tongue, few are those who know it in its written form. You must be very wise."

Daniel smiled. "So must you be, if you can read it."

She shrugged. "It is my duty. My service to the Mother Goddess is as archivist."

"Well, based on what I've seen so far, you do your job very well."

"Thank you. I do my best in service of the Mother Goddess."

Unable to help himself, Daniel winced at Aparna's obeisance to a Goa'uld.

To her credit, and Daniel's irritation, she noticed. "You do not approve of my devotion, Dr. Jackson?"

Deciding to do her the favor of being honest, Daniel replied, "No, Aparna, I don't. The Goa'uld aren't gods, they're parasites who take on human form and enslave and murder innocent people. Apophis kidnapped several humans, including my wife and brother-in-law. They were implanted with Goa'uld, forced to subsume their very existence to an alien consciousness with delusions of divinity. The hilarious part is that they were comparitvely lucky. The ones who *didn't* get chosen? They were killed and discarded."

"Well, of course," Aparna said. "Apophis is an *evil* god. The Mother Goddess would never do such a thing. All the Goa'uld in her service are hosted by mortals who have chosen that life."

Daniel blinked. That was, of course, true of Ramprasad, but only because he was a Tok'ra. "Really?"

Aparna nodded. "There are many acolytes who train all their lives to host one of the gods. The few who are chosen are always grateful for the opportunity to become immortal in the service of the Mother Goddess."

"That doesn't make it right."

"How could it possibly be wrong?" Aparna sounded genuinely confused, which Daniel found heartbreaking. "The *Kula* are cared for by the Mother Goddess. She provides us with food and shelter and health and happiness. She protects us — with her own divinity and with the Jaffa. None of the *Kula* are starving, Dr. Jackson, and none of us are unhappy."

"The people of this world were probably pretty unhappy when the Reetou killed them. She did a poor job of protecting you from them."

"Is that not why you are here, Dr. Jackson?"

Daniel actually smiled at her scoring that particular rhetorical point. "Fair enough, but I'm only here because Kali threatened the people of Bangalore."

Aparna frowned. "Bangalore is my homeworld."

"When Kali captured me and my teammates, she said that if we didn't cooperate — if I didn't conduct these negotiations and if Sam didn't do work in her lab — she'd wipe out the entire population of Bangalore."

Shaking her head, Aparna said, "You are either mistaken or lying, Dr. Jackson. The Mother Goddess would never do such a thing."

"I can't prove it to you, sadly, but I can assure you it did happen. Look, I'll agree that Kali isn't as bad as some of the other Goa'uld. Good for her for not actually kidnapping people and forcing them to become hosts. But it's just a question of degree. She's *not* a goddess, she's a living being just like any other, who happens to control powerful technology that she stole and adapted from another, older race."

Aparna shook her head, and Daniel realized that it was out of pity. "Do you think my devotion to the Mother Goddess comes from her power? I told you, she has protected us for millennia. I do not pledge myself to her service because she performs mighty feats, for I have seen others, including the Jaffa, perform similar feats. It is her dedication to our lives that compels me, Dr. Jackson." She took a breath. "Now then — since I may not aid you in translating, is there another method by which I can assist?"

Daniel just stared at her for several seconds. He had to admit to never seeing this before. Usually, the Goa'uld's subjects were cowed into submission. But Aparna's devotion came from a much more intellectual place.

Not that that made it any better. Slavery was still slavery, and even a well-treated slave still didn't have the power to walk away without consequence.

However, he knew he wouldn't win the argument with Aparna. So he just answered her question: "Some more water would be nice. Translating can be thirsty work."

She actually favored him with a smile. "Indeed. It is also easy to lose yourself in the act of reading and lose track of one's physical needs like eating and drinking."

"And sleeping," Daniel added, returning the smile.

"I will bring you a pitcher." She bowed her head and then left.

He stared at the doorway for several seconds after her depature before turning his attention back to the tablets.

She did indeed bring a pitcher, and the ice water was quite refreshing. As he sipped it, he read over the account of Ares trying to take one of Kali's worlds and failing.

Then he turned his attention to another tablet, which told of an expansionist campaign by Heru'ur. He moved in on many territories at once, challenging Bastet and Sobek as well as Kali. Individually, they were no match for even a fraction of Heru'ur's forces, but Kali's solution was to ally with the other two Goa'uld. Presented with a united front, Heru'ur backed off.

Interestingly, according to this archive, the betrayal of Sobek by Bastet and Kali was done only to prevent Sobek from doing likewise. In the joint confrontation against Heru'ur, he had taken the fewest losses and he thought that gave him a superior position. So at the feast celebrating their alliance and victory over Heru'ur, Bastet and Kali had him killed.

Most important, though, was the tablet that contained accounts of all of Kali's campaigns against the Reetou. Interestingly, every single one followed the pattern that Jacob had laid out — and that they had experienced in the SGC — three years earlier. Covert strike teams of five performing surgical strikes and then departing.

"Are you comfortable, Dr. Jackson?"

Daniel turned toward the doorway at the voice, which was not Aparna, but rather Kali herself. "Yes, it's a very gilded cage you've put me in."

She actually smiled. "Hardly that. This was Ramprasad's study. He often found it an efficacious place to work. His service will be greatly missed."

"Mmm." Daniel figured it was best not to focus on Ramprasad, since it wouldn't do to let Kali know that he was still alive and also a Tok'ra. Instead, he said, "I noticed in your rather detailed history of the conversion of Imphal into one of the worlds in your domain that there's no mention of how this place was built. Which isn't surprising, since it really isn't your usual style."

Kali nodded. "In fact, the structure was here when I claimed this planet. No doubt it was built into the side of the mountain because it made it more defensible. It has weathered many centuries intact, and it seemed the wisest place to put my headquarters on this world."

"Your headquarters. Which you almost never used, since this is only one of your worlds. Tell me, did anyone besides Ramprasad and a few servants get to come into your large, defensible stronghold? Or did you just leave them literally out in the cold?" Daniel's question was as much in response to Aparna's blind devotion as anything — he was hoping for something he could use in a later discussion with the archivist.

For her part, Kali's smile fell and she glowered at him, her eyes briefly glowing. "The winters on Imphal are cold ones, but the summers are quite pleasant. None of the *Kula* object to living outside the redoubt. And when a blizzard strikes, the people retreat here. I am not a cruel goddess, Dr. Jackson."

"In fact, you're not any kind of goddess, you're a parasite masquerading as one."

Shrugging, Kali asked, "What else defines divinity if not the devotion of those who worship? The *Kula* believe, and that is all that matters."

Daniel snorted.

But before he could comment further, Kali held up her right hand. "We could argue this point endlessly, Dr. Jackson, and it would serve no purpose. Your biases leave you room only for hatred for the Goa'uld."

"You don't know the first thing about me."

"On the contrary. Daniel Jackson, called 'doctor' due to your academic achievements in subjects relating to ancient history and linguistics. The Tau'ri military recruited you to assist in the deciphering of the workings of the *chappa'ai* that your people unearthed. You then travelled along with Colonel O'Neill and a contingent of Tau'ri warriors to Abydos where you killed Ra, and then remained there with your wife, Sha're, until she was taken by Apophis and made to host Amaunet."

Taking off his glasses to rub his eyes, Daniel said, "Fine, you know the first thing about me, and maybe the second or third." He replaced his glassses and stared right at her. "And you didn't record any of that information, since your archivist was unaware of it."

"Aparna is quite skilled at her job, but she is only in charge of the *public* records. Intelligence about my enemies is not something I would entrust to anyone who is not either Goa'uld or Jaffa. And not even all of them."

Daniel nodded, acknowledging the point, if not actually conceding it. "Still, you know I come by my hatred for you and your kind pretty honestly, all things considered."

"Yes. But I would posit that *you* do not know the first thing, as you put it, of my own history."

"Oh, I think I know enough. You were referred to — I'm sorry, *still are* referred to — as Kali the Destroyer. The actions of your Jaffa led to a word in my language that describes unpleasant, poorly behaved miscreants."

Kali smiled once again, and to Daniel's surprise, it was a rueful one, an emotion he never would have credited any Goa'uld capable of feeling. "Ah yes, a remnant of my early career, shall we say. I was originally in the service of Shiva and performed many unsavory acts on his behalf."

That actually surprised Daniel. "Really? That isn't in the records, either."

"No." Kali hesitated. "Intelligence about foes is not all that is kept out of the public records. I served Shiva before the Goa'uld first came to your homeworld. That story is not in the archives, as it is not relevant to the *Kula*. But I think you should hear it, Dr. Jackson."

"Oh?" Daniel found himself torn between his intellectual curiosity and his hatred. The former was champing at the bit to hear ancient history from someone who was actually there. The latter wanted Kali to leave the room as fast as possible, a feeling he always had when in the same room as a Goa'uld.

"Yes. After all, if you are to negotiate on my behalf, you must know for whom you are negotiating."

"I'm not negotiating on your behalf. I'm negotiating on behalf of those the Reetou are indiscriminately murdering."

"Then we have the same goal, Dr. Jackson," Kali said with more than a little smugness, "for I, too, wish to protect my people. And I believe it is important for you to know whence that wish derives."

CHAPTER ELEVEN

Earth—many thousands of years ago

THE *CHAPPA'AI* activated. Ra watched as Shiva came through, followed by his retinu.

"Welcome, Shiva," Ra said, limping toward the fellow Goa'uld even as the *chappa'ai*'s wormhole deactivated.

Shiva stared with concern at Ra's being hobbled. "It is good to see you, old friend, but if you need to go to the sarcophagus…"

Ra shook his head. "This body is dying. The Unas are physically strong, but they are susceptible to minor injuries. However—"

Then Ra stumbled again, and Shiva's companion stepped forward to catch him.

"Thank you," Ra said.

"This," Shiva said, "is Kali. She has served as my right arm for lo these many centuries."

"Then thank you, Kali," Ra said. "I must tend to this latest injury." He snapped his thick fingers and a mortal stepped forward. "This is my primary *lo'taur*. When I landed here years ago, he was the only one who did not run in fear at the sight of my *ha'tak*." He turned to the *lo'taur*. "Show Shiva and his servants to their quarters. We will gather for a meal in one hour."

The *lo'taur* bowed and said in a mellifluous voice, "Follow me, please."

Shiva, Kali, and their other servants followed through the stone corridor, which led from the *chappa'ai* to Ra's *ha'tak*. At each wall were several *lo'taur* who worked hard at the walls of the corridor. Peering more closely, Kali and Shiva both realized that the mortals were being put to work carving linguistic decoration into the walls. It would probably take months, but eventually, the entire corridor would be covered in hieroglyphs.

To Kali, Shiva said, "I believe that Ra finds the people of this world to be ideal slaves. See how hard they labor on the walls. They are many, and will serve us well."

Kali nodded. "They are barely able to construct their own tools. Our technology must appear as magic to them."

"Indeed."

The smooth-faced slave brought them to guest quarters on the landed *ha'tak*. The corridor had been constructed so that they went straight from the *chappa'ai* to the ship.

Shiva received his own cabin, as did Kali, though hers was less lavish. The other servants shared a third cabin.

For Shiva, there was a large bed and a half-dozen *lo'taur* to service his every need. His cabin also had several statues of Ra and a plate filled with delicacies.

In Kali's case, the cabin was smaller, no slaves awaited her pleasure, and there was only the one statue, but the bed was still large and there was still food and drink. That suited her well, as she had not eaten before departing, and the heat on this world made her thirsty.

Some time later, the *lo'taur* returned to announce that Ra awaited them in the dining hall. Only Shiva and Kali were invited. The other servants — some mortal, some Goa'uld — were told to stay in their quarters.

The dining hall was a rectangular space covered in gold inlay, with statues of all the System Lords lining the long sides of the room. Kali found the likeness of Shiva's statue to be lacking, but said nothing out of respect.

Only three places were set at the table, and Ra was already sitting at the head. The other two place settings were on either side of him. Kali waited and let Shiva choose where he wished to sit, as was appropriate. She took the third seat after he decided to sit on Ra's right.

Ra's host looked healthier than before, though he still moved slowly and with obvious pain.

"Welcome, my friends. Thank you for joining me here at the seat of the Goa'uld Empire."

Shiva and Kali exchanged glances across the table. "Then this is to be where the Goa'uld will rule?"

"Of course. The Ancients left *two* of their *chappa'ai* here. And there are other indications that the gate builders used this world as a base of operations. Plus the population is strong, yet obedient. Adaptable yet pliant. The *lo'taur* are the finest slaves I have ever seen."

A *lo'taur* came by and filled their mugs with an aromatic drink.

Taking a sip, Shiva asked, "Then you wish us to join you in ruling these people?"

"Those System Lords who have answered my summons have already staked their claims on this world. Anubis, Apophis, Bastet, Hathor — the entirety of the land near the great river is ours."

Shiva bridled, wondering if Ra had summoned him only to deny him territory and send him away again.

But then Ra's Unas host broke into a smile. "Worry not, my friend — there is more to this world than the great river. Cronus and Ares have ventured to the sea to the north. And to the east, there is a great mountain. Many potential slaves live in its valley."

As he spoke, several more *lo'taur* came into the dining hall bearing food.

"We will speak more of this after we dine. But I can assure you, my old friend, that you will find much of value in the land near that great mountain."

Nodding, Shiva grabbed his mug. "To the mountain!"

Shiva stayed some time in Ra's kingdom, travelling up and down the great river, seeing how he raised up the nomadic, desert-dwelling creatures from the muck, turning them into a mighty force of Goa'uld subjects. He also saw the domains of Anubis, Apophis, Hathor, and Osiris, seeing how they ruled the fiefdoms that Ra had granted them.

At one point, Shiva toured a giant farm, with Kali by his side.

Kali noticed that the farmers were not as devout toward Ra's leadership as others, and she mentioned this to Ra.

"You believe they are disloyal?" Ra asked her.

Shaking her head, Kali said, "I cannot be sure. But I believe that they bear watching."

Ra bowed his head. "My thanks, Kali. Shiva is lucky to have you in his service."

After a week had ended, Ra gifted Shiva with a *tel'tak* with which to travel to the great mountain.

The people there were instantly cowed and fell prostrate before the power of the Goa'uld — as any sensible mortal should. But even more, the people looked upon their Unas hosts and were frightened, for the Unas were broader of form than the Tau'ri.

Shiva was able to decipher the gutter tongue of the mortals and learned that they referred to their land as Bengal, that they lived in awe of the great mountain.

"The mountain is nothing," Shiva said. "It is merely rock that has formed in a manner that makes it *look* impressive. I can bring health to the sick and food to the earth. But I may also bring death to the living if they do not please me."

Two months after Shiva's reign in Bengal began, Ra summoned all the Goa'uld under his domain to a meeting in his throne room. The opulent room was filled with dozens of Goa'uld of all ranks –System Lords as well as minor Goa'uld who were servants to the gods.

The throne itself was empty at first. But once everyone had arrived, a fanfare announced the arrival of Ra's *lo'taur*.

To the shock of all the Goa'uld present, the *lo'taur* stepped up to Ra's throne and sat upon it.

Outrage flew through the gathered Goa'uld.

"What is this?"

"Kill the slave!"

"How dare he!"

But then the *lo'taur* spoke with a voice that was deeper and more resonant than that of any of the Tau'ri on this world. "*Silence*, all of you!" And his eyes glowed.

Shocked silence spread as fast as the outrage had moments ago.

It was Anubis who broke the silence. "Ra?"

"Yes, my friends. It is I, My Unas host has failed me, to the point that even the sarcophagus is of no use."

Shiva asked, "Then why not return through the *chappa'ai* and obtain a new Unas to host your magnificence?"

"Because it is not necessary. While the Unas are more physically powerful, they are also slow to heal. The Tau'ri may be lesser of strength, but they are greater of speed and adaptability. They heal faster from their wounds, and the sarcophagi are more effective on their bodies than they ever were on the Unas."

"Without the Unas' strength…" Shiva started.

But Apophis rubbed the chin of his Unas host thoughtfully. "What need have we of brute strength? We have millions of Tau'ri to serve us now. *They* will do our bidding. *They* will be our strength."

Shiva said nothing in response, but Kali could see that he was seething.

Ra rose to his feet. "This is the word of Ra! *All* Goa'uld will take Tau'ri hosts. Return to your kingdoms and find a Tau'ri you believe worthy of the honor of hosting our greatness."

Soon thereafter, the gathering broke up. Shiva went directly to the *tel'tak*, Kali barely able to keep up with his angry strides.

"What ails you, my lord?" Kali asked as they entered the vessel.

"Ra is a *fool*!"

Kali could see why he waited until they were safely on board, the airlock doors closed, before speaking, for his words were treasonous.

Slowly, considering her words, she said, "It does explain why he has favored that *lo'taur* so much, if he was grooming him for—"

"Be *silent*! We will never speak of such abominations again. The Unas are our hosts. That is the way of things. These Tau'ri are feeble and unworthy."

"But Ra decreed—"

"Enough!" To the pilot, he bellowed, "Take us back."

The *tel'tak* took off into the sky over the river.

Shiva turned upon Kali with a murderous expression. "Ra may *decree* all he wishes. The fools who serve under him here in the desert may do as *they* wish. In the great mountain valley, I rule, and I will *never* sully myself with such an imperfect host."

Once they returned to Bengal, nothing truly changed. Shiva had been correct that they were at a remove from the other Goa'uld—only Lord Yu's domain was geographically further from Ra's than Bengal, though Kali was curious to discover that Yu was one of the first to find a Tau'ri host.

After the palace had at last been finished, Kali asked one of the *lo'taur*, "How far down the valley are there people?"

"As far as the eye can see from the great plateau."

That piqued Kali's curiosity. "What great plateau?"

Eyes widening, the *lo'taur*, whose name was Priya, said, "How do you not know of the plateau? It is a day's travel up the great mountain, and it is like being atop the entire world, you can see so very far."

"Show me," Kali said, and Priya proceeded to draw a map for her in the sand using a stick.

Curious after this discussion, she went to Shiva in the throne room that the Bengali had made for him and told him of the plateau in question.

"Curious. You should take that *lo'taur* in the *tel'tak* and have her bring you there."

Kali smiled. "She suggested we hike there. It is only a day's walk."

"You did not entertain such a notion, did you? We are gods, we do not *hike*."

In fact, Kali had considered it, but she knew better than to contradict Shiva. "Of course, my lord, I simply mentioned it as an amusement."

The next day, Kali took Priya to the *tel'tak*.

"Where are you taking me?" she asked, suddenly scared as they approached the vessel.

"To the plateau." Kali said and her Unas host's eyes glowed. "Gods do not hike."

Priya hesitated before entering the *tel'tak*, and jumped in surprise when the airlock door closed behind her.

The same servant of Shiva who had flown them to and from Ra's kingdom also flew them this day. He sat in the pilot chair, and the vessel soon took off.

Walking to the front of the *tel'tak*, Priya stared in amazement as the ship rose into the air. "It is as if we are a bird!"

Kali was amused. "Birds fly by means of their wings. This ship flies by the might of the Goa'uld."

"Truly you are gods," Priya muttered, as if there could be any doubt. "I have seen vistas akin to this in the past, but always with the solid ground of the great mountain beneath my feet. To see it now with only this conveyance to carry me…"

Using her memory of the map Priya had drawn in the ground as a guide, Kali had little trouble navigating the *tel'tak*, and the servant followed her flight plan precisely.

Within half an hour, they had landed on the plateau.

To the servant, Kali said, "Stay with the ship."

Nodding, the servant put the vessel on standby. Meanwhile, Kali led Priya out onto the plateau.

Again, the servant jumped when the airlock doors opened of their own accord.

The plateau was only just wide enough for the *tel'tak* to land. However, it was long enough that there was sufficient room for Kali and Priya to walk and take in the magnificent view.

And magnificent it was. Kali had never seen anything as majestic and impressive as the view she had now of the Bengali settlements. Shiva's throne room was just a tiny speck in the distance, no different from all the other tiny specks.

The more she stared at it, the less magnificent it seemed, and the more frightening it became. As she saw how tiny and undifferentiated everything was at this distance, suddenly Kali did not feel at all like a god, or even like a Goa'uld. In the face of this giant mountain — the full height of which was several orders of magnitude greater than the upward distance that the *tel'tak* had achieved — she felt very insignificant.

It was not a feeling that sat well with her.

"You can see," Priya was saying, pointing southward, "that there are others who have not yet been shown the way of Shiva. If you can traverse the mountain with your mighty conveyance, then surely you may travel to those other lands, as well. Those others should not be denied your magnificence."

"Indeed they should not. Let us go to them, now. Quickly!" Kali spoke with haste, as she no longer wished to be standing on this plateau, nor be anywhere near the mountain. It was better, she decided, to admire its majesty from a distance.

She lumbered slowly toward the *tel'tak*. Priya moved much faster and with more grace. Ra was correct: the Tau'ri may not have been as strong as the Unas, but they were more adaptable and considerably more agile.

Just as they entered the ship, the very ground shook.

Staring at Priya, Kali asked, "What was that?"

"I — I do not know." Priya had been in awe before — now she was terrified. "I have come to this plateau many times. The ground has never shaken before!"

Turning to the servant in the pilot's seat, Kali said, "Take us out of here, now!"

"I do not believe we should do that, my lady."

A growl forming in the back of her throat, Kali asked, "What do you mean by that?"

"I mean that I believe the *tel'tak*'s engines are what led to the instability in this plateau in the first place. Should we use them again, I cannot predict the results."

"Perhaps," Kali said angrily, "but I can easily predict the results if you do not remove us from this plateau immediately." To emphasize her point, she raised her left hand.

Rather than face the wrath of Kali's *kara kesh*, the pilot began the startup sequence.

And then the ship shook from the impact of several large rocks falling on top of it from higher up the mountain.

"Rockslide!" Priya cried.

"Get us out of here!" Kali shouted at the pilot.

The servant tried his best, but more and more rocks came crashing down onto the *tel'tak*, including one that smashed directly into the front end of the vessel, which caved in, crushing not only the cockpit, but also the pilot.

Kali was mentally debating the efficacy of running out the airlock or taking her chances inside the *tel'tak* when suddenly Priya cried out, "My lady, look out!"

Priya was a tiny slip of a human and Kali's host was a powerful Unas. Nonetheless, Priya managed to throw her weight against Kali enough to knock her to the deck of the vessel, just as a large rock that had penetrated the hull whizzed past where her head had been. Priya herself also tumbled down to a prone form, and the rock that would have crushed Kali's skull instead landed on her legs.

And then another rock smashed through the new hole in the top of the ship and landed directly on Kali's chest.

She herself was undamaged, but her Unas host was past the point where she could heal her. The rock had completely caved in the Unas's chest cavity, and Kali could not repair the damage to her host until that rock was removed, which she did not have the strength to do. Facing the demise of her host, Kali did the only thing she could do: she escaped. Disengaging from the Unas's spine, Kali wriggled out the creature's mouth just as she took her last breath.

It took her several moments to readjust all five of her senses to being a tiny amphibian as opposed to a powerful biped. Her range of vision was now more limited — and also much closer to the ground. Being forced to engage in locomotion via slithering was quite irritating.

She needed another host. And with the pilot also crushed beneath the weight of one of the mountain's rocks, that only left one option.

Slithering toward Priya, who lay facedown on the deck, she saw that the *lo'taur* was bleeding profusely from her smashed leg. She would soon be dead. Kali would not allow one of their loyal subjects to die after bringing her this gift of the many lands available to them. Besides, it was not her fault that this rockslide happened — had they hiked as Priya had originally suggested, all would have been well.

Not only that, but Priya's actions had saved Kali's life, for had she not pushed her host's body out of the way as she did, she would have been struck in the head. The symbiote would likely not have survived such a blow. Kali owed Priya her life. That deserved a reward.

Finally, while Shiva had ordered her not to take a Tau'ri host, Ra had ordered her to do so. And Ra's word was supreme among the Goa'uld. Those who disobeyed rarely lived to regret that action.

Kali bit through Priya's back and tunneled into her spine.

Within a second, she had taken control. Priya's left leg was indeed completely shattered, but it was the work of only a few minutes to heal. As Ra had indicated, an injury that would have taken hours to heal with an Unas host she was able to cure in a fraction of the time.

The rockslide had stopped, at least, but the *tel'tak* was destroyed. The communications equipment was buried beneath several rocks, and what little could be seen was smashed to pieces. Kali had neither the ability nor the inclination to attempt repairs.

Besides, she now had access to Priya's memories of hiking to this plateau and back. It would take the better part of a day for her to hike down, but it was her only option.

It actually took more than a day—the rockslide had made the path that Priya had usually taken more treacherous and difficult to pass—but eventually Kali made it back to Shiva's throne room. She went directly there despite her rather unfortunate appearance—Priya had worn a lovely silk dress for the trip, but it was badly ripped and torn. And while Kali was able to heal any cuts and bruises, her face and arms were still streaked with dirt.

When she came before Shiva, he rose angrily from his throne. "How dare you come before me dressed like a savage! You will change into proper attire before—"

And then Kali's eyes glowed, and Shiva realized what had happened.

"Kali?"

"Yes, my lord, it is I." She quickly explained what happened on the plateau. "I had no choice."

"Indeed," Shiva said. "You must travel back to Ra's kingdom and use the *chappa'ai* to return to our homeworld and obtain a new host."

"I will not," Kali said.

Shiva straightened in his throne. "I beg your pardon."

Kali knew she had spoken out of turn, but it was now clear that Ra had been correct. "I am sorry, my lord, but Ra's words were true. This body is *far* more adaptable. I healed her broken leg in almost no time at all. I'm faster now, more agile. And I am still stronger than any around me, for I am able to supplement Priya's strength with my own."

"The Unas are even stronger."

"As Apophis said, what need have we of physical strength?" Kali asked. "We have *thousands* of subjects to do our bidding."

That got Shiva's attention, and his anger abated in favor of curiosity. "Thousands?"

"Yes, my lord. Before the rockslide, Priya showed me several villages to the south. There are many hundreds more people living there who have yet to be subjugated. I believe you should travel there and reveal to them the might of their god."

Nodding, Shiva said, "Perhaps I shall."

Within a year, many more of the Bengali had come under Shiva's rule. As with the first group they had subjugated, the people were frightened of Shiva's appearance. Some recoiled at the very sight of him, and when that happened, Shiva took to sending Kali in his place.

Ever since taking Priya as a host, the Bengali had started coming to Kali with their petitions. Shiva was always willing to entertain such from his subjects, but only on his own terms and when his whim took him in that direction. Kali was far more approachable. Many of the Bengali saw her as a melding of Priya (who was a respected member of the Tau'ri community) and Kali, and Kali herself did not discourage that notion. It meant that the people would come to her with issues, which she could then bring to Shiva.

For many months after this they were alone in the valley of the great mountain. Their subjects were devoted and growing ever-greater in number. And their rule was peaceful and good…

Then came the summer solstice. On the day when the sun spent the longest time visible in the planet's sky, Ra always held a feast for the Goa'uld.

"We will not attend," Shiva said. "Apophis, Anubis, Hathor, Osiris — they have all taken Tau'ri hosts, and no doubt Cronus and Ares and Olokun and the Morrigan have as well. I will not sit with Goa'uld who have embraced weakness over strength."

"It is *not* weakness!" Kali cried out. "I have needed the sarcophagus less than you. Ra was correct in his decree."

It was becoming an old, and tired, argument. Shiva had not changed his position. "No. We will not attend."

"And how will you explain to Ra why you have disobeyed his summons?"

Shiva had nothing to say in response to that — Ra's instructions were to be obeyed to the letter. Disobedience of Ra's directive regarding hosts was one thing. Reasons could be contrived — a worthy host had yet to be found, his Unas body had not deteriorated to the point where it was necessary — and this particular transgression was out of Ra's sight. But to not attend Ra's most important feast would gain notice — and incur Ra's wrath. Shiva was not prepared to be *that* seditious.

And so together they journeyed back to the banks of the great river, which Ra had taken to calling the Nile.

As Shiva had feared, almost all the other Goa'uld had taken Tau'ri hosts, though Kali was relieved to see that Shiva was not the only contrarian amongst them. Cronus and Ares also still had Unas hosts.

Upon sitting down to feast, Ra stared at the three who had disobeyed with the penetrating eyes of his Tau'ri host. "I believe I made my instructions on the subject of our new hosts very clear."

"Yes, my lord Ra, you did," Cronus said with a respectful bow of his head. "Your exact words were, 'find a Tau'ri you believe to be worthy of the honor of hosting our greatness.' The simple matter is, we have yet to find a Tau'ri who is so worthy."

Ra glared at Cronus before turning his eyes upon Shiva. "And you, Shiva? Kali has followed my instructions, yet you have not?"

"As Cronus speaks, so say I, my lord. Kali's Unas host was injured beyond repair, and so she took the nearest Tau'ri available as a host. I prefer my choice to be a more considered one. Rest assured, once I find a Tau'ri who is worthy, I will honor him."

Kali said nothing, knowing that the hypothetical day of which Shiva spoke would never come.

Shiva continued. "With respect, it is also a difficult search. The Unas were bred to host the Goa'uld. The Tau'ri are truly fit only to be our slaves."

"Actually," Hathor said, "they are fit for more than that. They are able to incubate our larvae. I have created several such among the Tau'ri, who now serve as our soldiers. As the ranks of our worshippers grow, it becomes imperative that we create soldiers whose loyalty is not in doubt."

Centuries later, Kali had become the queen to Shiva's king. The people of Bengal feared Shiva, thinking him to be a demon. His own growing discomfort with his fellow System Lords certainly aided in that. He had become more surly and unpleasant, and Kali's calming influence had been necessary.

Hathor's experiment had proven successful, creating the Jaffa. Every Goa'uld made use of her altered humans.

Kali became the voice of the Goa'uld to the Bengali. In front of Shiva, they cowered in fear, and while sometimes that effect was useful, more often a kinder, gentler face needed to be put on the Goa'uld rule of Bengal.

There was one day, though, when Kali realized that something needed to change.

"Ra has asked — " she started, but Shiva interrupted her.

"What possible reason do I have to do as Ra wishes?"

Slowly, Kali said, "He is the supreme System Lord. If you challenge him — "

"I do not challenge him — but I do not acknowledge his superiority, either. Let him rule the Nile. I shall rule Bengal."

"But Ra has asked that tribute increase."

Shiva snorted with his Unas mouth. "He is entitled to *ask*."

A long pause followed, and then Kali asked quietly, "What message shall I send back to Ra?"

"None. He has made his request. Let silence be his reply."

Predictably, Ra did not accept silence as a reply, and summoned Shiva to his throne room on the Nile. Shiva sent Kali in his place.

By this time, Shiva had several vessels in orbit, all of which were equipped with ring transporters. He had not brought a mothership to Earth, keeping them in reserve. Besides, the mountainous region of Bengal was ill suited to a *ha'tak*.

Kali simply transported to one of Shiva's ships, and then ringed down to Ra's palace. A *lo'taur* greeted her and escorted her to Ra's throne room.

Already present was Ares. He had taken a very tall, well-muscled human host with dark cruly hair and a dark beard. Where Kali had come in her finest silk raiment, Ares had kept it simple: a sleeveless leather vest, thick boots, leather pants, all black. The humans had come to think of him as the god of war, and looking at him now, Kali could understand why. He had embraced that part as thoroughly as Shiva had taken to his role as a demon.

"Why do you stand before me, Kali?" Ra asked. The soft face of his human host had hardened. "I summoned Shiva to the throne room, not you."

"Shiva has many matters of state to attend to. He asked that I come in his place." Quickly she added, "I am empowered to speak for him."

"And what do you say on his behalf?"

"That would depend entirely upon why you have summoned me, my lord."

"I see." Ra stood up from his throne and started to pace, his robes flowing behind him. "It is simple, Kali. I ordered tribute be increased. I am not singling your region out — all the System Lords have been so ordered. Only one gave an answer in the negative, and only one other has given me no answer at all."

"I — " Kali started.

Ra interrupted her by ceasing his pacing and holding up a hand. "We will discuss Shiva's lack of response in due course." He turned to face Ares. "Let us address the negative response first."

Kali turned to also look at Ares. For his part, her fellow Goa'uld looked impassive. Kali would not have considered Ares as one to defy Ra.

In his deep voice, Ares said, "As you instructed, my lord, I confronted Cronus and informed him that he would be wise to reverse his refusal."

So it wasn't Ares who refused, but Cronus, Kali realized.

"And did he?" Ra asked.

Ares let out a quick breath. "Not at first, my lord. Cronus has always been — stubborn. Since he continued his defiance, I acted in accordance with your instructions. A dozen Jaffa stormed Cronus's battlements upon Olympian Mountain and were triumphant. Cronus capitulated." Ares smiled beneath his black beard. "Expect all tribute from Greece to increase accordingly, my lord. Oh, and Cronus has also finally taken a Tau'ri host."

"Excellent." Ra resumed pacing again. "You have served me well."

Ares inclined his head. "Thank you, my lord."

With that, Ares turned and departed the throne room.

Kali swallowed as Ra studied her. "Now then. I still await Shiva's response to my instruction."

"Unfortunately, my lord, I have no response to give you, for just as Shiva provided you with no answer, he provided me with none, either."

While Ra continued to pace, Kali stood still. He finally came to stand face to face with her.

"You were once called the Destroyer, were you not?"

Kali looked away. "That was a long time ago, my lord, when I served as Shiva's right hand in battle. However, that function has not been necessary since we came to this world."

"But you still have the skills you learned in that role, do you not? They have not atrophied? They have not disappeared with the transfer from an Unas to a Tau'ri host?"

"I — " Kali hesitated. She knew where this conversation was going, and she needed to make sure that she knew where she stood. "Why do you ask, my lord?"

"As you heard from Ares, Cronus did not obey me and therefore he had to be dealt with. Shiva did not obey me."

"And he should be dealt with as well?"

Ra nodded gravely. "Yes, but the response can not be the same. Cronus is ambitious, but he knows his place. He will kneel before me. But Shiva rejects my authority. He is disobedient. And there is only one punishment for disobedience."

"Are you ordering me to kill Shiva, my lord?"

Ra smiled. "Is that a problem?"

"It is not. Shiva has refused to give up his Unas host. He has become more difficult. Indeed, our people see him as a demon, and he has endeavored to live down to that reputation."

Now Ra's smile grew wider. "I see you refer to the Bengali as 'our people.'"

She looked away. "I apologize, my lord. I assumed a station that is not my own."

"Would you like it to be?"

That got Kali to look directly at Ra, who had the same amused expression on his face.

Ra continued: "If you carry out this task then Shiva's holdings become yours. *All* of it shall be ceded to you upon his demise."

"In that case, my lord Ra, I do humbly accept your command. And I promise you that Shiva's death will be quick and efficient."

"I would expect no less from Kali the Destroyer." Ra dismissed her with a gesture. "Go and carry out your duty."

Kali bowed. "Yes, my lord."

Kali returned to Bengal and went straight to Shiva's throne room.

Two Jaffa guards stepped aside to admit her.

Shiva looked up at her entrance. "Welcome home, my love."

Kali bristled at the salutation.

"Tell me," he continued, "what unimportant tidings are there from the fool on the Nile?"

Kali stood before the throne and waited a few seconds before starting. "Ra told me a tale when I arrived," she finally said. "You know that Cronus and Ares were sent to the sea to the north to rule the people on the peninsula and the small islands there. When Ra made his decree that you all must increase your trib-ute, Cronus refused. He did not ignore the order, as you did, my lord, but actually told Ra no."

"Good for him."

"In fact, it was rather bad for him," Kali said with a grave expression, hoping Shiva would understand the gravity of the situation. "Ares sent his Jaffa to the Olympian Mountain, and Cronus capitulated."

Shiva rose from the throne, raising his arms in frustration. "The coward! Cronus should have stood his ground."

"Ra is the greatest of us," Kali started, but Shiva cut her off.

"Do not be a fool, Kali. Ra *claims* loyalty because he *claims* supremacy, but such coin is earned." Shiva started to pace back and forth. "This is an opportunity. Cronus can't have been happy about having to capitulate. Perhaps we need only talk to him, convince him to join in the fight against Ra? I already have Anubis on my side, it would be but the work of a simple conversation to convince Cronus to join us."

Kali started to join in the pacing, making sure to stay respectfully behind Shiva. "What makes you think that Ra *hasn't* earned that loyalty? Ares was in the throne room with me, reporting to Ra. I detected no reluctance on his part. Isn't it possible that he acted because he believes in Ra's leadership?"

Shiva turned to face Kali. "Ra took on a Tau'ri host. How does *that* prove that he's earned anything but contempt?"

Then Shiva made the last mistake he would ever make.

He turned his back on Kali.

She unsheathed her dagger and stabbed him directly in the back of the neck, severing his spinal cord and slicing his Goa'uld symbiote in twain.

As time passed, Kali — who now ruled the region in the valley of the great mountain alone — heard reports of many System Lords having trouble keeping the Tau'ri in line. The mortals grew in number, and grew also in sophistication. Some questioned the Goa'uld's divinity; others questioned the need for gods at all.

Kali knew that she had her loyal subjects — but she knew that not all her subjects were loyal. After killing Shiva, she'd made it clear that the people of Bengal were under her protection forevermore. The demon Shiva had been vanquished, and those who worshipped her, whom she had dubbed *Kali Kula*, would always be safe under her rule.

But not all worshipped her. While the *Kula*'s numbers remained strong, the percentage of the people in the Bengal region who considered themselves *Kula* shrank with each decade.

And Kali's domain was the least tumultuous. All throughout the world, from Cronus and Ares in the large sea to Yu and Ameratsu in the eastern regions, they were struggling to maintain their rule.

But the worst was on the Nile, where Ra's hold was slipping.

Eventually the humans rebelled, and so Ra departed, ordering all the Goa'uld to abandon Earth. Only their most devout worshippers came with them.

Kali immediately set up her new throne room on a world she named Bhopal and her Jaffa struck out onto several dozen other worlds.

She had very carefully made sure to keep the worlds she conquered far from those claimed by Ra, though still very much part of the ancient gate network.

Soon her empire grew. While she received many challenges, they were fewer than those of other Goa'uld. Mostly she made sure that the *Kula* remained safe.

And if the occasional challenge from the likes of Heru'ur made it necessary to ally with Sobek and Bastet — and then to turn on Sobek — then so be it.

CHAPTER TWELVE

P3X-418

KALI LOOKED at Jackson, who actually seemed fascinated by her story. She considered this a significant step forward from his contempt, which had grown wearisome.

"Interesting," Jackson said. "The stories I read on Abydos claimed that Ra took a human host as soon as he arrived on Earth." He smirked. "Then again, those stories didn't mention you or Shiva or any other Goa'uld at all."

"Hardly surprising. Ra preferred to think of himself as the be-all and end-all." Kali walked over to the picture window and stared out at the mountains.

"I will give you credit for one thing—that's quite a view."

"When I stand here, I am reminded of the mountains of Bengal."

"The Himalayas. They're a lot taller."

Kali turned to stare at Jackson. "True, but memories are now all I have."

"My heart bleeds." Jackson's contempt had returned.

"In any event, Dr. Jackson, I was content to remain out of the affairs of the other Goa'uld until you killed Ra. The chaos that ensued was overwhelming, and within a shockingly small time I found myself elevated to the rank of System Lord."

Jackson frowned. "Wait, you weren't a System Lord before?"

Kali shook her head. "No. Ra gave me Shiva's lands, but not his place on the council of the System Lords. That remained so until their ranks were so depleted that new blood was necessary. Cronus's death in particular prompted several of the System Lords to nominate other Goa'uld to fill out the ranks: Bastet, Olokun, myself, and others."

Jackson grabbed his mug of water. "Yeah, well, as interesting as this is, I'm kinda confused about something."

"And what is that?"

"Honestly, I'm not really sure what you hope to accomplish here."

"Peace."

At that, he spat the water onto the table. "Seriously?"

Tightly, Kali said, "I did not tell you of my history in order to weave a pretty tale for you, Dr. Jackson."

That was, strictly speaking, not true, as she had rather enjoyed telling it. It had been quite some time since she had told the stories of her rule to others. Long ago, she had done so regularly for the *Kula*, particularly in the days after abandoning Earth. But over the centuries, that habit had fallen by the wayside, and she hadn't realized how much she'd missed it until she started telling the tale to Jackson.

However, there had also been a more direct purpose to her doing so. "I have always prided myself on working *with* humans. I joined my human host in an act of compassion, and it is out of a sense of compassion that I wish to sue for peace with the Reetou. It is a large galaxy, and I see no reason why we cannot coexist."

"Wow," Jackson said with what sounded like amazement. "You're incredible."

"I beg your pardon?"

"First of all, there's *every* reason why you can't coexist. In fact, you *literally* can't coexist — that's why you need me to be your voice in these negotiations in the first place. Secondly, if the point of telling me those stories was to show me how compassionate you are, you kinda need to work on your storytelling."

Kali walked up to Jackson and stood over him, raising her left hand. "You will explain yourself."

Defiantly, Jackson said, "Or what, you'll zap my brain? Been there, done that." He rose to his feet and stood face to face with Kali, an act of impudence that the Goa'uld found impressive and insulting. "But sure, I'll explain why I think you're *nuts*. Compassion? You just told me that you're a killer, starting with that poor woman you've taken as a host."

"I saved her life!"

"Really? So I can talk to her, then?"

Kali shook her head. "Nothing of the host remains."

"Yeah, yeah, I've heard that line before. I argued against it when Zipacna defended Klorel on Tollana, and I *won*. Oh, and Skaara's living a happy, Goa'uld-free life on Abydos even as we speak. We won't even mention the Tok'ra. You say you're compassionate, you call yourself the Mother Goddess, but you're *personally* responsible for the continued enslavement of humans to the Goa'uld as hosts, and now you're trying to sue for peace by blackmailing me and my team into helping you by threatening the very followers you claim to be protecting and loving. You're *still* the Destroyer."

For a moment, Kali considered killing Jackson where he stood. She had eliminated humans for far less of an insult than he had delivered.

But she *did* need him to speak for her with the Reetou, and this very passion and ability to counterargue was what would be needed.

Besides, killing him would just prove his point.

So instead she smiled. "Excellent, Dr. Jackson. That rhetorical skill will prove very useful in your negotiations with the Reetou. And *do* recall that the threat you mentioned still exists. Finish preparing your presentation, doctor — the Reetou will arrive soon."

A Jaffa appeared at the doorway to the study and stood respectfully, waiting for Kali to acknowledge him.

Turning away from Jackson, unable to bear the sight of his sanctimonious face any longer, Kali looked at the Jaffa. "Yes?"

"Forgive the intrusion, Mother Goddess, but the *chappa'ai* has been raised from the water and put back in place. We have dialed the address provided by the Reetou, and they have confirmed that they will arrive within four hours."

"Excellent." She turned back to Jackson. "You have four hours,

Dr. Jackson. If there is anything you need, please ask Aparna."

"A ride home would be nice."

"All in good time, Dr. Jackson—all in good time." She turned and left the study.

Jackson would never believe it, but Kali truly did want peace. She had no need for conquest or to expand her empire. Indeed, the borders of her domain had hardly changed since the Goa'uld left Earth. She had severed ties with Ra not long after she killed Shiva for him, and he had let her be as long as she returned the favor. She had not given him the same insolence as Shiva, nor had she challenged his rule.

What changes there *had* been to her domains were due entirely to external threats, which she dealt with as necessary. Reluctantly, she allied herself with Bastet, whose territory was small, but whose Jaffa were dedicated and powerful—and clever. It was Bastet's impressive intelligence network that revealed Sobek's treachery, which in turn led to Kali and Bastet killing him.

But she preferred her Jaffa to be protecting the *Kula*, not fighting pointless wars against other Goa'uld. Surely the galaxy was large enough for them all? That was why she had voted to allow Anubis back in—the alternative was to suffer yet still more skirmishes with his forces. She was hoping that she could have the same mutual distance-keeping arrangement with Anubis that she'd had with Ra.

Two hours later, another Jaffa came to her with the news that the Tau'ri scientist had an update.

She moved quickly to the laboratory. While she preferred peace, she also preferred to have an advantage over a foe.

Upon entering, she saw several things at once: O'Neill holding an eradication rod and pointing it at a table containing the Reetou corpse her Jaffa had salvaged; Carter making adjustments to a device that looked as if it was cobbled together from several items that were never meant to be attached to one another; and one of her Jaffa standing guard.

"You have made progress," she said without preamble.

"Yes," Carter said. "It was the Reetou cadaver that actually gave me the breakthrough." She walked away from the device she had constructed and approached the Reetou. "We always assumed that the Reetou are a hundred and eighty degrees out of phase with our reality—but it turns out that it's more complicated than that. Based on my analysis, each of their individual cells are moving in and out of phase, at varying rates and speeds. That's why weapons fire can affect them sometimes—they're not insubstantial, because they're not completely out of phase, but it turns out that they're not always a full one eighty out, either. Now, the T.E.R.s work because they expose matter at *any* degree of phase, and the weapon component works on matter in any degree of phase as well. But they're still out of phase."

Kali shook her head. "Congratulations, Major Carter, you have learned more about the Reetou in a single day than all my top scientists managed to glean in weeks of work. I would kill them myself for their incompetence, except the Reetou have already completed that task for me." She looked up at Carter. "What I do not understand is why, if the Reetou is still out of phase, it ceases to affect my species after they're dead."

"No idea, I'm afraid," Carter said.

That surprised Kali. "You were able to learn the one thing but not the other?"

"That's a biology question." Carter shrugged. "I'm an astrophysicist. Matter going in and out of phase, I can tell you about. Why cells do that, and why it affects symbiotes, I couldn't tell you. If I had to guess, I'd say that when they're alive, they move in and out of phase at a much faster rate, and it's the speed of moving in different rates of phase that affects your symbiotes. But even if I'm right about that, I have no idea why you're affected by it, or how to fix it."

Kali was disappointed, but that concern was secondary. "While this is interesting, I was told you were going to demonstrate your progress."

"Yes." Carter walked back to the device she had made, moving past O'Neill, who was still holding the eradication rod.

"You are uncharacteristically quiet, Colonel."

O'Neill smirked. "Carter's in science mode. Better to just let her keep going. If I interrupt, she'll just take longer to finish with the technobabble."

"I'll try to keep it to a minimum, sir."

"No worries, Carter." O'Neill gave Kali a withering expression. "We're the prisoners here, after all."

Kali regarded O'Neill with contempt. She had respect for Carter and Jackson, for all that the latter was impudent. O'Neill had no such mitigating factor to his own impudence, and she was tempted to have her Jaffa shoot him again, just on general principle. She settled for saying, "Yes, Colonel, you are," matching his withering tone.

Carter pressed a button and the device started to hum, several pieces of it lighting up. "Once I realized that the cells went out of phase at differing rates, I realized that we needed to focus on getting them all in phase at the same time. This way, *any* weapon would work on them."

"Excellent."

"I'm hoping," Carter said after looking over various readouts on the device, "that this will do the trick. Basically, this device should create a field that pulls all matter into the same phase."

"Permanently?" Kali asked, very much wanting the answer to be yes.

Carter winced. "I'm afraid not. The power requirements to maintain the field are enormous, and get exponentially more so the bigger the field needs to be. Right now, I've limited the settings so that it will only affect this room. Even a naquadah generator would burn out after about an hour or two, and that would be shortened even further for a bigger field. But it's something."

Kali nodded. "For a single day's progress, Major, I have no complaints. I am sure that you could solve this power-consumption problem given enough time."

"Well, I also don't know what the effect would be on the fabric of local space, either. They — "

Holding up a hand, Kali said, "Enough! I was promised progress, and your spouting of theories is not that. I wish to see this device demonstrated."

"You bet." Carter gave one last glance at the various displays on the device, and then pressed a red button it its base.

PAIN! Agony like nothing Kali had ever suffered sliced through her, white-hot knives cutting through her abdomen. She doubled over, having never felt anything this horrible, this mind-numbingly awful in millennia of existence. Even the agony of having the rock slam into the chest of her former Unas host was as nothing compared to this. Her brain was barely able to form any kind of coherent thought as she found herself writhing on the floor of the lab, screaming.

Dimly, she registered that the Reetou on the table was visible. However, whatever it was the Reetou did to her kind, this device did it several orders of magnitude worse.

Summoning every ounce of strength, Kali forced herself to put one hand in front of the other to crawl her way across the floor. While she'd made others crawl before her on many occasions, this was the first time she herself had had to engage in this oh-so-demeaning activity since the rockslide that led to her taking this particular host body.

The pain overwhelmed the embarrassment as she screamed and crawled, making agonizingly slow progress toward the device.

After an eternity of spectacularly painful crawling, Kali finally reached the base of the table. She managed to raise her arm and then dropped it heavily onto the red button Carter had pushed.

And then, just like that, the pain was gone.

Snarling, Kali leapt to her feet to find that the only other person in the room was her Jaffa, also writhing on the floor in agony. There was no sign of Carter, or O'Neill — or of the Jaffa's *ma'tok* or *zat'ni'katel*.

The Jaffa scrambled to his feet, and Kali screamed at him. "Find them! Now!"

Nodding quickly, the Jaffa ran out of the room.

She called out after him, "And double the guard on Dr. Jackson!"

I am a fool, Kali thought. *I used the Tau'ri because of their accomplishments, because of their skills, and* still *I underestimated them.*

She stared at the device, then looked over at the table to see that the Reetou was invisible again. The eradication rod was also missing, and Kali supposed she shouldn't have been surprised that O'Neill had hung onto it.

At the very least, the device worked. She supposed that was something.

CHAPTER THIRTEEN

Aizawl

CAPTAIN Patel really hated the idea of walking through the Stargate in shackles.

The fact that they were trick shackles provided by Sergeant Siler that she could break out of with a flick of her wrist was only small comfort. She and Teal'c were walking onto a Goa'uld-controlled world. True, she had her P90 and a Beretta and a knife and several grenades and a mess of C-4. But all of that was hidden in her backpack, so they were not readily accessible should things go sideways on this planet ruled by Kali.

On the one hand, she was the one who rescued the Thakka, so she really had nobody to blame but herself for being put in this position. And he really was their best bet for getting to Imphal to rescue SG-1.

On the other hand, she was still walking through the Stargate into enemy territory. In fact, they weren't even a hundred percent sure that they were gating *to* Aizawl. The coordinates the Thakka provided matched those of a set of adjusted coordinates from the Abydos cartouche, but it wasn't scheduled to be checked by an SG team for another year. For all they knew, it was to Bhopal, Kali's homeworld, and Kali herself would be waiting for them with a dozen Jaffa pointing staff weapons at their heads.

The latter turned out not to be the case, at least. Patel exited the Stargate to find only two Jaffa pointing staff weapons at her head. They both had the circular black tattoo on their foreheads, and wore the robes-and-sash-over-armor that Kali's Jaffa seemed to favor. The gate itself was in a huge stone chamber covered in red curtains and gold beading. The room was incredibly chilly, so much so that it raised goosebumps on Patel's arms.

That alone concerned her, as she was wearing desert camo,

having been told by the Thakka that Aizawl was a hot and humid world.

Behind her, the gate closed with a *whoosh*, and the two Jaffa lowered their weapons at the sight of their First Prime. The Thakka was back in his armor, covered by his gold robes and red shoulder sash, and holding an inactive staff weapon. Of course, even without the ability to fire nasty blasts of energy, the weapon was modified with the word *staff* for a reason. Back when she first joined SG-7, she'd seen Teal'c sparring with Major Lagdamen using *bo* staffs. Lagdamen was a third-degree black belt in some martial arts style or other that was heavy on staffs and sais and swords. Teal'c had actually taught the major a thing or two about how to use a staff, and Patel had to assume that the Thakka had similar training.

The two Jaffa stood at attention and bowed their heads, putting their weapons back to an upright position. "Thakka. We had thought you lost on Imphal."

"No, though I must return there as soon as possible. I was diverted to another world, where I was able to capture these two prisoners, but when I attempted to return to Imphal, the *chappa'ai* did not engage."

The other Jaffa said, "The Mother Goddess has travelled to Imphal. We —"

The Thakka snapped, "I am *aware* that she is there, fool, why do you think I am going there instead of Bhopal?"

Patel swallowed. They in fact weren't at all aware that Kali had gone to Imphal, which reduced SG-1's survival prospects considerably. But the Thakka's improvised bluff that he knew all along indicated that he was still on their side, at least for the moment.

The Thakka continued. "I have captured Apophis's *shol'va*, along with one of his Tau'ri allies, and the Mother Goddess wishes to interrogate them personally. Especially *him*." Pushing Teal'c with his free hand, he added, "Move!"

Teal'c turned and gave the Thakka a murderous look, and then walked down the stairs from the Stargate. Patel followed.

As he led the two of them toward the room's exit, the Thakka said, "I will require a *tel'tak* with a cloak."

One Jaffa said, "There is one in the landing bay that was damaged in the battle with Anubis's forces. The maintenance crew cleared it for use yesterday."

"Excellent."

The other Jaffa frowned. "Why a cloak?"

Whirling around, the Thakka pointed his staff weapon directly at the Jaffa. "Who trained you, Jaffa? I wish to know the name of the incompetent who neglected to remind you not to question your superiors."

Bowing his head, the Jaffa said, "My apologies, Thakka, I was simply curious."

"A Jaffa's place is to obey, *not* to be curious." The Thakka raised his weapon, and then continued to walk them out the huge double doors, which led directly outside.

It was like hitting a wall of humidity, and Patel actually gasped as they exited. The structure that housed the gate was apparently climate controlled. But now they were walking a paved pathway that was being baked by a rather intense sun. Within seconds, sweat was beading on Patel's brow. This was the worst heat she'd felt since her best friend from high school had insisted on an outdoor wedding in the Chavez Ravine Arboretum in the middle of August.

The pathway was part of a latticework of paved paths that went between a number of structures of varying sizes. Assorted folks walked about, some Jaffa in robes and armor, some civilians in very old-fashioned clothing, all looking as if they were of Indian descent. It was like stepping into a bizarro Renaissance Fair in New Delhi or something.

However, Patel said none of this aloud. She was supposed to be a prisoner, after all, and it didn't do to mess with that. So she stepped lively alongside Teal'c, the Thakka right behind them with his inactive staff weapon.

The people, Patel noticed, gave them all a wide berth, particularly once they saw the gold circle on the Thakka's forehead. The only thing the subject of a Goa'uld feared as much as the Goa'uld they were ruled by was that Goa'uld's First Prime. In fact, they probably feared the First Prime more. The average Goa'uld subject rarely even *saw* the 'god' they served, but they likely saw the Jaffa a lot more in their day-to-day lives. They also probably had a lot more direct violence inflicted on them by the Jaffa under the First Prime's orders.

When the Thakka entered the rectangular building, no one questioned him. The two Jaffa at the doorway simply cleared a path for him and let him in. *It's good to be king*, she thought wryly.

She stayed alert, but everything was going according to plan so far. The Thakka had done exactly what he said he was going to do.

But she was still half convinced that something was going to go wrong. Because something always did. She'd had far too many hard lessons in that rule.

The first lesson had come on her first mission as a second lieutenant, fresh out of the Academy. She was part of the Air Force detail enforcing the no-fly zone over Iraq during Operation: Southern Watch, reporting directly to Captain Kenny Negassa. The first thing Negassa had said to her after introducing himself was, "Focus on the job while you're doing it. Think about what it means after it's done."

Six months after that, Negassa had been killed during a dogfight with Iraqi MiGs. Patel had been devastated, and came very close to resigning. But she managed to get past it, with the help of the company psychiatrist. She realized that Negassa was doing the job he'd signed up for. He'd known the risks, and he died doing his duty. That thought, and Negassa's words, were what had kept her going when comrades had died, up to and including SG-7.

Another lesson in the rule that something would always go wrong hit her when she'd been grounded following an inner-ear infection. Unable to fly, she'd figured that she'd be riding a desk until retirement. When she had received orders to report to Cheyenne Mountain in Colorado Springs, she'd thought it was going to be even worse: not just assigned to a desk, but to a very deep hole in the ground. The Pentagon's assurances that her new post was related to her high clearance rate, gained after Southern Watch, had fallen on skeptical ears.

And then she'd met General Hammond, and was shown around the SGC. Flying an aircraft — any kind of aircraft, whether it was a fighter jet or a 747 or anything in between — had been the greatest thrill of Patel's life, until she'd set foot on her first alien world.

"You'll get over that pretty quick, Patel," Lagdamen had said when she'd expressed her amazement at walking through a giant circle to another world, and he'd been right about that. That first world, which had the oh-so-exciting designation of P2A-798, had been a barren wasteland with humidity at about a hundred percent.

She still loved it.

Lagdamen had had his own variation on the things-will-always-go-wrong rule, which he told Patel on her first mission as SG-7's second in command: "Nothing ever goes according to plan once you walk through that gate. That's why we make backup plans and backup plans of our backup plans. The only way to survive this assignment is to be the most prepared son-ofabitch in the history of the world, and even then, you can do everything right, be ready for anything, and still come home in a body bag."

Castro had snorted, then, and said, "Nice pep talk, sir."

But Patel had just smiled. "That's what my old CO used to say about the Middle East." She hadn't added that Negassa had first said that to her the day before he was killed.

"Turn that up to eleven, and you've got off-world," had been Lagdamen's reply, and it was *that* that had truly scared her, for she hadn't believed there was anywhere in the universe as mind-numbingly insane as the Middle East.

Worse, Lagdamen had been absolutely correct. The galaxy at large made the sandbox she'd served in previously look like a day at the beach.

And here she was in another hot place, wearing desert camo just like she was when her F-14 got shot down in the Gulf. She'd ejected, and managed to land in a friendly zone, but the whole time she worked her way back to base, she'd been convinced that she was going to die. Back then, it had been Negassa's mantra to focus on the job that had kept her going.

But that at least was on the same planet as the rest of her support. If something went wrong here, she doubted that Hammond would even be able to send anyone through to get her.

Should've thought of that before you volunteered, she chided herself.

Then she remembered the charred corpses of Lagdamen, Castro, and Johnson.

The goosebumps came back as she entered the building ahead of Teal'c and the Thakka. Looking up, she saw a retractable roof over a cargo vessel.

A few moments later, they were inside the ship. The moment the Thakka closed the door behind them, Teal'c flexed his massive arms, freeing him from the shackles.

"Well done," he said with a bow of his head toward the Thakka.

The Thakka just scowled back. "I do not wish your praise, *shol'va*."

Patel also flexed her arms and then rubbed her now-free sore wrists. "I'm sorry you had to lie to your people like that."

He waved her off. "I have had to lie to my subordinates many times. It is the way of things." Then he smiled. "I simply do not wish praise from *him*."

"Fine, can you accept it from me? You did everything you said, and even hit that curveball about Kali being on Imphal."

"Yes, and that rather does change things," the Thakka said as he got into the pilot's seat. "My goal is to stop our mutual enemy.

If the Reetou are still on Imphal, then the Mother Goddess will dispose of them."

"And if she cannot?" Teal'c asked as he got into the copilot seat. For her part, Patel stood at the secondary console behind them. She wasn't rated to fly a cargo ship, though Lagdamen had encouraged her to take the time to do so at some point, since her inner-ear issue wouldn't matter in a spacecraft with an artificial atmosphere and inertial dampeners.

"Then I will rescue her from them."

Within minutes, the Thakka touched a control that opened the roof and then placed his hands on the control globe on the console in front of him. The ship slowly started to rise off the floor of the building.

It was strange to Patel, taking off without use of a runway, and only feeling the most minimal pull of gravity. The ship emitted its own gravitational field, had its own pressure. None of SG-7's missions had taken them onto cargo ships, so she hadn't had quite this experience before.

"Never thought I'd be able to do this again," she muttered.

Teal'c turned around. "You have flown in a *tel'tak* before?"

She shook her head. "No, this is my first time, but I meant fly in an atmosphere." She explained to the two Jaffa about her inner-ear infection. "I had to be doped up on meds in order to fly to Colorado to report to the SGC. But this…" She trailed off and just stared out the window, watching the ground of Aizawl grow distant below them, watching the clouds zoom by as the cargo ship achieved escape velocity.

Then they were in space, and it wasn't any different from her perspective than riding an elevator.

The Thakka was shaking his head, hands still on the globe. "So fragile."

"Excuse me?"

"You are not touched by the gods, *Kula*. As a Jaffa, I do not suffer from any infections, in my ear or anywhere else."

"Must be nice."

Teal'c added, "A Jaffa's reliance on a *prim'ta* is a great benefit in battle—but it is also a great weakness."

"I don't know, it seems pretty good to me," Patel said. "Like he said, you don't get inner-ear infections. And the blast he got hit with on P3X-418 would've killed me, and here he is walking around all nice and healthy."

"Yes, but without the *prim'ta*, we cannot survive."

The Thakka shot Teal'c a shocked expression. "Why would we ever be without a *prim'ta*? When it matures, we are simply given another one."

"Some are. And if one is not, then death is the immediate result."

Patel nodded. "Right, your whole immune system is removed when you get the pouch."

"Indeed."

"What does it matter?" the Thakka asked angrily. "*Worthy* Jaffa receive a new *prim'ta*. Unworthy ones do not deserve to continue to live." The Thakka snorted. "Which means your life will be at end when yours matures."

"Perhaps," Teal'c said with a surprisingly respectful bow of his head.

Before the conversation could continue, the Thakka said, "Preparing for hyperdrive."

Remembering what she'd read about in the files, Patel grabbed onto the rear console to steady herself. Based on the reports from various SG teams that had been on spaceships, going into hyperdrive took some getting used to. In particular, she recalled something she'd read in the SGC's copiouis files written by Dr. Bill Lee, which said that transiting to faster-than-light travel affected the inner ear, at least until the person went through it a few times and adjusted their balance.

Maybe I won't get used to it, she thought glumly.

Sure enough, the space outside the viewport went wonky, the ship itself seemed to buckle under Patel, and she almost lost her footing. The two Jaffa, however, were completely unaffected.

"Y'know, I never really thought about that," Patel said as she slowly recovered her balance. "The Goa'uld have to actually provide you with a new larva. That must cause problems when you try to recruit people for the rebellion."

The Thakka whirled around. "What rebellion?"

That made Patel look at Teal'c. "What, you haven't given him the sales pitch yet?"

"The Thakka does not believe that the Jaffa rebellion is real."

Patel snorted. "Seriously?"

"Teal'c is the only *shol'va*," the Thakka said with the same conviction that Patel had when she insisted to her mother that she believed in the tooth fairy — when she was six.

"He really isn't."

At that, the Thakka whirled around to stare at Patel. "You speak insanity, *Kula*."

"We just set up a whole bunch of rebel Jaffa on one of the worlds we control." Patel chose her words carefully, as orders were to be as circumspect as possible about the existence and the location of the Alpha Site. "The last mission SG-7 went on before the one where we — we met you was to help settle them in after their base on Cal Mah was compromised."

"Many Jaffa," Teal'c said, "have come to realize that the Goa'uld are false gods, unworthy of our protection."

"The Mother Goddess protects *us*, fool," the Thakka said disdainfully. "It is we who protect her subjects."

Patel stared at the Thakka. "I didn't see her doing much protecting on P3X-418 when the Reetou attacked. All your Jaffa died — you would've died, too, if I hadn't brought you back."

Without turning to look at her, the Thakka said, "And I am grateful for that, *Kula*, but — "

"*Will* you stop calling me that?" The words exploded out of her mouth. She hadn't consciously realized how much his using that term annoyed her until she snapped at him. "I'm *not* one of the *Kali Kula*. In fact, you couldn't pay me enough to be one. I don't want Kali's protection — I don't *need* her protection.

I'm a captain in the United States Air Force and a member of Stargate Command, and *that's* where my allegiance lies. With freedom and truth, not subjugation and lies."

"The Mother Goddess has *never* lied to us!" The Thakka's words were emphatic, but also, Patel thought, hollow. "There is no Jaffa rebellion! No Jaffa would ever go against their gods, it is unheard of!"

Teal'c raised one eyebrow. "In fact, such examples are commonplace, though they are usually followed by the false god exacting retribution. But the Goa'uld are *not* divine."

"How can you *say* that? They live forever, heal all wounds — "

"They extend their life via the sarcophagus, which any may use, and their symbiotes heal them as they heal us."

"Don't be absurd, only gods may use a sarcophagus."

Teal'c shook his head, and said almost pityingly, "No. The sarcophagus works the same on humans and Jaffa as it does on Goa'uld."

"It's true," Patel said quietly. "One time, my team went up against Cronus. Sergeant Castro was injured — a head wound. She probably had a subdural hematoma, and there was no way she was going to survive more than half an hour. Major Lagdamen picked her up and literally dragged her halfway across the mothership to get to the sarcophagus. I thought he was insane, there was no way she should even be moved, but he gave me an order and I followed it, guarding their six while we went through the corridors, leaving a trail of Castro's blood. When we got to the sarcophagus, he opened it up and put her in. I stood guard for about twenty minutes, and then the top just opened up on its own, and Castro was fine. I'd never seen anything like it." She snorted. "Could've used one of those yesterday. Castro's dead now, thanks to the Reetou, and so are Johnson and Major Lagdamen."

Now the Thakka was staring right at her and speaking in much quieter tones. "That look of wonder on your face, *Kula* — my apologies, Captain Patel. But you truly did see such a sight. A human using a sarcophagus."

"Daniel Jackson was placed in a sarcophagus by Ra himself," Teal'c said. "He did so in order to continue to torment him."

"Enough!" The Thakka held up a hand.

But Teal'c was relentless. "Everything the Goa'uld have told you is a lie. They do not see all or know all, but use technology to trick us into believing it. They are not truly immortal, for I have seen many of them die. They —"

"I said *enough!*" The Thakka took his hands off the control globe and made as if to rise from the chair. "Be warned, *shol'va*, that I will not tolerate —"

"The truth?" Patel said. "You may not think much of Teal'c here, but you said I was an honorable warrior. I don't know much about that, but I do know what I've seen. I'm not lying to you, Thakka, and neither is Teal'c. There *is* a Jaffa rebellion."

"And your presence would be welcome in our ranks," Teal'c added.

The Thakka stared at Teal'c, and then stared at Patel.

Then he turned back to face the viewport, placing his hands back on the globe. "We will speak of this no more."

It took the better part of a day for the cargo ship to travel to Imphal. Teal'c took over piloting when the Thakka went into the rear compartment for *kelnorim*, then they traded off, Teal'c doing his meditation thing while the Thakka piloted.

Patel made several attempts to discuss the Jaffa rebellion and the falsity of the Goa'uld while the pair of them were alone in the cockpit, but the Thakka rebuffed her.

At least, until Teal'c finished his own *kelnorim* and returned to the forward compartment. Then the Thakka asked, "How many Jaffa have joined this rebellion?"

Teal'c raised an eyebrow. "Then you do believe in its existence?"

Patel grinned. The big guy didn't normally go for sardonic, but he wielded it pretty well when he chose to. "Based on the last count we made when we were settling them in at our base, one hundred and nineteen."

"But that number is ever growing," Teal'c added, "and does not include the hundreds more who remain covertly in the service of their false god to further our cause."

"Look, it's up to you," Patel said. "You can believe us or not. But Kali *isn't* divine. A writer on Earth once said that any sufficiently advanced technology is indistinguishable from magic. The Goa'uld didn't even create most of the technology they use, they stole it from another ancient species. They use it to make themselves *look* like they can do magic. But it's just science, and anyone can wield it."

The Thakka was silent for several seconds before finally speaking. "We will go to Imphal and rescue your comrades and take our revenge on the Reetou. After that — we shall see."

"Very well." Teal'c sat in the copilot's seat.

Patel stifled a yawn, then decided not to bother and actually yawned. "How much longer till we arrive?"

"Four hours," the Thakka said.

Nodding, Patel adjusted her watch. "Fine, I'm gonna sack out for a bit." She hadn't planned on leaving these two alone for fear that they'd try to kill each other without her calming influence on the Thakka, but he seemed to have at least settled into some kind of reluctant acceptance that the universe wasn't quite what he thought it was.

So she went into the back and curled up behind a cargo container. She'd always been able to sleep anywhere for any length of time and be refreshed. It had served her well on hiking trips when she was a teenager, not to mention in the desert after her F-14 was shot down.

She just hoped that SG-1 was there to be rescued…

CHAPTER FOURTEEN

P3X-418

"WELL, *THAT* went better than expected," O'Neill said as he took the staff weapon and zat from the Jaffa that was squirming on the floor of the lab. He tossed the zat to Carter.

She caught it unerringly and said, "Yes, sir, though I think my theory about why the Reetou affect the Goa'uld may be wrong."

"I will somehow find it in my heart to forgive you, Major," O'Neill said as he gripped the staff weapon and activated it.

Carter removed a crystal from one of the devices she'd been playing with, slipping it into the Velcro pocket of her shirt. "This is all the data on the device. If we make it back to the SGC, we should be able to re-create it." She then grabbed the T.E.R. and holstered it.

O'Neill nodded his approval — the Reetou were still a threat, after all. "Let's move. We gotta find Daniel and then get outta here."

As they ducked into the corridor, Carter said, "Sir, the Stargate is still underwater, and the ring console on the island is still broken. The only ship is Kali's mothership."

"I admit the plan still needs some details filled in…"

The report of a zat startled O'Neill. He whirled around to see Carter lowering her weapon and a Jaffa, who had just turned the corner behind them, twitching on the floor.

"Good shot," O'Neill said. "Let's go."

With the ease of long practice, O'Neill and Carter moved into formation. First O'Neill stood fast and covered with his weapon while Carter moved forward. Then Carter stood fast and covered with the zat while O'Neill moved forward.

Typically, Kali's stronghold was a maze of corridors, with nothing labelled. *Of course,* O'Neill thought, *even if it was labelled, it'd probably be in a language that only Daniel could read.* They'd been through the stronghold before, but they'd been focused then on trying to find survivors. O'Neill hadn't paid as much attention as he should to the layout, just enough to know when he'd checked a room already.

When they reached a T-intersection, O'Neill moved ahead to check around the corner while Carter covered his six.

He saw four Jaffa standing in front of a doorway.

One of them caught sight of him and yelled, "*Kree!*" before O'Neill could pull his head back.

"Dammit," he muttered. Just as he turned around to tell Carter that they were seen, two more Jaffa turned into the corridor behind them.

Carter fired, taking one out. Both O'Neill and the other Jaffa raised their staff weapons into position to fire, but O'Neill moved just a bit faster, squeezing off a shot which struck the Jaffa just as his own finger spasmed on the control of his staff weapon. The Jaffa's blast fired harmlessly into the ceiling.

"*Really* wanting my P90 right now," he muttered. "We've got four more coming from that way." He jerked his thumb behind his head.

Then more Jaffa appeared behind the two they'd just taken down, and the one in front was familiar: it was the same one who'd been guarding them in the lab. *Which means the snake-head turned Carter's toy off. Happy joy.*

O'Neill signaled for Carter to move, and they dove to the floor, sliding toward the intersection. As soon as the Jaffa — now almost on top of them — came into sight, O'Neill fired the staff weapon. He didn't have time to take aim, but it was practically point-blank range, and it wasn't as if it was a precision weapon in any case.

Carter had been a few feet behind O'Neill, so it was half a second later that she fired her zat. Between them, they took down the three Jaffa.

"Didn't you say there were four?" Carter asked.

O'Neill nodded. "Other one probably went for backup. Go!"

They ran down the only corridor remaining. At a four-way intersection, two more Jaffa were to their left, while several more appeared to their right. They both fired blindly and kept running.

O'Neill gritted his teeth. There was no way they were going to find Daniel this way, and two people on unfamiliar terrain trying to outrun a platoon of Jaffa who actually *were* familiar with the terrain meant they were just living on borrowed time.

So they needed to change the terrain.

The corridor they turned down was a dead end, but there was a room at the end.

"If we're really lucky," he said as they ran toward it, "Daniel will be in there."

They weren't really lucky. O'Neill yanked the door open while Carter covered him. It was a storage room, filled with large boxes. Throwing the door shut behind them, he pointed behind one container and moved behind another.

Carter took up position where he'd indicated. "Now what, sir?"

O'Neill sighed, then noticed that there was a window. "Cover me," he said as he moved toward it, pushing the red curtain aside, revealing wooden shutters, which he unlatched and opened.

A burst of cold hit him, and he wished he still had the fleece — probably in some container along with his P90. The window looked out onto the village, conveniently enough. It was about a ten-foot drop out the window to a snow-covered, tree-lined incline that would take them into the village.

Carter whispered, "They're getting closer, sir."

"All right, Plan A is we stay here, hope we can hold out against every one of Kali's Jaffa as they step through the door. Plan B, we jump out the window and take our chances in the now-completely-empty village that's full of nice places to hide."

"Plan B sounds good to me, sir."

Nodding, O'Neill said, "Let's go."

Carter covered O'Neill as he hopped onto the window sill, dropped the staff weapon onto the snow-covered ground, looked down to judge the distance, then leapt off.

He landed and bent his knees as soon as his boots struck snow, then springing up from the crouch into a forward shoulder roll.

The first time he did this was in special ops training, taught to him by the even-tempered old sergeant who had served as his training officer.

O'Neill had been younger and more respectful then, so he hadn't actually said what he had thought: *Why the hell are we wasting our time learning to do a shoulder roll when we should just bounce up and shoot whatever bastard we're up against?*

Instead he had asked for permission to speak, which the TO had granted.

"Sir, what is the purpose of the shoulder roll at the end of the landing, sir?"

The TO had just stared at him for a moment before answering. "Jumping from a height gives you momentum, Airman. That momentum needs to be shed. Why, do you think there is a better way?"

"Sir, yes, sir."

"And that is?"

O'Neill had quickly looked from side to side before answering. "Sir, just bounce up and shoot whatever bastard we're up against, sir."

"Try it."

"Sir?"

The sergeant had pointed up at the large wooden staircase that they'd been jumping off the top of and going into forward shoulder rolls. "Try it."

"Sir, yes, sir!"

And so young Jack O'Neill had run up to the top of the stairs, jumped off the top, bounced back up from the crouch, and then lost his balance and fallen on his ass.

The other trainees had been too well disciplined to actually laugh at O'Neill, but he had seen a couple of their lips curl.

Again pointing at the staircase, the sergeant said, "Try it once more, Airman."

"Sir, yes, sir!"

O'Neill had gone back up, and this time when he bounced back up he fell on his face.

From that day forward, he made sure that he knew how to do a proper shoulder roll.

Of course, the training mat was flat and made of foam. On P3X-418, O'Neill was jumping onto snow on an incline, so his shoulder roll was probably not up to his TO's standards. Then again, the old bastard was long since retired, living in New Jersey, and spoiling his great-grandchildren.

Betcha never thought I'd be putting your training to good use on an alien planet, Sarge, he thought as he struggled to his feet and brushed the snow off.

He heard the electric sizzle of several shots from a zat, and he immediately ran for where he'd dropped the staff weapon.

A second later, though, as O'Neill was banging the staff weapon's center with his palm-heel to get the snow off it, Carter leapt out the window.

Her landing and shoulder roll were, he noticed, flawless.

"Ol' Sarge would be proud, Carter."

"Who, sir?"

"Never mind, let's move before the Jaffa decide to jump after us."

They started to move down the mountain. "I don't think they'll follow out the window, sir. Their armor—"

She was interrupted by a staff weapon, which hit the tree to their right.

"Talk later, Major!" O'Neill put the staff weapon on his shoulder, muzzle facing behind him, and started firing blind, hoping it would give the Jaffa pause enough to allow the pair of them time to put some distance.

It must have worked, as by the time they got to the base of the mountain, which was also the start of the village, there were no visible signs of pursuit.

They moved silently among the very same structures that they had been overtly searching for survivors only yesterday. This time, they were hugging the walls, trying to stay out of sight. The lack of pursuit could change at any moment.

"Sir," Carter whispered, pointing at one of the few two-story structures.

Nodding, O'Neill moved toward it. That required going around in a semi-circle in order to continue hugging the walls, as it were, and Carter covered him as he crossed the distance between a small house and the two-story structure, which turned out to be a library of some sort. There were books and scrolls and maps and things haphazardly tossed about onto shelves that lined all the walls, with two big tables with benches in the center.

"I'm guessing Kali doesn't use the Dewey Decimal System," O'Neill muttered.

One of the two tables was empty, but the other had two maps laid out on it. Peering at it, O'Neill saw that the top one was a map of the village, and under it was a detailed layout of the castle.

"And where was *this* when we needed it?"

Carter pointed to the rear of the library. "Sir."

Following her finger, O'Neill saw a spiral staircase. He nodded, and they moved toward it. He gestured for Carter to stay put, and she nodded, staying at the base of the staircase with her zat ready.

O'Neill moved quickly up the stairs to find a darkened storage area. More shelves like the ones against the walls, but up here they were in several rows, making for very little floorspace. The only light came from the two windows, one on the north side, the other on the south.

He whispered, "Carter!"

She looked up, nodded, and followed him up the stairs.

O'Neill moved to the south window, since that was the one that faced the mountain stronghold. He saw about a dozen Jaffa leaving from the front entrance to start searching the village.

"What's the plan, sir?"

The temptation to quote Indiana Jones's line about making it up as he goes was great, but O'Neill managed to resist. "Stay up here until the Jaffa are gone, then go back to the castle and spring Daniel." He winced. "The plan gets kinda fuzzy after that. I don't suppose you could fly the mothership?"

"I know enough about the systems that I could probably fake it — but I'd feel a lot better with Teal'c or my father around."

"Your faking it is better than most people's skill, Carter. I'll take it."

"Thank you, sir, but — "

Holding up a finger, O'Neill said, "Ah, ah! No 'buts.' I paid you a compliment. You say 'thank you, sir,' and there the sentence ends."

Carter smiled. "Yes, sir. And thank you, sir."

"That's better. You did good with the thingamajig Kali had you build."

"Honestly, sir, I didn't think it would have such a profound effect on symbiotes. I mean, don't get me wrong, I'm glad it did, but that wasn't my intention."

"There are times, Carter, when intentions matter less than results."

"Yes, sir — sometimes, maybe."

O'Neill smiled. "Well, I'm sure Daniel would have something long and boring to say about how the ends don't justify the means." He shook his head. "Damn, I'd like to hear one of those long and boring speeches right about now."

"Me, too, sir."

Watching as the Jaffa moved in formation to search the village, O'Neill put a finger to his lips and they waited in silence, trying not to breathe too loud. Then a noise came from downstairs, and they both turned to look at the top of the staircase. O'Neill pointed to the spiral staircase's landing. Carter nodded and moved toward it, zat at the ready.

The Jaffa weren't anywhere near close enough to already be in the library, so either these were other Jaffa O'Neill didn't know about, or other survivors of the Reetou attack they missed the last time, or another bunch of Reetou.

Or, as it turned out, Teal'c, Captain Patel, and the Thakka.

"Teal'c?"

All three of them looked up. "O'Neill!"

Quickly, O'Neill went down the staircase, followed by Carter.

"Well, *this* is a nice surprise," he said, keeping his voice low. Then he looked at the Thakka. "And a not-so-nice surprise. What's *he* doing here?"

"Getting us here," Patel said as she unshouldered her backpack. "Since the Stargate wasn't an option, the Thakka got us a cloaked cargo ship."

"Uh huh." O'Neill wasn't thrilled, but he couldn't very well argue with the results; the ends justified the means, after all.

Teal'c looked around. "Where is Daniel Jackson?"

Carter said, "We still have to rescue him from Kali. She wants him to negotiate with the Reetou on her behalf."

That got the Thakka's attention. "What?"

Quickly and concisely, O'Neill filled them in on what had been going on. He had considered asking Carter to do it, but while the major had many virtues, quick and concise explanations were not among them.

The Thakka actually snarled. Until he joined the SGC, O'Neill had never seen anyone snarl in real life before, but between the Goa'uld and Jaffa, he couldn't go a week without seeing at least five snarls.

"Negotiate? The Reetou killed an entire platoon of Jaffa, and would have killed me were it not for the Tau'ri. And now she would *speak* with them?"

O'Neill stared at the Thakka. "I'm sorry your boss is a jerk, except for the part where I'm not sorry at all. We need to rescue Daniel and get the hell out of here, and your cargo ship just got elected for the second part of that plan."

Patel had been rummaging in her pack, and was pulling out a couple of P90s and extra ammo. "This might help, Colonel."

Handing off the staff weapon to Teal'c, O'Neill grinned. "Oh yeah, youbetcha, Captain. Well done." He grabbed both P90s, tossing one to Carter.

"I also brought some C-4 and eight grenades," Patel added, handing two grenades each to O'Neill, Carter, and Teal'c.

The Thakka was shaking his head. "It has become clear to me that the Mother Goddess is not what I believed her to be."

"Ya think?" O'Neill said, sliding a clip into his P90. "Look — can you help us get into the castle up there so we can rescue Daniel?"

"Perhaps." He walked over to the table that included the design of the castle and started studying it. "Ramprasad and I used these to aid us on our plan of defense against the Reetou." He pointed to a spot on the mountain that had a small triangle on it. "This indicates a secret door to an underground passage that leads to the redoubt's lowest levels. Ramprasad and I had hoped to lure the Reetou to that passage and trap them with Jaffa on either side."

"Turkey shoot," Patel said. "Nice."

The Thakka shook his head. "It would have been, had we succeeded in luring the Reetou there."

O'Neill had finished locking and loading his P90. "All right, let's lay low here until the patrol passes us by. Then we'll head to the mountain to — "

"Jaffa! *Kree!*"

Turning, O'Neill saw one of the Jaffa had entered the library. He was pointing his staff weapon into the room, aimed mostly at Teal'c, but he was in a good position to hit any of them.

The Thakka stepped forward. "Lower your weapon, Jaresh!"

Jaresh hesitated. "Thakka? Why are you with these Tau'ri outsiders and Apophis's *shol'va*?"

"Teal'c is no traitor. I have learned that much we believed to be true has been a lie told us by a creature who masquerades as the Mother Goddess."

Jaresh stared at the Thakka, lowering his weapon. "How can you *say* that?"

Teal'c took advantage of the unguarded moment and fired his zat, but even as Jaresh fell to the floor, two more appeared in the doorway behind him. They looked in horror at their fallen comrade, and in anger at their First Prime. O'Neill realized that they'd probably heard and seen the entire exchange.

Confirming it, one Jaffa looked right at the Thakka and spat the word, "*Shol'va!*"

However, just as they were activating their staff weapons, both Carter and Teal'c fired their zats and took them both down.

"Looks like 'sneaky' just went out the window," O'Neill said. "Thak, you know the terrain, you take point."

The Thakka nodded, then turned to Teal'c and Carter. "Thank you both for not killing them. They were fooled by the false goddess as I was. They do not deserve to die for that."

"We've only got two zats," O'Neill said.

Staring at him, the Thakka said, "What did you call them?"

O'Neill raised his eyebrows. "Drop the '*ni'katel.*'"

Shaking his head, the Thakka said, "Are you so lazy, human, that you cannot speak an extra three syllables?"

"Yep," O'Neill said without hesitation or apology.

The Thakka actually smiled at that. "I admire your honesty."

"Well, I can die happy now. Point is, I can't guarantee that we'll be able to stun every Jaffa we'll see."

"I understand that, O'Neill. But — as I'm sure Teal'c has told you — Jaffa are trained soldiers. They know that death may come at any time when serving their — " He hesitated. " — their god. Nonetheless, I would prefer that killing my fellow Jaffa be a last resort, not a first one."

O'Neill glanced at Teal'c, who inclined his head slightly. That told O'Neill everything he needed to know — mostly that the Thakka was okay in Teal'c's mind, which was good enough for O'Neill. "We'll do the best we can. Let's move."

They went in formation, this time with the Thakka taking point, Teal'c right behind, then Carter, then Patel, with O'Neill bringing up the rear. The Thakka took them on what O'Neill thought was an unnecessarily circuitous route, but as they went, they saw no signs of the Jaffa patrols. Of course, those patrols had probably moved past the library by now, freeing O'Neill and his people to head in the general direction of the mountain.

It probably wouldn't have bothered O'Neill so much if it wasn't so *cold*. He and Carter had been moving quickly enough during the escape, adrenaline pumping, that he hadn't really noticed the cold on the way here. But now they were moving slow and stealthy, the chill was hitting his bones.

Despite his misgivings, though, he was impressed. He'd figured they'd be blasting their way through Jaffa, but the Thakka had kept them moving silently through the trees, avoiding the patrols completely.

But then, as they were reaching the treeline at the base of the mountain, Teal'c held up his arm, fist clenched. The other hand went to the Thakka's shoulder to stop him, since he couldn't see Teal'c's 'hold' gesture.

Teal'c pointed through the trees. O'Neill felt his eyes widen even as he saw Carter's do likewise, as they saw her father Jacob just *standing* there.

Then, about forty-five degrees to the right, O'Neill saw two Jaffa bearing down on Jacob.

He had no idea what Jacob was doing here — Teal'c and Patel appeared just as surprised as as he and Carter were — but there was no time to worry about that. He pointed at Teal'c and the Thakka and gestured for them to go around southward, then pointed at Patel and Carter and gestured for them to go around northward.

For his part, O'Neill moved straight ahead through the trees to Jacob. Since there were only two Jaffa on approach, the five of them would be able to flank them in short order.

O'Neill moved quickly but silently, taking up position behind a thick-trunked tree near Jacob's position. *And why the hell is he just* standing *there?* The two Jaffa were almost on top of him.

Jumping out from behind the tree, O'Neill pointed his P90 at the pair of them. "Don't move."

"Jaffa, *kree!*" one yelled and aimed his staff weapon at O'Neill.

"Oh, *kree* me a river," O'Neill muttered as he fired on full automatic.

Just as he did, Teal'c emerged and fired his own staff weapon at the other Jaffa.

Staring angrily down at the two dead Jaffa, Jacob yelled, "Dammit, Jack! What the hell're you *doing*?"

"I could ask you the same question. And you're welcome, by the way."

A voice came from right behind O'Neill, scaring him out of ten years of life. "That was foolish, human. The Tok'ra and I had the situation under control."

O'Neill whipped around with his P90 leveled, Teal'c doing likewise, only to see that it was Bra'tac who had spoken. He, of course, was less than ten feet from O'Neill, and the colonel hadn't even noticed him. *I hate it when he does that.*

Quickly lowering his staff, Teal'c inclined his head. "*Tek'ma'te,* Bra'tac."

Bra'tac moved toward Teal'c and they gripped each other's forearms. "It is good to see you, Teal'c." He broke the grip and turned toward O'Neill. "But your timing is poor. Jacob Carter and I had intended to lure these two Jaffa into a trap and then learn from them where the negotiations with the Reetou are to take place."

"What difference does that make?" O'Neill asked. "We're just gonna get Daniel and bug out. They can negotiate all they want — without him."

Jacob stared at O'Neill. "Just the two of you are gonna rescue Danny?"

"Not quite, Dad." Carter's voice came from behind Jacob, and O'Neill took great satisfaction in the fact that both Jacob *and* Bra'tac were startled by her and Patel's arrival.

Jacob broke into a grin. "Sam!"

"Good to see you, Dad." Carter lowered her P90 and she and her father shared a quick hug.

"Teal'c!" That was Bra'tac, raising his staff weapon.

Whirling around, O'Neill saw that the Thakka had also emerged from where he'd been waiting in reserve.

Quickly, Teal'c moved to stand between Bra'tac and the Thakka. "Master Bra'tac, *no*! He is with us."

Bra'tac, pointedly, did not lower his weapon. "He is Kali's First Prime."

"No longer," Teal'c said.

"The big guy's right, Bra'tac," O'Neill said. "The Thakka's on our side."

Stepping around Teal'c, the Thakka held his hands open, indicating that he was unarmed. "I have been convinced that the Mother Goddess is neither of those things."

"Very well." Bra'tac finally lowered his weapon.

A weak voice uttered, "*Shol'va*" from the ground.

Everyone turned to see that the Jaffa O'Neill had shot was still breathing.

"Lookee there, a living prisoner," O'Neill said with a glance at Bra'tac.

While Bra'tac didn't rise to the bait, Jacob went straight to the Jaffa, his left hand raised upward. For the first time, O'Neill noticed that Jacob was wearing a hand device.

Jacob's voice went all weird, which meant Selmak was behind the wheel. "You have far greater concerns than a First Prime who has betrayed your mistress. Where are the Reetou negotiations to be held?"

"Tok'ra *hasshak*!" And for good measure, the Jaffa let loose with a snarl.

The whole snarling thing is really becoming a cliché, O'Neill thought. Aloud, he said, "I'm guessing *hasshak* is bad?"

"Indeed," Teal'c said.

Selmak held his left hand over the Jaffa's head, but didn't yet activate the hand device. O'Neill noticed Carter looking concerned, but she didn't move.

Selmak said, "I will use this if I must. Do not force me to, Jaffa."

"You are not worthy to wield a *kara kesh*, Tok'ra."

"Oh, for cryin' out loud." O'Neill stomped over with his P90 raised, aiming it right at the Jaffa's head. "Let me just finish this jackass off and we can move on. Pretty sure your little mini-snake can't heal you from a shot to the head."

Another snarl. "The Mother Goddess has designated the tavern as the place where her Tau'ri proxy will speak for her with the Reetou."

"See how easy that was? Carter?"

O'Neill stepped back and Carter fired her zat at the Jaffa.

Teal'c said, "We are familiar with the tavern."

"Yeah," O'Neill said. "But if a mere human can ask a question here, who gives a rat's ass? Daniel's in the castle. We go rescue him—"

"In fact, human," Bra'tac said, "Dr. Jackson is likely in that tavern, as the Reetou are present on this world. They came through the *chappa'ai* less than an hour ago."

"The gate's operational?" O'Neill smiled. "Well, that makes our exit strategy a helluva lot easier."

"Not necessarily, sir," Carter said. "Our GDOs were taken. Even if we get them back..."

Teal'c said, "Captain Patel and I have GDOs with acceptable codes."

"Good," O'Neill said. "Then we go to the tavern, spring Daniel—"

Jacob interrupted. "And disarm the bomb."

That brought O'Neill up short. "The what, now?"

"The Reetou are collaborating with a Goa'uld named Belos,

who's got it in for the System Lords. He gave the Reetou a bomb that is out of phase until it detonates — and it only takes things out that are *in* phase."

"Okay, so we get Daniel out of there before the bomb goes off."

"Sir," Carter said, "remember what Kali said when she black-mailed us into doing her dirty work? She said there'd be several humans helping Daniel out."

"And," Jacob said, "there's no guarantee we'll be able to get Daniel out before the bomb goes off — and the explosion won't affect the Reetou at all."

O'Neill looked at Carter. "Major, can the — "

But as usual, Carter was already with him. "Yes, sir, the device will bring the Reetou into phase."

"What device?" Bra'tac asked.

Once again, O'Neill provided the exposition, telling Jacob and Bra'tac what Carter was forced to do while Daniel was preparing his negotiations for Kali.

Carter then picked up the ball. "If we activate the device in the tavern, the Reetou will be back in phase. They'll be as affected by the bomb as everyone else, and they'll have to dismantle it themselves." She looked at Jacob. "Should save us the trouble of having to find it."

Jacob nodded. "That sounds like a plan. And I've got a bonus." He held up his left hand. "The reason why I bluffed that Jaffa is that this hand device has been modified from its original purpose. It doesn't do the brain-fry thing anymore, but it does protect the wearer and anyone nearby from being affected by the Reetou."

Teal'c said, "That is a very valuable weapon."

"Yeah, well, Belos decided he didn't need it anymore after Bra'tac and I remonstrated with him."

O'Neill saw Jacob and Bra'tac exchange a nod, and wondered if the universe could survive those two old farts bonding.

"All right, here's the plan. Carter, you need to get back to the mountain and retrieve your gadget. Bra'tac, you go with her."

Both Carter and Bra'tac nodded.

"Patel, you take Thak and Jacob to the rings here in the village. Jacob, send them up to Kali's mothership, then destroy the ring assembly. Did you gate here or take a ship?"

"Cargo ship, why?"

"Then after you send them up, go secure your ship, make sure no one else can fly it."

"Already did that, Jack. It's SOP for the Tok'ra."

Nodding, O'Neill said, "Fine. Thak, you tell Jacob where you parked your cargo ship, and Jacob, you sabotage it. I want Jacob's cargo ship to be the only way to get to the island with the gate. Then head over to the tavern — we'll need your hand device's protection from the Reetou."

Jacob removed the hand device from his left arm. "Best take it now. Bra'tac and I tested it out before. Whatever Belos did to it removed its guts, and also means that anyone can use it even if they don't have naquadah in their blood."

"That doesn't suck." O'Neill glanced at Teal'c, who was staring at the hand device in distaste. Figuring Teal'c wouldn't want to use it, O'Neill took the device from Jacob and slid it onto his left hand. He winced. "Geez, that metal's *hot*."

"With the amount of power those things generate, sir, it's a miracle they aren't hot enough to burn the arm. In fact, with the symbiote's healing power, they probably *could* burn the arm without —"

"Carter!" O'Neill snapped, holding up his hand. Then, remembering what was now on that hand, he quickly lowered it, not wanting to blast anyone across the ground.

"It's okay, Jack," Jacob said with a grin, "like I said, *all* the guts've been taken out. Belos just left the power source intact to supply the Reetou protection. All the other goodies that you usually get in a hand device are missing."

"Right. I knew that." O'Neill shook his head. "'Sides, in this cold, it's kinda nice. Like a hand-warmer."

The Thakka gazed at O'Neill. "Tell me, human — what is it you would have the *Kula* and I do aboard the Mother Goddess's *ha'tak*?"

O'Neill gave the Thakka a look, wondering how he could possibly not know the answer to that question. "Blow it up." He then turned to Patel. "Captain, you're familiar with the specs of a Goa'uld mothership?"

Patel nodded. "Yes, sir. I spent quite a bit of time on Cronus's mothership. Also, I read up on your mission on Apophis's ship and I'm pretty sure I remember where you placed the C-4 to most effectively destroy it."

"Nice to see you did your homework, Captain. Hey, Carter, next time I complain about paperwork, remind me what Patel just said?"

Smiling, Carter said, "Yes, sir."

"Thak, you're her native guide, just in case. Set the mothership to blow, then ring back down to Jacob's cargo ship. Teal'c, you're with me — we're heading to the tavern, seeing the lay of the land, and also seeing if we can rescue Daniel without needing Carter's doodad."

Teal'c inclined his head.

Carter said, "Captain, how much C-4 did you bring?"

"A dozen bricks."

While O'Neill nodded his approval, Carter asked, "Mind if I swipe a couple from you? We might need it. And ten should be enough to take down the mothership."

Nodding, Patel reached into her pack and removed two bricks. "I only have one remote, though, so if you need it, you'll have to set it off manually."

"Understood."

"Let's go, people." O'Neill stared down at his hand as they moved out. The hand device just felt *weird*, and he hoped he'd be able to get rid of it soon. But if it kept Teal'c off the bench when the Reetou were around, it was definitely worth it.

CHAPTER FIFTEEN

Stargate Command

"CHEVRON one encoded."

Lieutenant Colonel Louis Ferretti paced back and forth in the observation room as Sergeant Harriman dialed P3X-418 for the nine millionth time.

"Chevron two encoded," the sergeant said.

Ferretti had only recently returned to the SGC to lead SG-17, having been reassigned to head up security at Area 51 when he was promoted to lieutenant colonel. Since the first year of the Stargate program, that classified Nevada research facility had become the destination for the various bits of alien technology that had been brought back to Earth by the SG teams. As part of the first Air Force team to go through the gate to Abydos back in the day, Ferretti had been a logical choice to run security. He would rather have remained in command of SG-2, but like his uncle — also an Air Force officer, recently retired — always said, "When you wear the blue tuxedo, you dance where they tell you."

But after two years in Nevada, Ferretti was itching to go back in the field, and so he requested a transfer from General Hammond.

"Colonel," Hammond had said on the phone after receiving the request, "I've heard nothing but praise for the job you've done at Area 51. The Pentagon is very pleased with your work."

"Yes, sir, and I'm very glad to hear that, sir. But I need to get back in the field. I owe it to Brown, Freeman, Reilly, and Porro. They went through the gate with us to Abydos that first time, but they didn't make it back, and we couldn't even bring their bodies home. They were *good* men, General, the best, and they wound up being the first casualties of the SGC before it even really existed. I'm happy to serve wherever you need me, but I'd like to ask that I be allowed to go back through the gate again."

Within a week, Hammond had put the paperwork through, and Ferretti had assembled an all-new SG-17 to replace the team that had been killed in action on Revanna.

Their first assignment: to be on standby in case they were able to dial through to P3X-418, and if they were able to dial that Goa'uld-occupied world, go through to back up Teal'c and Captain Patel in their attempt to rescue SG-1.

Next to him in the control room, Harriman said, "Chevron three encoded."

Every hour on the hour since Teal'c, Patel, and Kali's First Prime had departed, they had set the dialing computer to P3X-418. Every hour on the hour, Ferretti had been here waiting. And every hour on the hour, the master sergeant on duty — first Laura Davis, later relieved by Harriman when Davis's shift ended — had said, "Chevron seven still will not engage," and Ferretti left the control room in frustration.

"Chevron four encoded."

Siler had the MALP ready to go — again — in case they got through. Based on the UAV telemetry Carter had gotten the other day, they wouldn't be able to initiate radio contact directly through the gate, as it was on an island pretty far from the settlement. They'd need the MALP's booster on the other side in order to communicate with any of the SGC personnel's radios.

"Chevron five encoded."

Unless, of course, they were still on the island. But Ferretti was assuming that they wouldn't have been sitting on their asses waiting around. One way or another, Jack O'Neill would find a way to get to what passed for civilization on that planet.

"Chevron six encoded."

Truthfully, Ferretti was making a lot of assumptions. The first, of course, being that the Stargate would eventually be working again. And that SG-1 still had their radios. And that Teal'c and Patel made it to P3X-418. And that any of them were still alive.

"Chevron seven locked!"

Harriman sounded stunned when he said the words, and Ferretti stared through the window at the gateroom in wonder as the Stargate opened.

Leaning down into the mic, he bellowed, "General Hammond to the control room. Siler, send the MALP through."

Siler nodded, and activated the MALP.

Hammond came downstairs from his office and the briefing room. "Report, Colonel."

"We've dialed P3X-418. Sending the MALP through now."

The general nodded, hands clasped behind his back.

About a minute later, Harriman said, "Receiving MALP telemetry."

The screen activated to show two of Kali's Jaffa. One of them activated his staff weapon and fired at the MALP, at which point the screen went dead.

Sounding almost sad, Harriman said, "MALP telemetry lost."

Leaning into the mic, Hammond said, "Sergeant, keep the wormhole open and prepare a UAV. I want it equipped with a radio booster and I need it before this wormhole's thirty-eight minutes are up."

Siler didn't hesitate. "Yes, sir."

"Colonel Ferretti, I want SG-17 suited up. Have Lieutenant Satterfield examine the telemetry we *did* receive, and give me a plan that gets you through the gate with no casualties."

Nodding, Ferretti said, "Absolutely, sir."

Siler had the UAV ready in fifteen minutes, just as Ferretti came back to the control room, now suited up and in winter fleece. His second-in-command, Captain Anneliese Peruzzi, was alongside him.

"Ready to launch, General," Siler's voice said over the intercom.

"Launch the UAV." Hammond then looked at Ferretti. "Colonel?"

Ferretti blew out a breath. "We're working on a plan, sir, based on the size of the island and the fact that there are only two Jaffa."

"Assuming," Peruzzi added, "that they don't ring more Jaffa in."

Grinning, Ferretti said, "Captain Peruzzi is the team cynic, sir."

"Your cynic raises a good point," Hammond said dryly.

"Yes, sir," Ferretti said with a quick nod, "which is why Lieutenant Satterfield and Corporal Spencer are going over the telemetry with a fine-tooth comb."

Harriman interrupted. "Receiving UAV telemetry now."

They all went over to peer at the screen.

"Still only two Jaffa at the gate," Harriman added.

Smiling at Peruzzi, Ferretti said, "See? Nothing to worry about."

Peruzzi just shot him a look.

"Radio booster online," Harriman said.

Again, Hammond leaned into the mic. "This is General Hammond to any SGC personnel. Respond, please."

After a moment, a voice said, "This is O'Neill."

"Good to hear your voice, Colonel."

"Yours too, sir. I'm here with Carter, and we've got Teal'c, Patel, Thak, Jacob, *and* Bra'tac."

Ferretti and Hammond exchanged glances. Having the Tok'ra and the Jaffa resistance present on P3X-418 was unexpected.

O'Neill continued: "It's a regular party here. Patel was good enough to bring spare radios, so we can all talk to each other. The bad news is Daniel's still Kali's prisoner. She wants him to be her mouthpiece in peace talks with the Reetou."

"That's unusual," Hammond said.

"Yeah, I thought so, too, sir, but she seems legit in wanting peace. The Reetou, not so much. According to Jacob and Bra'tac, they're gonna use a bomb to blow up the negotiation — a bomb that won't affect them."

Hammond frowned. "How is that possible?"

"Something to do with their being out of phase — Carter could explain it, but with respect, sir, we *really* don't have that kind of time. We've got us a plan to stop the Reetou from blowing up a bunch of innocent people, and also Daniel. We've also got a hand device that'll keep Jacob, Bra'tac, and Teal'c from letting the Reetou turn their guts inside out."

"SG-17 is on standby if you need assistance," Hammond said.

Ferretti grinned and added, "Ready to pull your ass out of the fire again, Colonel."

"Then I take it the gate really is back in action?"

"That's right, Colonel," Hammond said. "We assume Kali had it fixed."

Ferretti's grin fell. "Right now, it's guarded by two Jaffa."

"Think you can neutralize 'em, Ferretti?" O'Neill asked.

"Working on a plan right now."

"I figured. I need you to take out those two Jaffa, destroy the rings, and hold that island."

Frowning, Ferretti saw a really big hole in that plan. But before he could articulate it, the general beat him to it. "Colonel, the rings are the only way on and off that island. How will you get there?"

"We've got us a Tok'ra cargo ship, General. But the Reetou came in through the gate, so if we destroy the rings it cuts off their only avenue of escape. We're going to fix it so that the Reetou can't set off their bomb, but also that we're the only ones who get off-world. Which will be even easier if Ferretti's holding the gate."

Looking at Hammond, Ferretti prompted, "General?"

Hammond only mulled for half a second. "SG-17, you have a go."

Ferretti grinned. "Yes, sir. We'll have that island within thirty minutes."

"You'd better, Louie, or I'll have your ass," O'Neill said over the radio, and Ferretti could just *hear* the colonel's smirk.

"Failure's not in the budget, Jack. We'll hold the line, you just get to the island." Ferretti then looked at Peruzzi. "Let's go, Major, we've got people to save."

There were five SGC personnel on that planet, plus two allies, and apparently some innocent civilians who had the bad luck to be the subjects of a megalomaniac — just like Skaara and the other folks on Abydos. Ferretti had no intention of letting them die if he could do anything about it.

CHAPTER SIXTEEN

P3X-418—Jacob Carter/Selmak, the Thakka, and Captain Patel

THE THAKKA led the Tok'ra and the *Kula* through the village toward the rings.

The *Kula*—or, rather, Captain Patel—looked at him with concern. "You all right?"

At that, the Thakka smiled. "I am pleased to see that you are concerned with my welfare, *Ku*—Captain, rather."

"And I am pleased to be called 'Captain'," she said with a smile right back at him.

"To answer your question, it will be some time before I am ever able to say that I am 'all right,' as you put it. For starters, every instinct in my body cries out to kill this Tok'ra."

The Tok'ra simply grinned at that. "You're welcome to try, Chuckles."

"Worry not—I accept that we now fight on the same side. But for all my life, I have been told that the Tok'ra are gods who have lost their souls. They are the sworn enemy of the Goa'uld, and therefore the sworn enemy of the Jaffa. That is a difficult instinct to overcome."

"Well, try to overcome it, will you please? The plan goes into the toilet if I have to kill you."

"You are confident, Tok'ra." The Thakka tried to smile, but his heart wasn't in it.

Patel said, "I guess this is all a bit insane for you."

"Somewhat. I had a friend named Gan." He shook his head with great dismay. "By uttering his name aloud, I am committing a capital crime, by the way. He spoke out against the Mother Goddess, wondering why she allowed my predecessor as the Thakka to stay in the position long after his ability to do so had deteriorated. He should have been allowed to retire, the way your comrade Bra'tac did. In speaking his mind, Gan was killed, his name struck from all records. The Mother Goddess forbade us from even thinking his name."

The Thakka let out a long breath as they moved past a residence. "But Gan was correct. My predecessor's foolishness lead to many losses, and eventually to his death at the hands of Anubis's forces. Kali was *wrong*—just as she was wrong about the Reetou. It is a very difficult thing to learn that your gods are not divine after all."

"I wish I could say I knew how you felt," Patel said. "My grandparents were all devout Hindus, but my parents weren't. In fact, my mother is a member of American Atheists, and my father mostly just doesn't care one way or the other. So I was never raised with any kind of religion."

"Once, Captain, I would have pitied you for such an upbringing." He laughed bitterly. "In fact, that time would have been only two days ago. Now, though, I envy you. You can never know the crushing disappointment I am feeling now."

Before Patel could answer him, the Tok'ra said, "Here we are."

Looking up, the Thakka saw that they were at the rings. The Tok'ra was moving to kneel down behind the console.

"The Jaffa on the *ha'tak* will believe me to be their First Prime," the Thakka said to Patel. "Leave your weapon slung behind your back."

Patel started to say something, then stopped. "Okay, I thought for sure you were going to make me give you my P90. Which wasn't going to happen. And we already broke the fake shackles."

"Should my bluff fail, I would prefer you to be able to wield your weapon—but the bluff will definitely fail if you are holding it at the ready."

Nodding, Patel said, "Fair enough."

The Tok'ra rose from behind the console. "Okay, I've set up a feedback loop—the next time this thing gets used, the energy buildup won't shut back down, and it'll overload. So get your butts up there, and we'll see you at the gate."

"Of course." The Thakka moved to stand within the rings, as did Patel.

Colonel O'Neill had altered their part of the strategy after they heard from their fellow Tau'ri. Instead of taking the rings to the Tok'ra's *tel'tak*, they were to go straight to the island with the *chappa'ai*, as it would be held by Tau'ri forces.

"Good luck," the Tok'ra said, and then the rings rose from the ground and sent them to the *ha'tak*.

To the Thakka's relief, the ring room was empty when they arrived.

Patel said, "We should start at the engine room. The C-4 will do the most damage there."

Nodding, the Thakka moved toward the doorway. No one was coming down the corridor, and he gestured for Patel to follow.

In a low voice, he said, "Many of the Mother Goddess's Jaffa are on the surface to guard her personage, and also to search for Colonel O'Neill and Major Carter. Her *lo'taur* are all on the surface as well. There should only be a small crew on board."

They moved swiftly and silently. The Thakka found himself admiring Patel's skills. Perhaps she wasn't truly *Kali Kula* — perhaps, no one was — but he felt that she was definitely worthy of his protection, for all that she probably didn't really need it.

And then they turned a corner and saw two Jaffa.

Patel already had her weapon behind her back, and the Thakka said, "Jaffa, I have escaped from the Tau'ri and taken one of their soldiers prisoner. Where is the Mother Goddess?"

Both Jaffa aimed their *ma'toks*. "*Shol'va!*" they cried in unison and opened fire.

CHAPTER SEVENTEEN

P3X-418—Major Carter and Master Bra'tac

SAM AND Bra'tac moved silently but quickly through the trees back toward the mountain and the secret tunnel the Thaka had described. Well, Bra'tac moved silently; Sam did the best she could.

Once they reached the area the Thakka had indicated on the map, Sam regarded the mountain face, covered as it was in brush and rocks, and tried to find the ingress point.

"One of these days," she said, "you need to teach me how to move like that."

Bra'tac actually smiled. "Your technique is quite adequate for a human of limited training."

Sam hesitated. "I was about to say that I wouldn't call the Air Force Academy 'limited,' but I've also heard Teal'c talk about what you put him through. Then again, you guys can afford to train more extensively when you've got a symbiote to heal any injury."

"Meaning what?" Bra'tac sounded genuinely confused and not offended, which Sam had worried about the minute the words came out of her mouth.

While continuing to search the rockface, Sam said, "Well, you can train harder and go through much more brutal exercises because you know that any injury you receive will heal quickly. We can't do that — if I sprained an ankle or broke an arm during my Academy days, I'd be out of commission for *months*. If the same thing happens to Jaffa, they're only down for a day at the most."

At that, Bra'tac looked thoughtful. "I had not considered that. Perhaps I have been too dismissive of the Tau'ri's prowess."

Grinning, Sam said, "It's okay. I mean, the larval symbiote is a part of you — I doubt you give it much thought day to day any more or less than you do a limb or an organ." Then she saw something that seemed out of place: a rock that was a perfect sphere. Rock formations were rarely symmetrical or orderly, and for that reason a smooth, solid sphere was unlikely — and it was even more unlikely for such a formation to just happen to be near the secret door.

She grabbed the rock and tried turning it, then pulling on it.

The latter did the trick, as a bit of rock slid inward about twenty feet, revealing a dark tunnel.

"Not bad," Bra'tac said with a nod.

Sam smiled as she switched on the flashlight attached to her P90. Cautiously, she entered, moving around the rock to slip into the tunnel itself.

The light was swallowed by the darkness eventually, but Sam saw enough to know that it was a long tunnel carved out of the mountain rock. "Amazing. This must have been artificially created. The floor is almost completely flat, and there are no stalactites or stalagmites that would indicate that it's a natural formation." She glanced back at Bra'tac, who looked even less interested than the colonel usually did. "Sorry," she added with a bashful smile.

"There is nothing for which you need apologize. It is impressive to find as talented a warrior as you who also retains the intellectual curiosity of the scientist. I see why your father is so proud, and also why Teal'c speaks so highly of you."

"Really?" Sam blinked. "That's — a surprise."

"That Teal'c would praise you or that your father is proud?"

"Both." She hesitated. "Well, okay, really only Teal'c. Three years ago, it would've been both, but Dad's changed since he blended with Selmak. It's like being a Tok'ra has brought out all his best qualities."

Bra'tac nodded. "Interesting. My dealings with the Tok'ra have been — limited. It is difficult to imagine a Goa'uld parasite making someone *better*."

"Well, it's working for them." Sam noted a curve in the tunnel ahead, and held up a hand. She moved alongside the cavern wall and peered around the curve with the flashlight. "Clear," she said. "Anyhow, since he blended, Dad has been friendly, proud, solicitous, less cranky, less mopey — it's been really nice."

"He was not like this when you were a child?"

"*No*, no, no," Sam said emphatically. "Before my Mom died, he was all gruff and bombast. If my brother or I did something wrong, we heard about it for weeks, but it was really rare that he gave us praise for doing something right." She sighed. "After Mom died, he was still gruff, but a lot more stoic — and a lot more cranky. He barely spoke to either of us. The house got *real* quiet after that. The dinner table used to be when we'd all gab at each other. Even Dad, when he was home, would do most of his talking over supper. I'd talk about homework, Mark would talk about music or girls, Mom would talk about something she'd read, or we'd all talk about something on TV or a movie we saw. But after Mom died, the only sound was us eating." She shook her head and turned to give the Jaffa a sheepish look. "Sorry. For some reason, I've been thinking about the past a lot today."

Bra'tac favored her with a gentle smile. "As I said, Major Carter, there is nothing for which you need to apologize."

As much to get the subject off her as anything, she asked, "How *did* you two wind up coming here together, anyhow?"

"I was attempting to recruit Imhotep's Jaffa to the rebellion when the Reetou attacked. I was the only survivor, and I tracked them to a world where they met with their Goa'uld benefactor. Your father had also arrived on that world based on intelligence provided by the Tok'ra who served with Kali."

Sam nodded. She hadn't had time to fully compare notes with Dad, but she wasn't surprised that Ramprasad's intel had led to the Tok'ra taking action. She wondered if Dad had specifically requested the duty once Ramprasad reported that seventy-five percent of SG-1 had been trapped on one of Kali's worlds, especially since his daughter was part of that percentage.

They came to a doorway with an ornate handle. Sam glanced

at Bra'tac, who nodded and got his staff weapon ready.

Sam tried the handle. It moved down easily and unlatched the door, which slid open toward her.

She cautiously moved through the doorway, P90 at the ready, but now with the flashlight switched off because the corridor into which the door led was well lit. She also recognized the corridor in question from their initial run through the stronghold looking for survivors, right after they found Ramprasad.

Turning to Bra'tac, she pointed twice toward the direction that would take them to her erstwhile lab.

As they got to the end of the corridor, Sam peered around the corner to see that four Jaffa were gathered at the base of the staircase that would take them up to the level where the lab was. The four were relaxed, speaking amongst themselves. Idly, Sam wondered what it was Jaffa talked about around the proverbial water cooler.

She looked over at Bra'tac, who nodded and unholstered his zat.

Following his lead, Sam did likewise.

Then Bra'tac moved out to the center of the corridor, which struck Sam as being spectacularly tactically unsound.

Normally, Bra'tac had a low, deep voice, but it got about an octave lower and several fathoms deeper as he shouted, "Jaffa, *kree!*"

All four of Kali's Jaffa snapped to attention at his commanding tone like a bunch of fourth-year cadets. Hell, Sam had to physically stop herself from straightening and putting her heels together.

Then Bra'tac raised his zat and shot two of them. Sam did likewise half a second later to the other two.

Walking slowly toward the four unconscious Jaffa, Bra'tac dryly said, "They are well trained."

Sam shook her head. She found herself reminded of the time her father was assigned to Andrews Air Force Base when she was a kid. Dad had been either a major or a lieutenant colonel then, she couldn't recall, but he had been giving his daughter a tour of the base. He'd been showing her around, checking out the hangars and the planes and the mess hall and the barracks — and then they'd turned a corner and saw four airmen playing cards. One of them hadn't shaved that morning.

Suddenly, he wasn't Dad anymore. He was an officer, chewing out four noncoms who had seriously screwed up. His back had gotten straighter, his voice had gotten deeper, just like Bra'tac's just now.

Even when Dad was chewing out Sam or her brother Mark, his eyebrows were always raised a bit, softening his face. But that day, with those SFs, the eyebrows were pointed straight downward, his eyes hardened.

Dad's eyebrows had stayed lowered like that pretty much exclusively after Mom's death…

Shaking herself out of her reverie, she and Bra'tac proceeded up the stairs.

As they got to the landing, she quickly got her bearings. They were close to the lab she'd been working in, and, with a gesture for Bra'tac to follow, she led the way along the silent corridor.

But just as they approached the doorway to the lab, a Jaffa came through it. His eyes went wide with surprise before he yelled, "*Kree!*" and opened fire.

CHAPTER EIGHTEEN

P3X-418—Colonel O'Neill and Teal'c

ONE OF the first things Teal'c learned while training under Master Bra'tac was that you could taste a victory in the wind.

It was not a perfect system, of course. There were times when victory seemed so sure he could taste it, only to have an unforeseen circumstance take it away.

But today, Teal'c could taste victory against Kali and against the Reetou. His plan had gone perfectly; he, the Thakka, and Captain Patel had reached Imphal without difficulty, and not only had they found O'Neill and Major Carter, but as an added bonus, Jacob Carter and Master Bra'tac were here as well.

Teal'c was sure that they would be victorious.

He and O'Neill slowly moved toward the tavern where they'd found Ramprasad. Teal'c noted that there were four Jaffa on guard, but at a distance.

Currently, the pair of them were crouched behind another structure that appeared to be a residence. O'Neill held up four fingers and whispered, "We've got four."

In a similarly hushed tone, Teal'c said, "The Reetou must be present in the tavern."

O'Neill activated the *kara kesh* he wore, which started to glow in the manner it did when a Goa'uld used it. "Stay close," he whispered over the hum.

Teal'c inclined his head. Intellectually, the Jaffa knew that it would have made more sense for Teal'c himself to wear the modified hand device. But too often had he and other Jaffa been the victim of petty attacks by the Goa'uld, who used the *kara kesh* as a quick-and-dirty punishment for any slight, whether real or imagined. Even wearing a modified device would feel too much like a betrayal.

As ever, Teal'c was grateful for O'Neill's perspicacity. He

understood Teal'c's discomfort without forcing him to speak it aloud. It was one of many reasons why he valued O'Neill so much as a fellow warrior and as a friend.

The four guards were at standing intervals, and Teal'c found himself disappointed in the training the Thakka had given his Jaffa. Roving guards would make the location more secure. On the other hand, no Goa'uld or Jaffa were present in the tavern, thanks to the Reetou, so perhaps Kali thought only a standing patrol was necessary. Indeed, she probably believed that the guards were primarily to keep Daniel Jackson and the other humans in, rather than to keep anyone out.

Teal'c would enjoy proving her wrong.

O'Neill held up three fingers, then two, then one, then clenched his fist.

Both of them leapt out from behind the dwelling and opened fire. Teal'c fired his *ma'tok* at the Jaffa closest to the door, while O'Neill aimed his P90 at the one to that Jaffa's left.

Teal'c's shot was true, and the Jaffa fell. O'Neill's rounds clattered on the Jaffa's armor, and several of his shots went wide and high.

"Damn hand device," O'Neill muttered, and then fired again.

From behind him, Teal'c heard a voice cry, "*Shol'va!*"

Whirling around, he saw two more Jaffa exit the dwelling they'd been hiding behind.

And behind them was Kali.

"Please drop your weapons," she said with a smile. "Or don't, and allow my Jaffa to kill you. Either suits me."

Teal'c glanced at O'Neill, though he knew what his response would be. Sure enough, O'Neill slowly unhooked his P90 from the strap and placed it on the snowy ground. Only then did Teal'c do likewise with his *ma'tok*.

Kali stepped forward. "I suspect, Colonel, that my first instinct to kill you was the proper one. I only truly needed Dr. Jackson and Major Carter. Letting you live has proven to be more trouble than it is worth." She then regarded Teal'c with anger. "And you have turned my First Prime against me, which can be added to your already-impressive list of crimes against the gods, *shol'va*."

Teal'c was surprised that Kali had such intelligence.

O'Neill voiced Teal'c's thought. "And you know about that, how, exactly?"

Kali glanced at one of her Jaffa, who held up an Air Force radio.

That caused O'Neill to wince, and Teal'c recalled that Kali had taken all the equipment that his SG-1 teammates had brought to the planet initially—including their radios.

With a smile, Kali said, "Yaresh here was the one who heard you speaking with your Tau'ri masters when passing the room where we kept your equipment. He brought it to me and allowed me to hear. Your primitive communications device was unable to glean everything, but I heard enough to know what your plan would be—and that my First Prime had turned on me. I believe I shall make Yaresh the new Thakka, since the old one must now die. My Jaffa will take him and the Tau'ri accompanying him on my *ha'tak*, as well as Major Carter and Apophis's other *shol'va* in the castle. And it is only a matter of time before we locate the Tok'ra Selmak."

Teal'c felt his heart sink. He had tasted victory in the air, it was within their grasp. Yet now, Kali had removed it from him.

Kali walked toward O'Neill. "And now thanks to your Tok'ra friend, I no longer require Dr. Jackson's services." She reached for O'Neill's left hand, but he pulled it back. "Please, Colonel, do not force me to remove the *kara kesh* from your corpse."

O'Neill let out a long, exaggerated breath and removed the *kara kesh* himself, handing it to Kali.

"Excellent." She handed the ribbon device to Yaresh. "You will protect your goddess from the Reetou, Yaresh. Serve me well in this, and you will indeed become the new Thakka."

Yaresh bowed his head. "I live only to serve the Mother Goddess."

Rolling his eyes, O'Neill muttered, "Oh, *please.*"

"Bring them," Kali said, leading them to the tavern.

Teal'c moved forward, goaded on by Yaresh and the other Jaffa, who remained behind them with their *ma'tok*s armed and ready. Kali led the way into the tavern, right past the two Jaffa corpses. Teal'c couldn't help but notice that Kali gave not a thought to the lives of those two Jaffa, and he considered and rejected pointing that out to Yaresh and his comrade.

Now was not the time to attempt to recruit for the rebellion. Besides, Yaresh would probably just say that the two dead Jaffa were pleased to have died in service to their so-called Mother Goddess.

It made Teal'c ill. So much death, so much carnage. Indeed, he knew exactly how much death and carnage, as he himself had been the cause of so much of it over the decades. He remembered every death he had been responsible for in service of Apophis, from the first Jaffa he'd killed in battle to the civilians he had massacred in Apophis's name. Even those who died due his inaction weighed on him, such as Sergeant Carol Weterings, the first Tau'ri Teal'c had ever met. She'd been taken from Cheyenne Mountain by Apophis as a possible host for Amaunet. Apophis's bride rejected Weterings, and Apophis casually murdered her while Teal'c stood by, helpless to stop it.

All those lost souls weighed on Teal'c's mind, and he knew that these two Jaffa, who senselessly lost their lives in service of a false god by the hand of Teal'c and his comrade, would do the same.

It was the burden he chose to bear when he joined O'Neill, Major Carter, and Daniel Jackson on Chulak. He did not regret that decision, but the sorrow never ended.

He knew it never would.

They entered the tavern, where Daniel Jackson sat at one of the tables, surrounded by six humans, three on either side of him, who were obviously servants of Kali. On the table in front of him was a pair of Goa'uld tablets, several more sheets of paper, and one small device that Teal'c did not recognize, though it appeared to be of Goa'uld design.

Upon Kali's entrance, two Reetou briefly became visible, standing opposite where Daniel Jackson sat. A series of clattering noises came from where they stood, and then the device Teal'c had not recognized uttered words in a mechanical tone: "What is the meaning of this interruption?"

Kali took a small bow. "Forgive me, noble adversary, but the time for intermediaries is past. I now have the means to continue these negotiations in person."

The device then let loose with a series of noises that sounded much like the Reetou language.

The Reetou remained invisible, but Teal'c could hear their reply in their language, which the translator rendered as: "We must consult for a moment. This development was not what was negotiated."

"Understood," Kali said with another bow. "The technology that allows me to participate directly only just became available to me. Take all the time you need."

Despite himself, Teal'c was impressed. Kali actually sounded humble and capitulating, two modes he had never seen a Goa'uld adopt except as a ruse. Of course, Kali's politeness may also have been a ruse.

Daniel Jackson looked over at O'Neill and Teal'c. "Uh, hi, guys. What's goin' on?"

"Hi, Daniel. How's things?"

"Oh, peachy until a second ago. Well, not peachy, but at least we were starting to have a dialogue. What's this all about?"

O'Neill shrugged. "Just trying to rescue you."

"Rescue me."

"Yeah."

"Not really going all that well, is it?"

"Not so much."

The Reetou suddenly spoke again. "We have consulted, and

agree to speak directly to the Goa'uld Kali rather than her emissary. The emissary is dismissed."

"Excellent," O'Neill said, "we'll just head on back to the Stargate and go home."

"Hardly." Kali looked at Yaresh. "Put Dr. Jackson with his friends."

O'Neill shook his head. "Coulda *sworn* you gave us your word that we'd be free to go once we did everything you asked us to do."

"Had you done everything I asked you to do, Colonel, I would have." Kali smiled sweetly. "But instead you attacked me and my Jaffa and have attempted to undermine my work." Then she turned back to the Reetou — or, rather, where the Reetou were supposed to be, they remained out of sight — as Yaresh picked Daniel Jackson up from his chair and put him alongside O'Neill and Teal'c. "These three are part of a team known as SG-1, a group of soldiers from the Tau'ri. I believe you are familiar with them, as they thwarted your attempt to destroy Earth?"

It was a moment before the Reetou replied. "We are familiar with the people of Earth, yes."

"Then, may I offer the three of them as prisoners for you to do with as you will in punishment for the Reetou deaths they caused? I am also on the verge of producing the fourth member of their team."

The Reetou again hesitated before replying. "That is an acceptable offer, pending the conclusion of these negotiations."

O'Neill visibly winced. Daniel Jackson let out a long sigh.

Teal'c frowned.

The taste of potential victory was growing bitter in his mouth.

CHAPTER NINETEEN

P3X-418—Captain Patel and the Thakka

PATEL DUCKED and rolled as soon as the first syllable of *"shol'va"* came from the Jaffa's lips. Not for the first time, she was grateful that the staff weapon took a couple of seconds to get into position, aim, arm, and fire. Had the Jaffa been carrying an Earth firearm, Patel would probably be dead with several bullets in her chest instead of rolling on the deck with staff weapon fire flying over her head.

She came up on her stomach and aimed and fired her P90 on automatic, which took out one of the Jaffa, while the Thakka fired with his own staff weapon to take out the other.

Shaking her head, Patel clambered to her feet. "Dammit, how'd they know about you?"

"I do not know." The Thakka walked over to kneel beside the two corpses. "I am sorry, Haj. You were a good warrior. As were you, Torret."

Patel appreciated what the Thakka was doing—these were *his* soldiers not that long ago—but there wasn't time for this. *Focus on the job while you're doing it. Think about what it means after it's done.* "We have to move. If the Jaffa know you've turned, we're not gonna be able to bluff our way out."

The Thakka turned and looked up at Patel.

Wincing, Patel saw a hollowness in the Thakka's eyes that she hadn't seen before. When she first met him on this snowy world, he'd seemed devoted, and on the cargo ship as she and Teal'c wore him down, he was angry.

Now he was sad. Worse, he looked defeated.

In her best imitation of Major Lagdamen, she barked, "We don't have time to mope, soldier. Move!"

He nodded. "Of course. The engine room."

They moved quickly toward their destination. Miraculously,

they encountered no Jaffa. She was worried that the Jaffa would be able to sneak up on them, since Kali was the only Goa'uld she knew of who carpeted her corridors.

She quickly placed C-4 in all the optimal places. They moved on to several other locations and were amazingly left alone.

This is going way too smoothly.

Just as she had that thought, they approached the bridge, to find four more Jaffa visible through the open hatch.

Dammit, I knew *it was going too smoothly.*

She looked over at the Thakka and shook her head. Putting C-4 in the *pel'tak* wasn't absolutely necessary. While you could control all ship's functions from the bridge, none of the actual critical systems were located there. The only reason to blow it up was to keep anyone on board from trying to accomplish anything like piloting or sending out a communiqué.

But that comparatively minor advantage wasn't worth a four-against-two fight that they'd probably lose. They were lucky with the previous two Jaffa, and Patel stopped counting on luck being useful the day Captain Negassa was killed.

She tried to convey all that with the shaking of her head at the Thakka. Then she motioned for them to move away, toward the ring room.

Instead, the Thakka set his staff weapon against the bulkhead and touched several of the hieroglyphs on it. When he was done, he stood in the entryway to the bridge without actually going inside. The staff weapon remained out of his hands against the bulkhead.

What the hell is he doing?

He held up his arms. "Jaffa!"

All four Jaffa turned around. One raised his staff weapon. "*Shol'va!*"

"Please, my loyal Jaffa, hear me! I know you believe me to be a traitor to the Mother Goddess — and perhaps I am. But that is because my eyes have been opened to the fact that Kali is no goddess."

Patel stayed out of sight, thinking that this was very much *not* the time to try a recruiting drive, but helpless to do anything.

Well, not *completely* helpless. She could just leave, head to the ring room and leave the Thakka to his boneheaded play.

But no, that wasn't the mission. And besides, the Thakka *had* turned. He was one of the good guys now. Patel had seen the members of the Jaffa rebellion that they'd installed on the Alpha Site — the exposure of Kytano as Imhotep had been a devastating blow. Having the First Prime of a System Lord on their side would be a huge shot in the arm. More so if he brought some of his friends along.

So she stayed to the side of the entryway, P90 at the ready, hoping that the Thakka knew what the hell he was doing.

From the sounds of it, he wasn't making much headway. One of the Jaffa said, "How dare you speak that way! I looked up to you, Thakka — the day you were chosen as the new First Prime, I was the first to cheer. Now I look upon you with disgust and shame."

The Thakka still had his hands up. "Disgust and shame are indeed appropriate, my friend, but it should not be directed at me. The Goa'uld are *all* false gods, including the Mother Goddess herself. She is *not* all-knowing, *not* all-seeing. If she was, she would have known I would betray her."

"She did, *shol'va*! That is why she sent you on this fool's errand to Imphal, to sacrifice you so a *loyal* First Prime could take your place."

Patel rolled her eyes. She gave the Thakka an *are we done here?* look.

"A pity," the Thakka said. "Let us hope she is all-knowing enough to save you."

And then he lowered his outstretched right arm to touch one of the hieroglyphs, which shut the hatch.

He turned to Patel. "That will only keep them trapped in the *pel'tak* for a few minutes, and they will alert the other Jaffa to our presence." Then he held up a hand, just as Patel was opening her mouth to object. "I realize it has made our position more precarious, but these are warriors I fought beside. Some of them I trained with, others I trained. I had to at least *attempt* to bring them to our side. I owed them that much respect."

Patel's argument died on her lips. "Fine. Let's get to the ring room and blow this popsicle stand."

"What is a popsicle?" the Thakka asked as he grabbed his staff weapon.

She laughed. *Blow this popsicle stand* was one of Lagdamen's favorite phrases. She hadn't even realized that she'd adopted it until the Thakka asked her the question. *I guess he's not the only one who owes respect to comrades.*

As they jogged down the carpeted corridor, Patel said, "When we get back to Earth, I'll show you, but basically they're flavored ice." At the Thakka's dubious expression, she added, "They're *really* yummy. Teal'c *loves* them."

She actually had no idea what Teal'c's feelings were on popsicles, but she figured that would help.

They made it to the ring room without incident

"Small favors," Patel muttered, then added more loudly: "Guard the door."

As she went inside, the Thakka shouted, "*Kula!*"

Before she could even respond, she saw him leap in front of her, as he had done the last time the pair of them were at a ring terminus, and just like the last time, he took weapons fire meant for her.

As he fell to the deck, she saw a Jaffa holding a smoking staff weapon.

Whom she then shot with her P90 on automatic.

She didn't even wait for the Jaffa to fall before kneeling down at the Thakka's side. He was lying on his back, clutching his belly. "Let me see."

Removing his hands, Patel saw that the staff weapon had struck him right in the pouch that housed the Goa'uld symbiote. His entire belly basically looked like it had been through a meat grinder and then set on fire. She didn't think there was anything *left* of the larval Goa'uld.

He muttered, "*Shel kek nem ron.*"

Then he went limp on the deck.

For about three seconds, Patel just stared at the Thakka's body.

Then she pulled the timer for the C-4 out of the pocket of her desert camo. *At least I get to give him a Viking funeral.* She looked over at the dead Jaffa who shot him. *Even have a dog to lay at his feet.*

Of course, Viking funerals would've been more appropriate for Norse gods rather than a Hindu one like Kali, but the hell with it.

She set the timer for one minute, then moved both bodies out of the circumference of the rings. After entering the code, she activated the timer just as the rings rose from the deck and whisked her down to the Stargate.

CHAPTER TWENTY

P3X 418—Lieutenant Colonel Ferretti and the rest of SG-17

FERRETTI waited for the Stargate to open and then he walked up the ramp toward the event horizon. He said, "Go!" and he, Major Peruzzi, Lieutenant Satterfield, and Corporal Spencer all threw flashbangs into the wormhole.

Looking over at Satterfield, he saw that she was mouthing numbers, so she was counting down how much time it would take the flashbangs to go through the wormhole, materialize on the other side, and go off—hopefully blinding those two Jaffa in the process.

Then Ferretti glanced over at Peruzzi, and shook his head with amusement. *If only me five years ago could see me now.* While his parents raised him, it was his mother's brother who'd had the biggest influence on his life. Uncle Freddie had flown bombers for the Air Force in Vietnam. Ferretti looked upon Colonel Manfred Louis Monferato as a true hero, and as a boy he hung on Uncle Freddie's every word.

And a dozen of those words, spoken often, were, "Don't know what they were thinkin', lettin' women into the Air Force."

Because Uncle Freddie said it, it had to be true. Never mind that Ferretti's own mother, the colonel's sister, kept saying he was full of it, that women had always been part of the Air Force since it was formed after World War II. "It's not like it went downhill after they let women in 'cause they *always* let women in."

Mom and Uncle Freddie argued about that a lot.

Ferretti, though, always listened to Uncle Freddie because he was the colonel and he flew bombers, and Mom was just Mom, and he didn't listen to her when she said vegetables were good for him, so why listen to her about that?

His attitudes were rarely challenged when he went to the Academy or after he graduated. Nor were they during his entire time in the service, up to and including a classified mission that took him to an alien world called Abydos.

It wasn't until a year after that, when he met Samantha Carter, that he realized he was being an ass. Kawalsky and Ferretti hadn't wanted Carter along on the mission, as they figured she'd be a liability — though she did share Ferretti's love of Major Matt Mason astronaut action figures.

The SG-2 team that Ferretti had inherited from Kawalsky was all-male, and during the year he'd been in charge of it, he kept it all male, stubbornly insisting upon following Uncle Freddie's credo.

But once he transferred to Nevada, and he started reading all the reports as they came in, he realized just how often Carter in particular not only pulled SG-1's fat out of the fire, but saved the whole damn planet. After another year, he started to realize that maybe Mom was right and Uncle Freddie was full of it.

As a result, when Hammond gave him the go-ahead to put the new SG-17 together, the only thing Ferretti looked at were the service records, not the names. Peruzzi had served with distinction in the Gulf as a pilot, and lately had been serving at the Pentagon under Major Davis, but was also being promoted to major and had requested a transfer to a field position. Satterfield was a recent Academy graduate, one of four from this year's class who had been tapped for the SGC. She'd been waiting for an opening — tragically, one of those openings was created by her classmate, Lieutenant Kevin Elliot, who had been part of the previous version of SG-17 and was killed with the rest of them on Revanna.

As far as Ferretti was concerned, the fourth person had to be a jar-head. Given the types of threats SG teams faced, he wanted at least one person on the team whose primary purpose was muscle, and one of Uncle Freddie's bits of advice that

Ferretti still thought was useful was: "Best man to watch your six is a Marine." The best Marine available, based on the service records Hammond had given him, was Corporal Avery Spencer, who was part of one of the gate room security details. Like the others, he was a recent promotion.

Satterfield stopped counting and said, "Now, sir!"

"Let's *go!*" Ferretti cried, and the four of them ran toward the wormhole.

"Godspeed, SG-17," Hammond said over the mic just as Ferretti reached the event horizon.

He hesitated for just a second before crouching down to step through, wanting to come in low in case the flashbangs didn't work.

Sure enough, as soon as the four of them came through the gate, staff weapon fire went over their heads and into the wormhole.

"Take cover!" Ferretti cried, leaping off the stone ramp to the left, watching as Peruzzi and Satterfield did likewise to the right, while Spencer took cover underneath the DHD.

Ferretti looked over the island, peering through the snow.

There was no sign of actual Jaffa. The staff weapon fire had come from two different places on this small island, but it had happened fast enough, and over his head, that he hadn't been able to pinpoint it.

Luckily, Satterfield came to his rescue. From the other side of the ramp, she thumbed her radio, Ferretti hearing her voice more clearly over the radio clipped to his clavicle than he would if she tried to shout over the ramp. "We've got one hiding behind the rafts, and the other behind the ring controller."

Peruzzi's voice came over the radio next. "I told you the flashbangs wouldn't work." After a second, she added, "Sir."

Ferretti smiled. "Fine, Major, next time, you come up with the brilliant strategy."

"I'd rather complain about yours, sir," Peruzzi deadpanned.

The two Jaffa popped out from their cover like jacks-in-the-box and fired their staff weapons. Ferretti ducked behind the ramp. The blast hit the ramp itself.

But before the blasts even hit, Spencer also broke cover long enough to fire several rounds, then ducked back behind the DHD.

The exchange of fire continued for a few more minutes. Ferretti, Peruzzi, and Spencer fired their P90s, while Satterfield did likewise with her zat. The Jaffa fired their staff weapons. Nobody hit anyone, but the ramp, DHD, and ring controls all took plenty of fire.

However, the rafts — which were already pretty beat up — were taking plenty of damage from the P90s.

Thumbing his radio, Ferretti said, "Peruzzi, Spencer, concentrate all your fire at the rafts."

"Sir!" Spencer broke cover and fired. Peruzzi did so half a second later.

Within about ten seconds, the rafts were being cut to ribbons, and the Jaffa back there was forced to break cover and run toward the ring controller.

As soon as he did so, Satterfield fired her zat at him. He cried out with a loud, "Urk!" and fell to the snow-covered ground.

The other Jaffa didn't miss a beat, breaking cover again, leaning on the ring controller and firing. Ferretti ducked quickly behind the ramp.

"Hey, Jaffa!" he shouted. "You may wanna reconsider your position!"

He waited a few seconds to see if he replied.

Unsurprisingly, he didn't.

So Ferretti went on: "There's four of us. There's one of you. Now I'm not the world's greatest mathematician, but I'm pretty sure that puts the odds in our favor."

The Jaffa responded by shouting something in the Goa'uld language.

As usual, to Ferretti, it sounded like a cat horking up a hairball. Satterfield was the team's linguist, so when the Jaffa was done shouting, Ferretti thumbed his radio. "Satterfield, what'd he say?"

"I'd tell you, sir, but I promised my grandmother I wouldn't use those words anymore."

"Noted."

"I have an idea, sir," Satterfield added. "He keeps resting his arms on the ring controller when he fires."

"Yeah, so?"

"Hang on, sir."

Spencer took another shot at the ring controller. As soon as he did, the Jaffa resurfaced and fired again. Satterfield risked breaking cover and fired her zat at the ring controller. The electrical blast hit its mark, sending a charge all through the controller — as well as anything touching it. Like the Jaffa. Who convulsed and then fell to the ground.

Ferretti ran over to the ring controller, P90 at the ready. "Spencer, with me!"

The Jaffa was facedown in the snow and not moving.

"Nice work, Lieutenant!" Ferretti called back to the ramp. Then he looked at Spencer. "Corporal, do me a favor and get ready to trash the living hell out of that ring controller."

Spencer smiled. "Yes, *sir.*"

While he got to work, Ferretti went over to check the other Jaffa, who was also unmoving.

"Major Peruzzi, please secure these two fine gentlemen while Lieutenant Satterfield takes their weapons away."

Peruzzi smiled wryly. "You always give me the fun jobs, Colonel."

Before Ferretti could come up with a smartass reply of his own, the rings activated.

Spencer, who had been kneeling down at the ring controller planting C-4, immediately leapt to his feet, P90 at the ready.

The rings popped out of the snow, glowed, and then went back underground. Captain Kirti Patel was now standing in the center of them.

Patel immediately saluted upon seeing Ferretti. "Colonel."

Returning the salute, he said, "At ease, Captain — and nice timing. Stand down, Spencer, and get back to work."

"Yes, sir." Spencer did as he was told.

Having finished securing the Jaffas' wrists with zip-ties, Peruzzi turned to face the captain. "Weren't you part of a two-person team?"

Patel nodded. "The Thakka didn't make it. He saved my life." She glanced at her watch, then looked up.

Ferretti tracked her gaze and saw a bright light in the sky, followed a second or two later by a loud detonation.

"Good work," he said. "Of course, when *I* blew up a Goa'uld mothership, I had a nuke. Made a much bigger boom."

"It didn't fit in the backpack, sir," Patel said with a tiny smile.

Grinning, Ferretti said to Peruzzi, "I'm gonna dial the gate, report to Hammond. Let's hope everyone else did their jobs as well as the captain here."

CHAPTER TWENTY-ONE

P3X-418—Major Carter and Master Bra'tac

BRA'TAC felt the fiery sizzle of the *ma'tok* as it struck his left arm even as he fired his *zat'ni'katel* with his right.

The Jaffa fell to the floor, and only then did Bra'tac clutch his left bicep where it was wounded. Pain sliced through his arm, but he knew his *prim'ta* would heal his wound in time.

Major Carter slowly moved to the laboratory door and checked inside, leading with her weapon. "Clear," she said a moment later. Then she turned to Bra'tac and asked, "Are you all right?"

"I will be fine. A Jaffa is not defeated until after he is buried." He smiled grimly. "And occasionally not even then."

Smiling, Major Carter entered the laboratory, Bra'tac right behind her. She immediately moved toward a table and removed two different devices from it. It was unclear to Bra'tac if both were separate components of the item they came for, or if the two served different purposes. Ultimately, he also cared little — he trusted the Tau'ri woman to know her business, trust that, as far as Bra'tac was concerned, she'd more than earned over her time in the fight against the Goa'uld.

"Got it," she said. "Let's go."

They retraced their steps — including going down the staircase and stepping over the Jaffa they'd surprised — unmolested, but then as they approached the doorway to the passage, Bra'tac heard running footfalls that grew ever-louder. They ran in formation — which bespoke excellent training — but were also definitely heading directly for Bra'tac and Major Carter's location.

Which meant the time for stealth was past. They'd been moving slowly and carefully to avoid being detected, but it was obvious now that Kali's Jaffa had either detected them despite their efforts, or were otherwise alerted to their presence.

"Quickly!" he said, now running toward the door.

Major Carter was right behind him, though her speed was reduced somewhat by her desire to keep her weapon ready, a precaution Bra'tac appreciated.

They reached the entrance to the tunnel before the Jaffa were in sight. Bra'tac noted that on this side, it was less obviously a door, with the molding of the wall blending in and the seams difficult to see unless you were specifically looking for them. He admired the design.

Once they both went through, Major Carter closed the door and then reached into one of her pockets and removed one of the rectangular blocks the Tau'ri favored for demolition. Bra'tac had always found the humans' explosive to be primitive and unnecessarily destructive, but he had to admit that it had its uses.

Major Carter crouched down and placed the explosive just under the door latch, where it attached itself easily. Then she removed one of the devices she'd taken from the laboratory and attached it to the explosive.

She got up and quickly started jogging down the corridor. "Let's move. The C-4'll blow as soon as someone opens that door."

Nodding, Bra'tac followed her at a run.

A few seconds later, Bra'tac heard the click of a door opening, followed immediately by the deafening report of the explosive detonating, which was in turn followed by Bra'tac being thrown violently to the ground as if he'd been pushed in the back.

He naturally landed on his left side, exacerbating his injury a hundredfold.

Bra'tac lay on the cold, hard rock for a few seconds, trying to move past the pain of his *ma'tok* wound, not to mention from the fall. *I am, perhaps, growing too old for this.*

Major Carter clambered to her feet and offered Bra'tac her hand.

Gratefully, Bra'tac reached up and clasped her forearm with his right hand and used her as an anchor to pull himself upward. She stumbled a bit — Major Carter was tall for a woman, but still had less strength than a male warrior, and Bra'tac *was* wearing armor — but managed to retain her footing as Bra'tac got to his feet.

She looked up. "There was no way the explosion would budge this mountain, so all the force of the explosion got sent down this tunnel. Sorry about that."

"I will live — probably," Bra'tac said with a smile. "And if I do not, I will die in a noble cause."

Major Carter smiled. "Personally, I prefer option one."

"As do I. Come, let us rescue Dr. Jackson and be away from this place."

Nodding, Major Carter led the way toward the exit.

Just as they reached the curve in the corridor, Bra'tac heard the sound of footfalls. "We are still being pursued."

Major Carter turned to look at him in surprise, but after half a second, she nodded. She hadn't heard the pursuit, but she trusted that Bra'tac could. "Can you run?"

Rather than answer verbally, Bra'tac simply started running. With a small smile, Carter followed right behind him.

The hidden rock-door was still set in from the mountain when they arrived, leading back outside into the chill air of Imphal.

"Close the door quickly!" Bra'tac spoke urgently as he ran out into the snow, Major Carter right behind.

"Hang on," she said as she stopped and pulled out one of her grenades.

Bra'tac nodded with approval. He had not thought highly of the Tau'ri's small, ball-shaped explosives at first, but he had to admit to himself that it was mostly because of how O'Neill had used them to show up Bra'tac when they were trying to sabotage Apophis's *ha'tak* when it was in Earth's orbit. Bra'tac had an elaborate plan for how they would rappel down into the shield generator to destroy it, rendering the mothership helpless. As Bra'tac was in the midst of spelling that plan out, O'Neill had removed two grenades from his pocket, pulled their firing pins, and dropped them. Four seconds later, the shield generators were destroyed.

In truth, O'Neill was a doughty warrior and he and his subordinates in SG-1 were among the finest people Bra'tac had ever known. It had taken him a while to come to accept that.

Now, Major Carter pulled the rock that would bring the door back forward to hide the entrance. But she placed the grenade against the side of the opening, which prevented the rock face from moving all the way into the shut position.

"As soon as they reopen the door," she said, "the firing pin will come out. We, ah, we should run."

"No." Bra'tac took a deep breath and looked around. There was a large oak tree nearby, at which he pointed with his weapon. "There."

Without waiting for her to acknowledge him, he jogged over to the tree. Major Carter followed him, and they took up position behind the oak.

He heard the muffled voices of the Jaffa as well as their approaching footfalls through the tunel entrance. Then the rock door started to once again slide inward and Major Carter's grenade fell down into the snow.

Three Jaffa appeared at the entrance, their leader running ahead, yelling, "*Kree!*"

But behind him, one of his men cried out in alarm. "Jaffa!" Too late, he had noticed the grenade on the ground.

It exploded, cutting both Jaffa to ribbons. Their leader, however, was merely thrown to the ground by the concussive blast.

Bra'tac broke cover and ran toward the fallen Jaffa. But before he could get there, the Jaffa had gotten to his feet, still clutching his staff weapon.

He broke into a huge grin. "You are clever, *shol'va*. But know that, no matter how many Jaffa you kill, the Mother Goddess will remain supreme."

"She is neither mother nor goddess, nor is she supreme. She is a false god, like all the Goa'uld. You have one chance, my friend. Join me. The Jaffa Rebellion has grown and you would be welcome in our ranks."

The Jaffa shook his head. "You wantonly kill my comrades, and then try to recruit me? You are a fool, *shol'va*." He armed his *ma'tok*. "I will kill you where you stand."

Using only his right arm, his left still wounded, Bra'tac also armed his staff weapon, bracing it under his right armpit. It was less efficient than holding it two-handed, but at this range his shot need not be precise. "If you fire, I will fire. We will both die."

The Jaffa shrugged. "Then I will die well, in defense of the Mother Goddess. It has been my hope since I first reached the Age of Prata, that when I die, I do so in her service. You, however, will die poorly, a traitor to your god and all the gods, alone in the snow."

Bra'tac shook his head. "There is another possibility you have not considered."

"And what might that be?"

From behind him, Major Carter stepped out from behind the oak, wielding her gun. "Me. Put the staff weapon down."

Laughing derisively, the Jaffa asked, "Or what? You'll kill me?"

Major Carter nodded. "Those are your options, yes. And before you start in on the fact that I'm a woman, keep in mind that your two buddies over there were killed by *my* grenade."

"A cowardly attack is one thing," the Jaffa said, "but to kill a man who stands before you? There are women who I believe would be capable of such a thing, but you are Tau'ri. All Tau'ri are weak." He turned his *ma'tok* toward Major Carter. "And I will prove it by—"

He was interrupted by Major Carter shooting him in the chest and head. He fell to the snow, which was stained red with his blood.

She walked over to his corpse and stared down at him, her expression indecipherable. Then she looked over at Bra'tac. "We should get moving."

"Agreed."

Before they moved off, she looked back at the corpse again.

"I'd honestly expected better from someone who worshipped a female god." She sighed. "C'mon, let's get moving before—"

She was interrupted by a bright flash in the twilight sky. Looking up, Bra'tac saw a new star erupt in the sky over Imphal.

Major Carter looked at Bra'tac and smiled. "Looks like Captain Patel and the Thakka did their job."

"Indeed. Let us proceed."

The sun was beginning to set, which was good. No technology ever developed had changed the fact that, when on the surface of a planet, the times of the rising and setting sun were the most difficult in which to engage in direct battle. The poor visibility at those times gave the advantage to those who moved secretly in the shadows, as they would need to do to reach the tavern.

They moved as silently as they were able toward the village — limited by Bra'tac's injury and Major Carter's lesser stealth, but such was the way of things.

When they passed by one of the residences, Bra'tac noticed something wrong in the way the wind moved. There was a clearing up ahead, but the wind was blowing around it as if there was a structure present.

As he was holding his *ma'tok* in his right hand, he reached out to grab Major Carter's shoulder with his left, which sent phantom knives slicing through his bicep.

My prim'ta *is taking longer to heal these old cells*, he thought ruefully.

The major turned to look at him, and he indicated the clearing in front of them with his head. She nodded, and raised her P90. It was obvious to Bra'tac that she couldn't detect the disturbance that he sensed, but that she also trusted his judgment.

And then the airlock door to a *tel'tak* suddenly appeared from nowhere and opened to reveal Jacob Carter, who was motioning for them to enter.

Relieved, Bra'tac ran toward the airlock, and Major Carter followed, lowering her weapon and putting it in its standby mode.

Neither they nor the Tok'ra spoke until the airlock was shut, at which point the entrance was once again protected by the cargo vessel's cloak, leaving it fully invisible.

"Glad you two made it out in one piece," Jacob Carter said. "And it looks like Patel and the Thakka did okay."

Major Carter reached for the communications device attached to her vest. "I'll check in with Patel, see if—"

Holding up a hand, the Tok'ra said, "Don't, Sam. We've got us a big problem: Jack and Teal'c got caught."

As he spoke, Jacob Carter called up a holographic image taken from the *tel'tak*'s external sensors. It showed the tavern where the Reetou were meeting with Dr. Jackson. Through a window, they could see that it was Kali, now calmly speaking with seemingly nobody, her *lo'taur* by her side, while O'Neill, Teal'c, and Jackson stood at the rear of the tavern, guarded by four Jaffa. O'Neill was no longer wearing Belos's *kara kesh*, but Bra'tac noted that one of the Jaffa was.

Jacob Carter continued: "Transphasic sensors indicate five Reetou in the room — along with the explosives."

Major Carter winced. "Any idea when they'll go off?"

He shook his head. "Sorry, Sam, no way to tell. From what Bra'tac and I overheard, though, they could go off anytime, and the Reetou won't be harmed."

Bra'tac nodded his acknowledgment. "We must move quickly if we are to move at all."

"Right. We'll have to get in there with this." Major Carter pulled the other device they liberated from Kali's stronghold out of her pocket. "Dad, can you use the cargo ship's communications to talk directly to Colonel Ferretti's radio on the island?"

"Assuming he's there, yeah, I think I can. Gimme a sec." Jacob Carter went to the controls and manipulated the communications systems with a deft hand. "Colonel Ferretti, this General Carter, respond."

Bra'tac shot the Tok'ra a look. Even though they had discussed it earlier in the *tel'tak*, Bra'tac had temporarily forgotten that Jacob Carter held a position within the same military structure as his daughter, O'Neill, and Hammond of Texas. Indeed, he carried the same rank as Hammond.

A static-filled voice sounded over the *tel'tak* speakers. "Ferretti. Good to hear your voice, General."

"Likewise. I've got Major Carter and Bra'tac here. Sitrep, Colonel."

Bra'tac had no idea what a "sitrep" was, but it apparently was a prompt for the colonel on the other end to provide a report. "Gate is secure, the Jaffa are zatted and fit to be zip-tied, and the rings are a smoking pile of junk."

Nodding, Jacob Carter said, "Good work, Colonel."

Major Carter stepped forward. "Ferretti, is Captain Patel there?"

The captain's voice now sounded. "I'm here, Major, but the Thakka didn't make it. The mission, though, was accomplished."

"So we saw. Good work."

Colonel Ferretti came back. "How 'bout you, Carter?"

Bra'tac noted that the colonel sounded anxious. He also noticed that two more of Kali's Jaffa had just entered the tavern and were trying to get the Goa'uld's attention.

Major Carter replied to the question: "Colonel O'Neill, Teal'c, and Daniel have been captured by Kali. Bra'tac, my father, and I will get them out. You'll need to keep holding the gate till we get there, sir."

"You need backup? Major Matt Mason's ready to ride to Sergeant Storm's rescue."

At that, Bra'tac shot Major Carter a look. "Who are Matt Mason and Sergeant Storm?"

"Private joke," she smiled. "Negative, Colonel, you and Lieutenant Long stay put."

Bra'tac wondered if Lieutenant Long was a member of Ferretti's team, or another part of that private joke.

"The Reetou could set off their explosive any moment, sir," Major Carter continued. "As soon as we rescue the others and are all on the cargo ship, we'll signal you to dial the gate."

Now Bra'tac saw that the Jaffa had succeeded in getting Kali's attention and was speaking frantically at her.

He also noticed that Major Carter had very carefully phrased her comments to the colonel so that it didn't come across that she was giving orders to him. After all, this Ferretti person was of a higher rank than she. He admired her respect, which she managed without sacrificing the efficiency of the campaign.

"You got it, Carter. Bring 'em home."

"Yes, sir."

After signing off, Jacob Carter regarded his daughter quizzically. "Major Mason and the others? Those were those astronaut dolls I got you when you were a kid, right?"

"Yeah." Major Carter looked away sheepishly. "Ferretti had a set of his own when he was growing up. It's kind of been a running gag between us ever since we brought Daniel back from Abydos."

Bra'tac pointed at the holographic display. "I believe Kali has been informed of the fate of her *ha'tak*." At this point, Kali had risen to her feet and was speaking angrily to the Jaffa.

Major Carter shook her head. "We need to move. If the Reetou realize that Kali's lost her mothership, they'll take advantage and set off the bomb sooner rather than later."

"Assuming they don't have it on a timer," Jacob Carter added.

"We can't take the chance. I've got another brick of C-4. If I can use it as a distraction, it should get most of the Jaffa out of there." She looked at Bra'tac. "Do you think it'll get them all out?"

"Of the four currently in the tavern," Bra'tac said, "I believe three will investigate an explosion of the type you propose. The one wearing the *kara kesh* will remain to protect Kali from the Reetou."

"Okay." She lifted the device she'd taken from Kali's lab. "This affects symbiotes as much as the Reetou do normally, and I have no idea how it'll interact with Belos's hand device, so I'll need to be the one to go into the tavern."

Bra'tac quickly said, "Then I shall plant the explosive."

"Like hell," Jacob Carter said.

At that, Bra'tac straightened. "I beg your pardon?"

In response, Jacob Carter grabbed a tool off the console and threw it to Bra'tac's left. "Here, catch."

Bra'tac attempted to raise his left hand to catch the tool, but he was unable to do so as the pain of his wound shot through his entire arm. The tool clattered to the deck behind him.

"I rest my case," Jacob Carter said. "I'll set off the C-4, you sit there and let your symbiote heal that arm." He pointed at the pilot seat.

Gritting his teeth, Bra'tac reluctantly forced himself to agree with the Tok'ra. "Very well."

Major Carter smiled and put a friendly hand on Bra'tac's right shoulder. "It's okay, Bra'tac. We'll get 'em. You be ready to take off as soon as we're all on board."

He nodded. "I will do my part."

"Thanks." Then she turned to her father. "As soon as you set off the C-4, I'll go in."

"You got it, kiddo. Let's get to work." He grinned. "We'll do Major Mason proud."

CHAPTER TWENTY-TWO

P3X-418—Colonel O'Neill, Teal'c, and Dr. Jackson

THE GOOD news, as far as O'Neill was concerned, was Kali obviously didn't overhear the part of their radio conversation with the SGC on the subject of the explosives that the Reetou had planted in the room.

The bad news was that they were still in the room with the explosives, and they had no idea when they'd go off. When they did, they'd take out Kali, her Jaffa, her slaves, and himself, Teal'c, and Daniel, plus anyone else in range of the explosive.

And not take out the Reetou. Which sucked.

Worse, O'Neill had no idea how the rest of the plan was going. There was no word on the other two teams. Kali wouldn't necessarily fill him in on the fate of the rest of his people. She might do so, of course — Goa'ulds were never happier than when they were gloating — but O'Neill couldn't afford to assume that no news was actually good news.

Which meant he had to proceed as if Carter, Bra'tac, Jacob, Patel, and the Thakka were captured or dead and the three of them were on their own.

The problem there was that any move they made might result in the Reetou just setting off the damn explosives. That put the invisible bugs in the driver's seat as far as O'Neill was concerned.

Which left him with damn few options.

O'Neill *hated* it when he had damn few options.

"Teal'c," he whispered, but before he could get any further, one of the Jaffa nearby moved forward.

"The prisoners *will* be silent," the Jaffa said in a low, even tone so as not to disturb the "Mother Goddess" while she spoke with the invisible insects.

"Will we now?" O'Neill asked.

The Jaffa simply glared. O'Neill supposed he was lucky — usually when he mouthed off at Jaffa, they hit him with one of those pain stick thingies. A stern look and talking-to was a refreshing change.

He didn't say so out loud, though. That would be pushing his luck. Not that O'Neill wasn't willing to push his luck far more than was healthy, but on this occasion, it probably wasn't the brightest move.

Two more Jaffa came into the tavern, and O'Neill's heart sank. The last thing he needed were *more* bad guys in the room.

Kali was in the midst of jabbering at the Reetou, which the doodad was translating into what passed for the bugs' language. Then the bugs screeched and chittered and then the doodad translated it for her. It was all very slow and cumbersome and was giving O'Neill a massive headache.

"How'd you put up with that?" he whispered to Daniel, deciding to risk incurring the tut-tutting of the Jaffa.

"Wasn't easy. Why do you think I've learned how to speak so many languages?"

"Wild guess—you're a linguist?"

Daniel smiled. "Well yeah, but the archeologist's curse is to have to wait for the translation when you're talking to the locals. Lot easier—and faster—to just learn the language yourself. At least when you're as good at languages as I am, and I always had the aptitu—"

The Jaffa stepped forward again. "The prisoners—"

"—will be silent, yeah yeah," O'Neill said.

"Forgive me, Mother Goddess," one of the new Jaffa finally said when there was a pause in the action, as it were, at the table, "but I bear urgent news that cannot wait."

Kali didn't stop looking at the Reetou. "Forgive me. I *am* the ruler of a massive interstellar empire, and there are times when I must tend to it."

After a moment, the Reetou response came from the doodad: "We will recess."

Then Kali got to her feet and walked away from the table.

"What *is* it?" she asked angrily.

"I'm sorry, Mother Goddess, but — " The Jaffa looked stricken, which meant that he was about to give what Kali would consider bad news — which meant it would probably be good news for O'Neill and the rest of his team.

"Speak, please, and quickly. I am quite busy here, and — "

"The *ha'tak* is destroyed!"

Yes! O'Neill barely managed not to say that out loud.

"What?"

O'Neill decided to go for it. "Coulda sworn you said you were gonna stop the rest of my team. Crap job so far."

"Be silent!" Kali barked at O'Neill. She turned back to the Jaffa. "Send the patrols that are searching for the Tau'ri to the rings and have them secure the *chappa'ai*."

"Ooh, that's a *great* idea!" O'Neill said. "You'll definitely want to do that."

"I said be silent!"

Daniel whispered, "May not wanna push your luck, Jack."

O'Neill just stared at him. "I'm sorry, have we met?"

"Fair point."

Teal'c chose that moment to start talking. "The Thakka has already seen you for what you are — a false god."

The Jaffa who'd brought the news about the mothership going boom, turned to move threateningly toward Teal'c. "Do not speak your lies, *shol'va!*"

Whatever snappy comeback Teal'c might have had was cut off by the big explosion that shook the ground and the tavern.

"Jaffa, *kree!*" Kali bellowed, pointing at the exit to the tavern. "Yaresh, remain here."

All the Jaffa — except for Yaresh — left the tavern, leaving just the three SG-1 members, the half-dozen slaves, Kali, Yaresh, and five Reetou.

And if it wasn't for the five Reetou, O'Neill might have considered making a move. But they could've been armed, for all he knew, plus they had that damn bomb.

Kali moved back to the table. "My apologies for these delays."

The Reetou screeches came back as: "There is no need to apologize. These negotiations are obviously meaningless to you — and they are to us, as well. The Goa'uld are parasites who must be removed from the galaxy, as must the bipeds you take as hosts."

"Now hang on a sec!" O'Neill said, but Daniel stepped in front of him.

"Honored negotiators, I thought we had discussed this before Kali replaced me as mediator. The hosts are not to be blamed for the actions of the Goa'uld."

O'Neill glanced over at Teal'c and mouthed the words *honored negotiators?*

Teal'c, naturally, remained impassive.

Kali whirled on Daniel. "*This* was how you negotiated on my behalf?"

Daniel smiled. "You made me promise to negotiate for you. You didn't make me promise to be good at it."

Moving toward Daniel, Kali held up her left hand. "I have had enough of—"

And then she doubled over in pain. Across the tavern, Yaresh did likewise.

The five Reetou, meanwhile, became completely visible.

They screeched and screamed, and the doodad said, "What is the meaning of this?"

O'Neill, though, just grinned. All of a sudden, his headache was completely gone. "Carter? That you?"

Sure enough, Major Samantha Carter entered the tavern, P90 at the ready. "Right here, sir."

"Sweet!" He turned to the Reetou. "To answer your question, O 'honorable negotiators,' the meaning of this is that we've made you just as in phase as the rest of us. Which means the little bomb that you put in here hoping to kill the snake-head and as many humans and Jaffa as you could take with her, is now gonna kill all five of you, too."

Daniel smiled. "I can't imagine the Reetou rebels will be

particularly thrilled with that."

"Oh, they definitely won't." O'Neill recalled Jacob and Bra'tac mentioning something about how pissed the Reetou were at how many of them died here on Imphal when they wiped it out. Apparently, they didn't have the Jaffa's proclivity for suicide missions and dying well and all that other crap.

"We are only five," the doodad said after more screeching. "We are willing to give our lives."

"Sir," Carter said, and O'Neill followed where she was looking to see a white oval underneath the table.

"I'm guessing that's the thing that goes boom?"

"Yes, sir. Should I disarm it?"

"Nah, just shoot it."

Carter swallowed, but just said, "Yes, sir," and aimed her P90.

A huge screech followed by, "Wait!"

O'Neill grinned. "Aaaaaand the bluff is called. Here's what's gonna happen, kids. You're gonna sit right here and not move, or we'll shoot you. You're in phase now, so we *can* shoot you. We're going to leave the planet. After that — well, you just do whatever it is you guys do."

Carter grabbed her radio. "Dad, I've got the colonel, Daniel, and Teal'c."

"Little busy here!" came Jacob's frantic voice, and O'Neill could hear staff weapon fire. He also swore he heard a ragged cough.

O'Neill looked at his team. "Let's go."

Kali's Jaffa had put O'Neill and Teal'c's weapons on the tavern's bar, so they went there to grab them. As Teal'c took hold of his staff weapon, O'Neill checked the clip of the P90 — he had about half the magazine left — and shouldered it.

For his part, Daniel grabbed a zat off Yaresh, who was too busy writhing on the floor in agony to object. Kali was doing likewise nearby, and O'Neill had to admit to enjoying seeing a Goa'uld helpless for once.

Daniel turned to the six slaves and said, "It's not safe for you here. You should come with us."

The slaves looked at each other and then one of them looked at Daniel.

"It's all right, Aparna," Daniel said to her. "We'll help you."

"Very well," she said with an enthusiastic nod.

Carter was leading the way out of the tavern. "This way, sir."

A chill washed over O'Neill as he stepped outside. The sun had gone down, and it was about ten degrees colder than it was when he and Teal'c had been approaching the tavern earlier.

Carter headed south at a run, and O'Neill and the others followed, with Daniel keeping Aparna and the other slaves close to him. After only a couple of seconds, O'Neill could hear the staff weapon and zat fire that he'd heard over the radio. It was, perhaps not surprisingly, given the explosion, not far from where the plumes of smoke were rising.

Sure enough, they soon came within sight of a small fire with billowing smoke that used to be one of the village's buildings, and about thirty feet west of that, five Jaffa hiding behind other, intact buildings, poking their heads out periodically to fire their weapons in the general direction of the smoking ruin.

The electric hum of a zat came from behind the burning building, which told O'Neill where Jacob was hiding. Still, even factoring in the fire, O'Neill wasn't too clear on why the five Jaffa were being so cautious against one Tok'ra.

Another zat shot came from a different part of the fiery mess, and O'Neill realized what Jacob was doing, and why the Jaffa were being cautious — and, for that matter, why he heard Jacob cough over the radio. He was moving around inside the periphery of the fire, making it look as if there was more than one person firing on them.

Well, now there was. "Yo, dumbasses, over here!"

Several of the Jaffa turned toward O'Neill's voice, at which point he and Carter both fired their P90s, Teal'c fired his staff weapon, and Daniel shot his borrowed zat.

Four of the five Jaffa went down. The fifth, showing uncharacteristic good sense, threw his staff weapon to the snow-covered ground and removed his zat from its forearm holster and threw that to the ground as well. He raised his arms, and cried, "I surrender!"

All four members of SG-1 turned their weapons on that Jaffa, who stood steadily with his arms raised without flinching. O'Neill admired the grit, at least.

"Oh, Jacob," O'Neill said, "come out come out wherever you are! We got the bad guys!"

A second later, Jacob emerged from the smoke, covered in soot, coughing so much he sounded like a chain smoker with a head cold, and with several charred holes in his clothes.

"Dad!" Carter cried and ran over to help her father out. "You okay?"

He waved her off. "I'll be fine." He coughed a few times, then: "It looks worse than it is."

"It'd almost have to," O'Neill said.

Another cough. "Selmak's takin' care of it. Hell, running around inside the fire was *his* cockamamie idea. Worked, too, I don't think I could've held off five Jaffa otherwise." That prompted *yet another* coughing fit.

O'Neill glanced at Teal'c. "Don't suppose you and Patel packed lozenges?"

"We did not."

"Didn't think so."

Daniel was still staring at the Jaffa. "What do we do with him?"

The Jaffa said, "You are Teal'c — the leader of the Jaffa rebellion?"

"I am Teal'c," was all he said in reply.

"I wish to join you. The Goa'uld are false gods. Yaresh told me that the Thakka has joined your rebellion, and I wish to do the same."

O'Neill guessed that this guy was there when Yaresh found their radios. "Do you, now?"

"I will do whatever you ask to prove my desire to join you."

Turning to Teal'c—he was the expert on this stuff—O'Neill prompted, "Whaddaya think, T?"

"Daniel Jackson—shoot him."

"Wait," the Jaffa started, but Daniel fired his zat, and he went down.

O'Neill stared at the unconscious form of the Jaffa. "That was unexpected."

But then Teal'c walked over and picked the Jaffa up into a firefighter's carry. "We will bring him to the Alpha Site, where Master Bra'tac, the other Jaffa rebels, and I will all determine if he is worthy to join us."

Daniel frowned. "And if he isn't?"

"He will regret it."

"Okay, then."

Carter was supporting her father, who was still coughing up a lung. "Sir, we should get moving. The device will deactivate soon, and we should be gone by the time Kali is able to send more Jaffa after us."

Nodding, O'Neill said, "Let's move."

The Carters led the way to where Jacob had parked the cargo ship. O'Neill took up the rear, keeping the six slaves protected as they lagged behind Daniel and even a burdened Teal'c. The colonel was a little worried when they ran into a clearing and just stopped, but then an airlock appeared out of nowhere.

He shook his head. "Those cloaks get me every time."

They all ran inside the cargo ship, where Bra'tac was sitting in the pilot seat.

"All aboard who's coming aboard, Bra'tac," O'Neill said. "Hit it."

"It is good to see you all alive and well," Bra'tac said as he touched several controls that closed the airlock and got the ship underway.

Helping Jacob into the copilot chair, Carter then thumbed

her radio. "Colonel Ferretti, we're on our way."

"Good news or bad news, Major?" Ferretti asked.

O'Neill said, "You don't get rid of me that easy, Louie. The gang's all here, plus half a dozen locals that need saving. Let's go home."

"You got it, Colonel. Dialing the gate now."

Nodding, O'Neill moved to stand at the console behind the pilot seat. He felt like something was missing — something important that hadn't happened yet, that needed to before they could gate home.

Bra'tac turned to glance at O'Neill. "Not bad."

That was it, he thought with a smile. *Now* they could go home.

Slowly, Kali got to her feet, the agony that coursed through her entire body, radiating out from between her shoulder blades, finally beginning to subside.

She looked around the tavern, but she only saw Yaresh. "What happened?" the Jaffa asked.

"The Tau'ri." Kali practically spat the words. "I offered them an arrangement that benefitted everyone. And they betrayed me! I should have known better than to trust those who are worthy only to be slaves or hosts." She shook her head, trying to clear it, then walked over to the table where the translator still sat. With the infernal device that Major Carter had created no longer functioning, the Reetou were now invisible. The translator had been shut off, probably from being inactive for too long. She reactivated it and spoke. "Honored negotiators, are you still here?"

Her words were translated, but no response came.

She sighed and turned to Yaresh. "Jaffa, *kree*."

As she exited the tavern, she said to Yaresh, who followed in step behind her, "You shall be the new Thakka, Yaresh. Gather all the Jaffa who remain and bring them to the throne room."

"I will obey, Mother Goddess," Yaresh — or, rather, the

Thakka replied.

A high-pitched whine started to fill the air. It came from behind them in the tavern.

And then the very air around Kali exploded, and she felt her host body burn...

CHAPTER TWENTY-THREE

Stargate Command

DANIEL Jackson was very grateful to hear his boots clang against the ramp in the gate room of the SGC. More than dialing Earth's address, more than transmitting the GDO code, it was that sound of sole on metal that told Daniel that he'd made it back home. Every alien world had stone steps or ramps made of other material or metal stairs or something else. Only on Earth in Cheyenne Mountain was there the mesh-metal ramp that made that wonderful echoing clangy sound when you stepped on it.

The ramp was pretty crowded: all of SG-1, all of SG-17, Captain Patel, Bra'tac, Jacob, the six *lo'taurs*, and three unconscious Jaffa — the one Daniel had shot on Teal'c's instruction and the two that SG-17 had taken prisoner.

Of course, General Hammond was waiting for them. Ferretti had dialed the gate and sent his GDO code as soon as Bra'tac took off, so by the time they got to the island — getting a lovely view along the way of the giant flaming meteor careening toward Imphal that was all that was left of Kali's mothership — Hammond had ordered the gate room security team to stand down and was awaiting their arrival at the bottom of the ramp.

Also present was Janet Fraiser, ready to tend to any wounded, along with several of her staff. She made a beeline for Teal'c.

"These Jaffa were all struck with *zat'ni'katel*s. They must all remain sedated until we may bring them to the Alpha Site for interrogation."

"I'll take care of them," Janet said, then turned to one of her staff. "Get some more stretchers for these three."

The medtech nodded and ran off.

Janet then approached Bra'tac and Jacob and smiled. "You two look like hell."

Jacob grinned back. "Always admired your bedside manner, doc."

"I know you both have symbiotes, but get to the infirmary anyhow."

Bra'tac nodded. "Of course." Then he turned to the general, and waved his right hand over his head. "Hammond of Texas. It is good to see you."

"The feeling is mutual, Master Bra'tac — you too, Jacob."

"Thanks, George," Jacob said. "But I think we'd best follow doctor's orders, 'cause I'm feelin' like crap."

Sam smiled. "I'll walk you two to the infirmary now."

Hammond gave Sam an approving nod, then looked at Jack and Ferretti. "I take it the mission was a success?"

Jack shrugged. "Well, we all got home, and we're more or less in one piece, so yeah. Plus, y'know, Carter figured out a way to make the Reetou visible, so that was kinda nice."

From behind Jack, Captain Patel quietly said, "One of us didn't make it."

Daniel winced.

"What was that, Captain?" Hammond asked.

Patel spoke up. "The Thakka didn't make it, sir. He died taking a staff weapon for me on Kali's ship." She shook her head. "That's the second time he saved my life."

"I'm sorry. Debrief in one hour." Hammond, to Daniel's mind, didn't sound particularly sorry. But then, the Thakka *was* a First Prime. He was an enemy combatant, and that wasn't someone Hammond was going to waste a lot of time mourning.

Of course, if he was saving Patel's life, then he'd obviously had *some* kind of change of heart. He hadn't gotten the whole story yet, as Jack and Teal'c were too busy being Kali's prisoner to fill him in on what he'd missed since Kali holed him up with a bunch of tablets. Had Teal'c convinced him to join the rebellion?

Though if he was dead, it didn't really much matter anymore...

Sam had already left with her father and Bra'tac, and Jack

was talking with Ferretti now — probably talking about the good old days when they were both just regular Joes fighting the good fight for the U.S. of A., or whatever it was old Air Force buddies talked about. Teal'c was having a conversation with Peruzzi and Satterfield from SG-17, while the fourth SG-17 team member, a bald Marine whose name Daniel didn't know, was leading the six *lo'taurs* out of the room toward their debrief. Aparna was one of them, and he gave her an encouraging look. She nodded back. He had a feeling that her knowledge of Kali's history would prove useful to both the SGC and the Tok'ra.

Patel just looked miserable standing in the middle of the room and finally exited quietly.

Daniel followed her.

"Captain Patel," he called out as he reached the corridor.

She stopped, turned around, and faced Daniel. "Is there something I can do for you, Dr. Jackson?"

He caught up to her and gave her his warmest smile. "It's Daniel — and that was going to be my question for you."

"Thanks, but — well, this is something I have to deal with on my own."

"No — no, it isn't. We're a team, Captain. And we've all had to deal with death. I watched my wife die."

Patel winced. "I'm sorry, Doct — Daniel, of course you do understand it, but — " She blew out a breath that sounded like a pipe bursting. "Honestly, what I'm having the most difficulty with is the Thakka. I mean, I feel awful that Major Lagdamen and Elena and Anwan died, but that's part of the deal when you sign up. They were my teammates and my friends, and I'm going to be mourning them for a *long* time, but I know how to deal with that. I've lost people I've fought alongside in the past — the first one was six months after I graduated the Academy. It sucks, it's awful, but I have the mental means to deal with it. But the Thakka — I guess I just don't know how to process losing him. I didn't even *like* him, and he saved my life — twice! He's dead because of me."

"He was also alive because of you." Daniel said the words without thinking, but he realized as he did so that it was true. "From what you told us after you guys went through the gate the first time, the Thakka probably would've been killed by the Reetou if SG-7 hadn't been there. And I'm guessing Teal'c talked him into joining the rebellion?"

Patel nodded. "We both did. That was the odd thing, he listened to me a lot more than he listened to Teal'c. He kept viewing me as one of the *Kali Kula*, even after I asked him repeatedly not to."

"Not surprising," Daniel said, remembering Kali's story of the origin of the *Kula* and how much emphasis she herself put on protecting her people. "You gave the Thakka a gift, Kirti. In fact, you gave him two."

"He said something."

Daniel frowned. "Hm?"

She shook her head. "When he died, he said something in Goa'uld. I didn't understand it — Elena was the linguist, I'm afraid the Goa'uld language just sounds like Klingon to me."

Biting his tongue, Daniel didn't comment. He'd seen a lecture by the linguist who'd created the Klingon language for the movie studio, and had had his own issues with the silly made-up language. "Do you remember the words he spoke?"

Closing her eyes, Patel seemed lost in memory for a second. "Shell kick nimron?"

Nodding in a total lack of surprise, Daniel corrected her pronunciation. "*Shel kek nem ron*. It means 'I die free'."

Patel's eyes widened. "Really?"

"It's what rebel Jaffa prefer their last words to be. Personally, I'd rather my last words were thanking everyone for the well wishes on my hundred and ninetieth birthday, but that's just me." He put a hand on her shoulder. "Look, what I'm about to say probably doesn't feel like it means much — in fact, it probably doesn't feel like it means anything. The Thakka spent his whole life living a lie under an oppressive monster. He may have died, but at least knew the truth when he did. More to the point, he went out on his own terms. First Primes generally are killed in service to the Goa'uld they're subjects of. But the Thakka died doing something that mattered to *him* rather than something that mattered to Kali."

"So you're saying I should be happy that he died?"

"God, no, that's crazy." He shook his head. "But it will get better with time. When Sha're and I were together, every thought I had was about her. After Apophis took her, every thought I had was about rescuing her. And right after she died, every thought I had was about how much I missed her. But now? I've gone entire days without thinking about her. Doesn't mean I don't miss her, but eventually we heal. Even if we don't have a symbiote inside us."

That got her to smile. "I suppose. Thank you, Daniel — you've given me a lot to think about. Including whether or not I want to stay here."

"You're thinking of quitting?"

"Perhaps. That's what I need to ponder. My first CO said something to me that I've always held onto. 'Focus on the job while you're doing it. Think about what it means after it's done.' Well, it's done, and I'm thinking about it, and — well, I know that I most assuredly to *not* want to go back through the gate. I don't think I could face going with another team."

"Well, I can't tell you what you should do, but I can tell you what you *shouldn't* do."

"What's that?"

"The worst thing you can do right now is make a major life decision when your emotions are all churned up. At the very least, sleep on it."

"That's good advice." She smiled, though the smile didn't make it all the way to her eyes. "Again, thank you, Daniel. If you'll excuse me, I want to head to the mess before the debrief, see if they have any popsicles."

"Uhm, okay," Daniel said, watching her leave.

For his part, Daniel wasn't in the least bit hungry. He was more curious about what happened to Kali and the Reetou after the bomb went off — if they had survived.

Not enough to go back to P3X-418 or anything, but he did wonder what might have transpired between them...

EPILOGUE

Stargate Command—two weeks later

"UNSCHEDULED off-world activation!"

Hammond looked up from his desk. He'd been hoping for a quiet day catching up on his perpetually overdue paperwork. But he supposed that Major Davis at the Pentagon was just going to have to wait for the latest reports from SG-3, SG-9, and SG-13.

By the time he came down to the control room, Sergeant O'Brien said, "Reading Tok'ra IDC, sir."

"Open the iris." Hammond immediately went down the next flight of stairs to the gate room. He hoped it was simply Jacob coming to visit his daughter — there was still enough of the day left for it to remain quiet.

When he'd first been assigned to Cheyenne, it had been intended to be Hammond's last post before retiring. But now his originally planned date of retirement had come and gone and he was still here. Back then, when he'd relieved W.O. West, the outgoing general told him that the tedium would only be relieved by the boredom. Sure enough, he'd spent a lot of days wishing for a bit of excitement.

Then Apophis had attacked and excitement — if that was the right word — became an everyday occurrence. Now he prayed for a little boredom now and again.

Entering the gate room he saw, not Jacob Carter, but rather a young man he'd last seen on the base three years earlier. He'd grown considerably since then, though he still was completely hairless.

"Charlie! Welcome back to Earth."

The young man who'd been genetically engineered by the Reetou as a facilitator between the out-of-phase aliens and the humans had been taken by the Tok'ra. Last Hammond had heard, he'd been blended with a symbiote, thus healing him of the many illnesses that his hastily constructed human body was ill-equipped to handle on its own.

"It is good to see you again, General. I actually bear news regarding the Reetou. Is Jack here?"

Hammond nodded, and looked up at O'Brien through the window. "Have Colonel O'Neill report to the briefing room."

"Yes, sir," the sergeant replied.

Within minutes, O'Neill had joined Hammond and Charlie at the table upstairs. "Good to see you, kiddo. My, how you've grown."

"My growth is consistent with human growth, Jack."

"Of course it is. Still — how you been?"

"I am well. I was blended with a symbiote named Jentol." Charlie lowered his head, and then his voice deepened and distorted in a manner that Hammond had gotten depressingly used to these past five years. "Charlie has proven an excellent host, though it took some time for me to heal his many ailments. The Reetou's work was — slipshod."

"Hey, cut them some slack, they were desperate," O'Neill snapped.

"Colonel." Hammond spoke the word in his best *calm down* voice.

To his credit, O'Neill nodded and relaxed in his chair.

Jentol lowered his head again, and then Charlie's voice returned. "For obvious reasons, the Tok'ra High Council assigned me to keep track of Reetou activity. After Ramprasad made his report, I was able to contact the government-in-exile. The campaign against Kali resulted in many lost lives. The change in tactics was due to a change in power in the rebellion's leadership, but those alterations had too many casualties for the Reetou to be comfortable with, given their stated goal of preserving their species."

"Funny, that," O'Neill muttered.

Hammond asked, "What was the final result of their fight against Kali?"

"The five Reetou who went to negotiate with Kali were trapped on Imphal. All the vessels on the world had been destroyed, and the Reetou's attempts to traverse the icy waters failed. Kali herself was badly injured by the explosive provided by Belos, but her Jaffa summoned another *ha'tak* to Imphal, and she was healed by her sarcophagus. However, her forces have been badly weakened by both the Reetou and you Tau'ri. Olokun and Ba'al have already taken several systems on the outer edges of her territory, which she ceded without a fight."

"Darn," O'Neill deadpanned.

There was a phrase Charlie had used that piqued Hammond's interest. "You said 'government-in-exile'?"

"Yes, General." Charlie actually smiled, something he hadn't done the entire time he was at the SGC during the previous Reetou attack. "The reason why I was not present when Ramprasad made his report is because I was busy relocating several key members of the Reetou Hierarchy to a distant world. They are attempting to rebuild Reetou society away from the Goa'uld. It is our hope that they succeed."

Hammond nodded. "Major Carter has been working to duplicate the technology she created that brought the Reetou temporarily into phase with us — she's also trying to eliminate the side effects to Goa'uld, Tok'ra, and Jaffa. If she's able to, perhaps our people will be able to properly communicate."

"That is my hope as well, General. In fact, I would like to see the major's work, if I may."

O'Neill rose to his feet. "Carter's in her lab now, sir. I'll be happy to escort Chucky-boy here."

Again, Charlie smiled. "I would like that."

"Dismissed, Colonel."

"Thank you, General." O'Neill smiled. "So the Reetou are getting their acts together and a System Lord's been royally screwed. I've had worse days."

Hammond watched as O'Neill and Charlie left the briefing room, the latter asking how Dr. Fraiser was doing.

The general had to agree with the colonel. He'd had worse days. It would've been better if the mission had been accomplished without the loss of SG-7 — and with more actual additions to the Jaffa rebellion. While the Thakka had died, one of the three Jaffa they'd brought back from P3X-418 had signed on. The other two claimed that they were interested in joining the rebellion, but in truth they were attempting to infiltrate it in order to curry favor with Kali, at which they failed, badly. Teal'c had the pair of them sent back to Aizawl, each unconscious from a zat strike.

Still, in their ongoing war with the Goa'uld, this had to count as a victory. Even better, it might have been the last they saw of the renegade Reetou.

He got up and went back to his office. There were still reports to be read on this nice, quiet day.

Tomorrow, he was sure, would go back to exciting.

ABOUT THE AUTHOR

Keith R.A. DeCandido received a Lifetime Achievement Award from the International Association of Media Tie-in Writers in 2009, which means he never needs to achieve anything ever again. Somehow, he managed not to write any *Stargate* fiction until 2014, when his short story "Time Keeps on Slippin'" was published in Fandemonium's *Far Horizons* anthology.

He's very pleased to add *SG-1* to the many other TV shows he's written fiction based on, also including *Star Trek*, *Sleepy Hollow*, *Supernatural*, *Doctor Who*, *Farscape*, *Heroes Reborn*, *The X-Files*, and many others. He's also done fiction based on games, movies, and comic books, most recently the *Marvel's Tales of Asgard* trilogy of novels.

His original fiction includes the fantasy police procedural series that started with *Dragon Precinct* in 2004 and has continued to several novels and short stories, as well as a cycle of urban fantasy short stories set in Key West, Florida, and a series of urban fantasy novels taking place in New York City that will debut in 2016 with *A Furnace Sealed*. Dark Quest Books recently published his short-story collection *Without a License: The Fantastic Worlds of Keith R.A. DeCandido*.

Keith is also a second-degree black belt in karate (he not only trains but also teaches several classes a week to both kids and adults), a prolific blogger (he has been doing rewatches of shows in both the *Stargate* and *Star Trek* franchises for Tor.com since 2011, in addition to his own blog at kradical.livejournal. com), the percussionist for the parody band Boogie Knights, and probably some other stuff too, which he can't remember due to the lack of sleep.

Stay in touch...
Follow us on Twitter
@StargateNovels

Find us on Facebook at
facebook.com/StargateNovels

Sign up for our newsletter
at StargateNovels.com

THANKS!